A CONSPIRACY OF POISONS

J. G. Jeffreys

A Conspiracy
of Poisons

WALKER AND COMPANY
NEW YORK

First published in the United States of America in 1977 by the Walker Publishing Company, Inc.

ISBN: 0-8027-5359-0

Library of Congress Catalog Card Number: 76-57848

Printed in the United States of America

10 9 8 7 6 5 4 3 2 1

EDITOR'S NOTE

A full account of "wourali" comes in the 1885 edition of Waterton's *Wanderings in South America* edited by the Reverend J. G. Wood and published by Macmillan. Waterton's first journey to Demerara was in 1812, but there is no doubt that wourali was known to at least a few travellers for some time before that date. The Mr Sims Sturrock called on can only have been the first of the family of theatrical agents recommended in a curious little handbook intended for would-be actors; *The Road to the Stage*, published in the second edition in 1835. "Mr Sims," it says, "holds the situation held for so many years by his father; to the manners and acquirements of a gentleman he adds an intimate knowledge of the profession."

Apart from these I have not been able to find any further references to Sturrock's adventures in August 1804; but this may be due to the fact that he obviously changed several names to save himself from what he calls 'embarrassment'. Rumours of invasion were certainly current throughout that summer, and the kidnapping and murder of the Duc d'Enghien by Napoleon in March just as certainly gave rise to fears that he might attempt some such daring demonstration against this country; fears perhaps all the more acute from the uncomfortable memory of a quite remarkably inept conspiracy to assassinate the First Consul—as he was then—in which the previous administration under the pathetic figure of Henry Addington had been implicated. Pitt's government in 1804 was only a little less muddled and earned no more respect. In the event so far from being crowned by a startling *coup de main* Napoleon's rather absurd review at Boulogne on August fifteenth was washed out in the early evening by a torrential thunderstorm.

B.J.H.

ONE

'Pray, Mr Sturrock,' said my publisher, tapping his fingers on the desk, 'pray,' says he, 'let us have a work of more weighty matter. We have had to this present an account of some bumpkin highwayman at the village of Roehampton; diverting no doubt, but with little instruction in it. We have had also a narrative of our London bankers in which you were somewhat less than respectful, and be damned the state we're in today it don't pay to cock any snooks at those gentry.' He looked as if he was about to intone a prayer to Mr Coutts or the Bank of England and continued, 'And latterly you have presented a frivolous romance of a singularly bold and unbiddable young woman; true enough a Philadelphia heiress and so demanding proper respect, but a most unfemale creature otherwise. Damme, it won't do,' he finished. 'In short let us have a reminiscence with more meat to it and more respect for your betters. We're a respectable house, Mr Sturrock, and your toss pot adventures with bawds, trollops, doxies and cut throats won't do.'

That is the way these flint eyed and brass browed rascals address their poor scribblers, and for me the more uncalled for as I am not by any means one of the snuffish and ink spattered rogues begging for a crumb myself, but a chief ornament of the Bow Street Patrol—known to the vulgar as the Runners, the Robin Redbreasts, or the Thieftakers—a master of our new Art and Science of Detection, and a proper figure of a man in bed or out; of modest manner but handy with my pistols or my fists, and of a proper philosophical turn of mind when I feel like the exercise. It is a mere foible or vanity in me to set down one or another of my adventures now and again, and I do it mostly to please the ladies and several gentlemen who have already spoken kindly of my genteel memoirs. It was so to please them

7

now that instead of giving a particular round answer, as I well might have done, I affected to ponder for a time and at last said, 'There is the matter of the Frenchy spies, sir. A most mysterious and frightful business as might have spelt our ruin and defeat by Bonaparte. To be sure there's a whore or two concerned, indeed it's damned near all whores; but only of the very best kind.'

'I daresay it'll do,' he admitted, 'if you've nothing better to offer. But see you mind your manners and your whores.'

So with that permission we are in the stormy and unseasonable summer of 1804; all Europe at odds with the Corsican villain showing his claws again, and people still talking everywhere of the most wicked kidnapping and murder in March of the Duc d'Enghien, Prince Louis Antoine Henri de Bourbon Condé. You will no doubt recollect that discovering or affecting to discover a Royalist plot to have Master Bonaparte done away with suspicion fell or was placed upon this unfortunate gentleman—who was presently residing in neutral Baden and engaged in no more warlike conspiracy than paying court to a certain fair young lady—and the Monster's vengeance was swift and cruel. At his orders and riding by night a party of gendarmes crossed the Rhine secretly, surrounded the prince's house and carried him back in chains to the Château of Vincennes, by Paris; where at two thirty of the morning after a trial in which no defence was allowed he was dragged down to the moat, shot dead by a firing party, and buried in a grave which had already been prepared. *The Times* newspaper had several very proper observations to make on the matter, and there was scarcely a dry eye left among the ladies of England when it was reported that the noble young man had died uttering the last words, 'Adieu, my Clementina.'

It was a villainous business which had much to do with my own tale following, for if kidnapping and murder were to be the new weapons of war who might dare to consider himself safe? Talk of invasion was on all lips, daily reports of the audacious rascal's fantastical camp on the downs of Boulogne, rumours of great rafts driven by windmills and a monstrous bridge to span the straits, whispers that if you listened carefully

8

at night about the Kentish coast you could hear the tapping and hammering of engineers driving a tunnel under the sea itself, and yet more rumours that London and Portsmouth were alive with Bonapartist agents. And not to be outdone on our side Volunteers, Fencibles, and Militia were mustered from all patriotic gentlemen resolved to sell themselves dear when they could master the niceties of their drill and stop falling over their muskets.

Even my Master Maggsy was taken with a fit and declared for enlisting with the St Mary le Bone Volunteers or the Hanover Square Armed Association. But I soon disabused him of that whim, telling him plain that so far from doing the heroic in front of servant wenches he'd be as good as an army corps to the Frenchies, for our own gallant fellows would retreat in disorder at the very sight of him with a Brown Bess in his hands. 'Depend upon it,' I said, 'we shall have work enough to do in our own trade. Any day now there'll be a call for Jeremy Sturrock.' And so it turned out.

There are some affairs which come at you like a ship of the line with all sails tight and broadsides roaring, while others creep up like thieves in the night. This was of the last sort, at least in its beginnings. It was a sweltering Monday night about nine o'clock of August tenth with another storm brewing up, and we had just returned to London after a trivial matter of some impudent highwayman at Putney Heath, of no great importance save that it had kept me out of London since Saturday noon and caused me to miss Divine Service at St Giles Church yesterday; a matter I attend to with some care unless there happens to be a pugilistic contest or other sporting event announced, as in the Bow Street Patrol it pays you always to keep Providence well on your side.

To start with then you are to see Maggsy and me—though somewhat uncertainly in the thick air, smoke and candlelight— seated at a settle and rough table in the Brown Bear Tavern along with a certain Mr Popham Snadge, who had come up to me no more than a minute before and most earnestly desired and requested me to relate to him the remarkable story of my early life for publication, so he said, in *The Gentleman's Maga-*

9

zine; a most respectable journal. As to the Brown Bear I shall say little of it now for I have explained it several times before, but in brief it is a flash house close by the Bow Street Office; the haunt and meeting place of as pretty a pack of rogues, villains, pimps, dips, sweaters, and receivers as ever you saw, and not by any means to be recommended to ladies, gentlemen with gold watches, or canonical visitors from the country. Nevertheless it suits me well enough as I often pick up odds and snippets of curious information here, while One Eyed Jack, the landlord, still contrives to keep a fair to middling drop of claret in spite of the war, no doubt smuggled, and the saucy trollop of a serving wench minds her manners with me; though now and again turning a naughty eye on Master Maggsy, as she seems to fancy the little monster. God knows why; I wouldn't.

This Mr Snadge was unknown to me, having been waiting for us to appear and then present himself; nor did I take to him all that much as being a kind of mule between a lean and over obsequious school usher, yet with an uncommon knowing look in his eye, and a Grub Street scribbler, though better turned out than most of that rumble guts and down trodden tribe. But to tell the truth I took little notice of him, even had it been possible in dim and murky light and babel of voices, rude jests and singing, as it is becoming not uncommon for me to be invited to give some account of myself to one or another of the newsprints; a courtesy of which I am always particular obliging. So the fellow was dipping his pocket quill into the little ink bottle he carried hung on his coat like so many of these reporters, scribbling away for dear life, when One Eyed Jack approached bearing a folded paper sealed with wafer and saying, 'Be hanged, Mr Sturrock, I very near forgot this. Was left for ye yesterday noon; and said to be in haste.'

'And hanged you might well be before you've done, Jack,' I replied with the utmost pleasantness, surveying the superscription written in a not ill formed feminine hand to "Mr Sturrock, at the Brown Bear or elsewhere; most urgent and privit". 'Who brought this?' I enquired. 'Anybody you know?'

Gazing at me sideways out of his single eye, and that no

maiden's dream of love, Jack shook his head. 'Never see the cove before. Might've been a servant of sorts, but not of no account. Demands "Where's this Sturrock?" and when told you ain't here says "Be damned, I was begged to place it in his own hands. But I can't spend all day about it, so do you pass it him yourself, master." And upon that gives an uncommon leery grin and finished, "You can tell him she's a particular tasty piece if he fancies a ride; ain't never a tastier nor longer golden hair in the whole length of Haymarket." '

'That was yesterday noon, was it?' I asked. 'And you very near forgot to give it me now? Begod, Jack, you'll forget your head one of these days if it ever happens to come loose at the neck.'

He made an observation which I shall not repeat and took himself off in attendance on his undesirable customers again, while I opened the paper to study the few lines of writing on it and our Mr Snadge scratched and muttered, 'Now, Mr Sturrock, if you'll be pleased to attend a minute, sir.'

With only half an ear to him I pulled one of the candles closer to study this mysterious letter with greater care. It was written neat enough, though on poorish paper, and it said, 'Mr Sturrock; Being at St Giles Church this day but not coming upon you there I now send this in haste. I have heard of a secret matter of great import and desire to acquaint you of same, as I wish no part of it for my own life. Please to come privit and discreet after dark by ten this night and oblige; Henriette d'Armande. At the top lodging, 11 Coventry Court, Haymarket, next against the livery stables.'

Simple enough it looked, without hint of the terrible events to come, but no gentleman refuses such an appeal from a lady, and I announced, 'Mr Snadge, with respect to you and the *Gentleman's Magazine* I have fresh business now to hand and fear we must make ours short and sweet. So here's the plain tale. I was born poor yet middling honest; in short of a costermonger and market woman, but decided at a tender age that there was no advancement in that trade. Thereupon I fell in with a Spitalfields silk weaver's family where I lodged as a youth until an occasion when I set about completing the youngest daughter's

11

education under the kitchen table one night, and was so cast incontinent into the street with the toe of the silk weaver's boot up my breech.'

"Well, I dunno,' Mr Snadge observed, 'but that's hardly the *Gentleman's* tone, is it?"

'Dress it up as you will,' I told him handsomely, and continued, 'Upon this I next turned to a study of the law by attending the Courts of Justice to keep warm, as I recollect that year was a bitter winter. Furthermore I attended to my reading and lettering and learned an uncommon fine style of our noble English language from an ancient screever who affected to have been a close companion of the late Doctor Samuel Johnson in his youth.'

'That's good,' Mr Snadge nodded, scribbling like fury and scattering ink from his little bottle, 'that's uncommon fine. Private tutorials by a lifelong *amicus curiae* of the great doctor. What's a screever, Mr Sturrock?'

I gazed at him in some surprise, explaining, 'A screever is a rascal who makes his living by writing begging letters, touching epistles, testimonials for dishonest servants, and any other sort of conning or cozenry which requires a nice turn of phrase.' Reflecting that he was a devilishly odd reporter if he did not know that, I went on, 'So equipped I next fell in with a sodden old lawyer's clerk who employed me to write for him when he was too drunk to hold a quill; but a man of keen wits otherwise, and from him I learned yet more of the Common and a good deal of damned uncommon Law. A most useful and improving association until the rascal fell into a flux and died weeping gin. Upon which I took myself to the office of the Bow Street Courts and enlisted in the Runners to embark on a career which has excited general admiration, being now the first practitioner of our new Art and Science of Philosophical Detection, and also being one of the personal bodyguards to His Majesty the King when called upon. You might almost say a friendly acquaintance,' I added, 'as it's nothing for the good kind old gentleman to exchange a word or two with me now and again. "What, what, what?" says he, "it's you again, Sturrock, is it?" '

Properly impressed Mr Snadge continued to nod and scribble,

and resolving to have done with it and be shot of the fellow I indicated my horrible small companion—now lifting his snub snout out of his pot of beer—and finished, 'And this is my clerk, messenger and general orderly; a most singular contumacious and bloodthirsty little monster. One, Maggsy; of no other name, being of parentage unknown.'

Mr Snadge took that gamely enough, though gazing at the creature as if he could barely believe his eyes; and you could hardly blame him. But he asked kindly, 'Well, my little man, and how old are you?'

I looked on with some interest, more than half expecting to see him get his nose flattened for that address as the child is never one to stand on ceremony, but to my vast surprise Maggsy answered promptly, 'Fifteen as near as anybody can tell, and a most cruel, tragical and pitiful life, being a poor chimney boy at one time and sold to Mr William Makepeace the Practical Chimney Sweeper for a crown piece. But what with singeing my arse climbing the hot chimneys, being smoked out like a badger when I got stuck, and Mr. William Makepeace lamming the hide off me when he was in the gins, I concluded to run away and be a tinker. It's an uncommon romantical tale and I'll tell it you all for a shillun.'

'Be damned, you will not,' I interposed. 'The gentleman don't have time, and no more do we. But that's true enough, Mr Snadge. The rascal was found sheltering from the snow on a dung heap at the King's Head Inn, Roehampton, where some several years since I was enquiring into the matter of a certain titled lady's jewels. He was well on the way to the gallows or transportation no doubt, but out of the softness of my heart I caused him to be doused in the horse trough to cleanse him a bit and thereafter took him into my service.'

'Out of being up to the back teeth in mulled claret more like,' Maggsy observed, much put out at being stopped short in his opera.

Mr Snadge rose, saying, 'I'm obliged to you, sir,' putting away his quill in its case and stoppering his ink bottle. I would have liked to make a better tale of it for *The Gentleman's Magazine*, and liked it better still had Mr Snadge taken his turn to pay for another pint of claret, but my mind was more on that letter. It was still lying there under my hand and seemingly of some interest to Mr Snadge also, for his eyes lingered on it an instant and he looked about to ask another question; but these reporters are all a damnation inquisitive tribe, and it might have been merely the habit of his trade. Whatever it was he thought better of it, repeated only, 'I'm uncommonly obliged,' and then after several more civil leave takings set to shouldering his way out through the reek and the thickening crowd to the door.

'You would spoil it, wouldn't you?' Maggsy demanded aggrievedly. 'I could've milked a shillun out of him as easy as rolling Nan over. Not as I took much cock's eyes to him,' he added darkly. 'If you ask me he ain't nothing like so simple as he looks.'

'We'll have less talk of rolling over that trollop at your age,' I admonished him. 'She'd eat you alive. And Mr Snadge's simplicity or otherwise hadn't escaped my notice either, but it's no concern of ours. We've got more important business on hand, so let's set about it.'

I urged him on his way with a light touch of my cane, and we left the rude clamour of the Bear to turn our steps westwards under a lowering and smoky sky and a growl of thunder above the rattle and clatter of the streets; through the torches and flares of Covent Garden into the darker and narrower alleys beyond, out in safety to the more modish spaces of Leicester Square, and so on to the elegant glitter of the Haymarket. It was by then near enough ten o'clock and the nightly bustle at its height; carriages, phaetons, and sedan chairs, gentlemen off to their clubs and houses of entertainment, ladies attended by servants and grooms, soldiers and the commoner sort looking for what they could pick up, street arabs, sweepers, and vendors adding their cries to the hubbub, and all a spectacle under the blaze of candles from countless shops and fashionable establishments.

But Coventry Court was close and silent, a crooked leg passage of stablings and tall old buildings huddled against each other, a few dim lit windows and a lantern or two which served only to make the shadows more obscure. A rabble of chairmen

14

arguing at one ordinary after the surly manner of their kind, at another a patch of light spilling out on the cobbles with half a dozen coachmen drinking and waiting for their carriages to be called to the theatre; a stable boy in close conversation with a wench on the steps of a doorway, and four or five more sitting by a candle over dice on an upturned pail. It was no worse than a hundred other mews courts but Maggsy announced, 'I don't reckon much of this lot neither; here's a fine place to get yourself filleted. If you ask me, you're looking for trouble again, Mr Sturrock; God's Pickles, you can sniff out trouble quicker'n a dog can smell muck.'

There was trouble indeed, though when we came to it the house itself was commonplace enough. Plainly a lodging for whores—any man of experience can pick 'em out on the instant—and like most such places with an ancient crone nodding and snoring in a kind of little cupboard under the stairs; but sharp as a vixen, for as we approached she opened one wicked eye and demanded, 'What d'ye want?'

'Mademoiselle d'Armande,' I told her.

'She's receiving a'ready,' the hag answered snappishly. 'Young gen'leman went up not a minute back.'

'She'll receive me too,' I said. 'I'm expected.'

The creature stuck out a claw from her shawls saying, 'It'll be a shillun; gen'lemen commonly gives me a shillun to pass up. Be damned,' she cackled on a blast of porter, 'Miss Hoity-toit's driving a trade tonight. Was two not an hour since, and next this young 'un, and now you.'

I was about to advise her where she might go for her shilling when there was a sudden noise from above. It might have been a cry or a curse; then a door banging and footsteps coming down the stairs at a rush and seemingly tripping over every other step in their flight. 'We're late,' I started but then wasted no more words, thrusting the woman aside and careering up myself with Maggsy at my heels as fast as the other was descending. There was just enough light to see by from a little night glim placed on each landing and before you could stop to draw breath, as we turned one corner and he another, a dark figure with its coats flying came tumbling at us with a crash which

15

damned nearly pitched us all over in a heap. He let out a fresh curse on that, and I said, 'Whoa there, my man, steady your leaders. What's this then?'

'Have done, you rogues,' the hag screeched from below. 'I won't have no fighting. I'll call my man and have you put out.'

'Be quiet there, you old bags,' I commanded her. 'This is the Bow Street Patrol,' and then taking a fresh grip on the man, with Maggsy clinging to him like a terrier, repeated, 'What's this I say? Been up to mischief, have you?'

That calmed the rascal. At the mention of Bow Street he stopped struggling and gave me a chance to take stock of him. A youngish fellow and handsome enough in his way; dark hair, straight eyebrows and squarish chin, what might be a devil may care manner when not so agitated and even maybe a touch of the foreigner; pretty well dressed, though not extravagant, and plainly not short of a guinea or two. All in all, I concluded, about half and half towards a blood; not quite gentry but near enough. He looked down at Maggsy and tried a laugh. 'God's Blood,' he enquired, 'does it bite? Or do you tell it to lie down? Bow Street, did you say?'

Maggsy made his own answer to that impertinence, while I answered sharply, 'The Runners,' and roared down at the old crone, 'By God, woman, if you don't stop that damned yellocking I'll have you in Newgate quicker'n you can take another breath.' This silenced her too, and I continued to our young sprig, 'Now then, I'm seeking Henriette d'Armande.'

'Begod,' he answered coolly, 'you'll have to seek a cursed long way then. But it's no affair of mine and I'll not detain you from it.'

'No, sir,' I said in my soft and terrible manner, 'we'll have you come with us.'

'Why, God damn your eyes,' he started but then stopped to survey me again and thought better of it. 'Let's have it done with then,' he added pushing Maggsy aside and turning unwillingly to lead the way up the next flight of stairs. 'If you must know,' he flung back over his shoulder, 'she's dead, poor bitch, and none too pretty of it. But I say again it's no affair of mine.'

16

Down below the old hunks was muttering and cursing as we went up past the next landing, where one door was opened a crack and then closed again as we passed and behind another a woman's voice cried, 'It's only drunken roisterers, you fool,' for that is the secret habit of these establishments. You'll never find one where the inmates don't go to ground at the first hint of mischief. We might have been alone in the place as we came to the top where there was a crack of light showing under one last door. This I put my foot against and thrust open myself, urging our reluctant guide in front of us.

It was a biggish apartment for a garret; heavy with close air and female perfume, and though there were several candles placed in their holders only one was burning; that set on a little table by the head of the bed and casting its soft glow on a still, silent figure lying about midway between this and the door; as if it had been trying to reach the bed itself. As might be expected Master Maggsy was the first to speak. 'What done for her, I wonder?' he demanded, 'God A'mighty, look at her face.'

Driving the monster back with a touch of my cane, ordering him to light the other candles to see what we were about, I paused to survey the poor creature myself. Not more than five and twenty, I judged—though it takes a better man even than I am to be certain of a woman's age these days—she was half on her back with one arm stretched out and the palm of the hand upwards, dressed in respectable outdoor apparel and walking pattens, a light cashmere shawl pinned by a heavy brooch at her breast, and a bonnet with the ribbons loosened which seemed to have rolled a little distance away as she fell. The clothing was of a nice middling quality and not unbecoming, and she herself had been out of the common pretty, with a particular care to her appearance at one time; a good oval face and full mouth, hair the colour of well ripened corn, and eyes grey inclining to blue.

If whore she was, and there appeared little doubt of it, she was of a better quality than you would expect to find in this house. But the most dreadful features were the strange pallor of her cheeks, the lips drawn back in a mysterious smile, and a look of such helpless anguish and terror in the eyes as I hope I may never see again. It was as if she had perceived Death himself reaching out his hand for her and known herself powerless to stop him.

The fresh candles Maggsy lit added no kindness to the scene, and in their light our man gazed down at her and muttered something on a harsh breath. 'I'll tell you again,' he cried, 'it's no affair of mine. I had no part of it; God damn it, I wouldn't. She was a taking piece.'

'If you ask me,' Maggsy announced judicially, 'she snuffed of the grues. God's Weskit, I seen all sorts, but never one like that before. Mr William Makepeace the Practical Chimney Sweeper used to say there's things that can strike you dead with but a single look.' He peered about over his shoulder apprehensively. 'D'you reckon there's a ghosk or a monster or something up here?'

'Only you,' I told him, turning again to the other man and adding, 'Now then, let's have some sense and short answers. I'd say she fell forward first on her face and she's been turned over since. Was it you?'

'It was not,' he protested. 'I came in with never a thought carrying a bottle of wine for us both.' He jerked his head at an armchair, where there was an unopened bottle lying on the seat as if tossed down in haste, and continued, 'She was expecting me. The door was half open and I damned near walked over her. I'll tell you plain, one look at that was enough. I fancy I must have let out a cry I was so put back.'

'So you did,' I observed. 'And very natural. It'd be a vexatious discovery after what no doubt you was expecting. But we all have these disappointments now and again. Did you light that candle?'

'It was already burning,' he avowed. 'That I'll swear to.'

'You'll very likely swear on Newgate drop before you've done,' I promised him kindly. I mused on the candles for a minute, and it was plain enough. Those Maggsy had lit were new, put fresh in their holders today, while by the length of it the other must have been burning for an hour or more. It might mean much or little, but there were more pressing matters for now, and I

18

said, 'Give me a hand to lift her.' Though the fellow was somewhat unwilling he took her by the heels and between us we laid the poor mortality on her bed, which must have observed many a different scene; then I commanded, 'Bring those candles closer.'

With the two of them holding these on each side, a sudden uneasy draught causing the shadows to waver and creep in the corners of the chamber, I set to work to examine the woman; and to be plain and short discovered nothing. There was no taint or stink of anything untoward or acidulous, no sign of staining or burning about the mouth—as she might have swallowed something which disagreed with her—and no sign of wounding, pistol ball, stabbing or other mistreatment. Save for the dread filled look in her eyes there was nothing to be seen; only one small cut, scarcely more than a scratch on the inside of her left wrist. But that should not have harmed a baby and it might even have been caused by the pin of her own brooch; you can inflict worse on yourself being careless about sharpening a quill, and this must have been done some hours since for what trace of blood there was, seemingly wiped away with a kerchief, had dried long ago.

Discontented and perplexed I drew back at last saying, 'You can cover her up; and you, Maggsy, fetch that ugly hunks from below. These old Jezebels are commonly as sharp as ferrets, and I'll have it out of her about the two other gentlemen who came here.'

Even as I spoke there was what sounded like another cry in the silence of the house. It seemed to be cut short suddenly and up here there came the moan and rattle of a breath of wind on the tiles outside and a fresh distant grumble of thunder. 'What was that?' the child demanded fearfully. 'I don't like this lot, nor I don't like this Coventry Court neither; I told you, she snuffed of seeing something as didn't ought to be here. Mr William Makepeace used to tell of a doxy who fell into convulsions and snuffed horrible on catching sight of the Devil, and he should've knowed. And who was it give a screech then? That's what I ask.'

'You'd best go to find out,' I advised him. 'If you see any-

19

thing half as ugly as yourself, depend upon it he'll die first.'

He went off complaining and cursing, taking one of the candles for comfort, while I drew a cover over that pitiful face and then turned to survey our young man once more. Unless he was a better actor than any they have at Drury Lane—though that would not be difficult of late—he was innocent I concluded. I fancied also that he was more affected than he chose to show, and asked, 'What was she to you? I'd say by your cut that what you most look for in women is common to all of 'em; so was she just another trot? Or something more?'

He was recovering fast for he cried, 'Be damned, I'll thank you to keep a civil tongue in your head. She was a whore plain enough, but not of her own choice and a better sort than most. She came over from Paris in '93, escaping the Terror.'

I studied him pityingly. 'And no doubt a slip of some noble family? She'd be about fourteen then. D'you mean to say you swallowed that one? God help you, they've all got some such tale. But let it pass. Tell me instead, who and what are you? And we'll have the truth, my man, for your own sake.'

'No reason why you shouldn't,' he answered pertly. 'Rodney Pottle; articled to the law firm of Pottle Soskins and Pottle, Lincoln's Inn. And, by God,' he added, 'if the old man ever comes to hear of this he'll put a guinea in the bank and have me live on the interest.'

'I wouldn't be surprised,' I observed. 'You're a damned uncommon articled apprentice, even for the law. But if you do as you're told and answer questions maybe he don't need to hear of it. Now then; you're sure it is Henriette d'Armande? And how long have you known her?'

He glanced at the shrouded figure lying silent on the bed. 'It's Henriette sure enough. I've known her about a week. Was at Vauxhall Gardens. She seemed to be running from somebody in the press by the Rotunda and came slap into my arms. Then nothing would suit her but I should engage a hackney on the instant and bring her back here.'

'So ho,' I mused. 'Well, Vauxhall's become a vulgar place of late. I never go there myself. Now did she. . . ."

But before I could frame the question there came yet another screech; and this time the unmistakable melodious and dove-like tones of Master Maggsy with his feet clumping up the stairs at a gallop, and an instant later the door flung open to reveal him like a statue of Doom with a candle. 'Be damned,' I cried, 'what's this now?'

'Not a lot,' he answered, 'oh no, not much. Save you won't get nothing out that old trollop. One thing it ain't a ghosk, and I'm thankful of that; not unless ghosks goes around with pig stickers tucked up their weskits. Corpussed,' he announced briefly.

'What's this?' I repeated. 'Another vexation?'

Thrusting him aside I started down those damned stairs with Mr Pottle coming after me and Maggsy clattering behind exclaiming, 'It vexed her all right; God's Whiskers, it would me too. There on the floor she is, a welter of blood and a hole as big as Puddle Dock in her guzzler.'

Nor was it an inapt description, though coarse. The creature was lying with a filthy stain spreading about her on the stone flags and one glance was enough, for the villain who had done this had been quick and certain and knew his business; whatever that woman had seen tonight she would never talk about. Wasting no time on her I stepped nicely over the mess of blood to the door, which was now swinging half open and letting in a gust of rain. But there was nothing to be seen out there either. Not a soul in sight; a carriage or two and horses waiting at the far end of the narrow court, the few lanterns and patches of light flickering and splashing in the sudden downpour, the shadows even blacker, and all else gone to shelter. We should have no good of chasing and hallooing out here, for our villain would be streets away by now with nobody to see him go, and I drew back inside to give some vent to my feelings.

By now also some of the secret people in the house were creeping out of their holes; a few faces peering over the banisters, and one fellow on the first landing demanding, 'God's sake, what's this?'

'Murder, my man,' I told him shortly. 'Now get back, all of you, and keep quiet. There's nobody leaves this house tonight before I give the word; and if you're late home to your wives you may tell 'em it's the compliments of Bow Street.' I did not expect much of anybody here either, but the power of the law must be upheld, and when one or two made some expostulation I roared, 'Back, I say, or I'll have all of you in a damned sight colder lodging than this.'

There are few care to argue with me when I take that tone, and turning afresh to Maggsy and Pottle I continued, 'Now you two; fetch the watchman and the Parish Constable if you can find the useless rascals, and notify the mortuary men and coroner's officers. Maggsy knows what to do,' I told Mr Pottle, and added, 'likewise I want you back here, and if you know what's good for yourself and the firm of Pottle Soskins and Pottle you'll make no mistake about it. And on your way you can ask up and down the court whether anybody was seen here just before the rain started. Though I doubt you'll get much out of that.'

So sending the pair off in spite of Master Maggsy's further complaints about the rain and some monster lurking in the darkness with an all too ready knife, I locked the door behind them, took the key, and returned to my own business. The old woman was not worth a second look—she was no oil painting at the best of times—and I passed back up the stairs in a profound manner, affecting never a second glance at the eyes watching me from the cracks of one door after another. But I stopped at the last, as I judged precisely under Henriette d'Armande's chamber.

This one alone was still closed, with certain scufflings, murmurings, and giggles from within, and I cried, 'Open here, and look sharp; this is the Bow Street Patrol.' Then with that genteel notice, to give them decent time to collect themselves, I put my foot hard against the lock and burst it in.

It flew back to reveal a pretty connubial picture. A wench sitting up on the bed as pert as a buttercup with a monstrous hairy fellow, a countryman by his looks, reclining beside her and both sharing a pot of porter. They was somewhat discomposed by my unceremonious appearance and the fellow started up roaring, 'Who the hell are you? God blast your eyes, get out of it before I break your neck.'

22

'Easy now,' I admonished him. 'It ain't a soft joint to crack. Didn't you catch what I said, or haven't you ever heard of Bow Street?' I produced my baton and crown to prove my credentials, and continued, 'Cover yourself up, you ain't near as pretty as your mistress. There's been murder done here, or a brace of murders, and it's not seemly to appear like that.'

The wench let out a squeak and I said, 'One Henriette d'Armande up aloft, and a very provoking way of doing it too, and the other that old woman who kept the door.'

The trot seemed more engaged than affected, crying, 'What? Old Mother Grope? I always said somebody'd do for her one of these days. But what's this about Henriette?'

'Just what I've told you,' I said. 'Neither more nor less. So let's have some quick answers. What d'you know about her?'

'Why nothing,' she replied. 'Save she's Miss Hoity-toits.'

I reflected on that for a minute. 'A cut above you lot, was she? And how long's she been here; in this house?'

The naked trollop looked at me wickedly out of the corners of her eyes and then in provocation pushed the sheet back further with a not unshapely leg. 'How of damnation should I know? A bit above a week I fancy.'

'And where did she come from?'

The hairy fellow cursed, pulling up the cover to himself as fast as his doxy pushed it off, but the wench was a hard bitch even with murder in the house for she answered, 'Lookee now, Master Thieftaker, it's naught to do with us. Me and my friend've been busy this two hours or more; and reckon to be busy for another two if you'll let us be, for Mr Barber's a bold rogue and likes his oats. All I can tell you is Mother Grope had some tale Henriette was one of Madame Rosamunda's girls.'

'He don't look all that bold,' I observed. 'Madame Rosamunda, is it? Then what the devil was the wench doing in a house like this?' That seemed another mystery, for Madame Rosamunda's elegant establishment in James Street was well known; a most particular salon for the nobility and gentry, and some uncommonly fanciful nightly entertainments there if only half the tales told about it were true. 'What was she doing here?' I repeated.

23

Miss Pert stretched and arched herself, hitching up her tits, put her hands behind her head and yawned, saying, 'I wisht to God you'd have done. Between you and Mr Barber I shan't get no sleep tonight. She most likely fell out with Madame. That's easy enough, so I've heard.'

'You're uncommon cool about it all,' I mused. 'I wouldn't wonder if we have to get you to Bow Street to find out why; if you're still alive by the morning. Get this in your noddle as easy as you get other things elsewhere, you trollop; there's been two murders done already and there might be more. And you one of 'em.'

'What?' she screeched, jerking herself bolt upright and toss-ing her shaggy swain out on to the floor, where he fell to curs-ing again and scrabbling for his britches and shirt; a most unlovely sight. 'God damn you, why didn't you tell us so be-fore?' she demanded.

'That's better,' I said. 'Now we'll have quick questions and short answers. You say you've been here the better of two hours. So did you hear anything up there? Moving about, conversa-tion, a sudden cry as if the woman might have been taken with sickness or a fit and called for help?'

She shook her head. 'Never a sound. I'd ha' thought there was nobody there. But was two went up a while back. And an-other not long since; and then a damnation racket of traipsing and running.'

I cut her short. 'We know that. How many of you are there in the house?'

'Five,' she replied. 'And Mother Grope. She takes a shilling or two from gentlemen to admit 'em. And there's William Tooley lodges here.'

'He'll be the bulldog? So where is he now?'

'Ain't he there? Be damned, here's a nice thing; murder and thieftakers, and our man not in the house. Boozing most likely.'

'It's a vulgar habit of such fellows,' I observed. 'Do you pay this old woman for your lodging?'

The trot gazed at me in astonishment. 'God's sake, no. She's a mere servant. We pay to Madame Rosamunda.'

'So ho,' I mused. 'Madame Rosamunda again. That lady

24

seems to have a finger in some tasty pies.'

'The fat sow's got more than a finger,' she replied. 'She's up to her arse in 'em.'

On this there came a thunderous banging at the door below and I descended once more, this time to admit the Parish Constable and a watchman; one little less than half drunk and the other a bit more than half simple. But that is the common sort with these poor rogues; they were good enough for all that was needed now, and leaving them to their business I returned myself to a round of questioning the other lodgers and their customers. To be short about that I discovered no more than I had already learned from the love birds upstairs and received a great deal of pertness and impudence as I was about it; one fellow so far forgot himself that I was forced to remonstrate with him ungently, and left him moaning, cursing and spitting out teeth in the arms of his ministering angel while she made several observations which I shall not repeat. There is no respect for the law in London these days.

Before I had finished this Master Maggsy and Mr Pottle came back; seemingly boon companions by now and by the look of them had taken a drink or two on the way, which if I knew Maggsy Mr Pottle must have paid for. A few sharpish observations soon calmed their exuberance however, the more so as I sent them out immediately again to look in the beer houses along the court and elsewhere for the man William Tooley. This was something more from which I did not expect much even if they found the fellow—save that it must have been he who brought Henriette d'Armande's note to the Brown Bear—but it got the pair of them out from under my heels and left me at leisure to search her chamber.

Neither was there much to find here. Not all that many clothes, though again of a better sort than the gaudery with which some of these cheaper daughters of Venus adorn themselves; yet a few articles of feminine underwear in uncommonly fine and elegant material but old, much faded, carefully repaired, and even monogrammed with the letters "H.A." done curiously in newer and brighter silk. A few trinkets, but none of much note, seven sovereigns and some odd silver coins, a pretty little

25

Prayer Book bound in blue morocco, and a small writing case or box in inlaid wood. This contained several fancy quills, all well sharpened down and treasured for a long time, wafers, and paper of a poorer quality than the box itself; the same kind as that on which she had written to me. There was nothing else; no scrap of other written matter either in this case or elsewhere in the chamber. My only other discovery was a square of folded pasteboard wedged under a short leg of the table by the bedside, seemingly to make it stand more firmly; an admission card to a subscription rout at the Assembly Rooms, Bath, and dated some six months before.

It was little enough on which to shape a history of the poor soul, but I fancied I could read certain outlines. I sat musing for a time on these pathetic remainders until the tramp of Maggsy's dainty feet heralded his return with Mr Pottle. His news also was much as I expected. The man Tooley had been seen, as he often was, in two of the nearby beerhouses tonight but he was nowhere to be found now.

It was then long past twelve and I said heavily, 'Let it be then. If he's gone to ground we've lost him tonight, and if he's not we'll find him tomorrow. There's little more we can do here; it's for the mortuary men now.' Even Master Maggsy perceived that this was no time for poetics and remained wisely silent while I continued, 'Now, Mr Rodney Pottle, there're certain questions I mean to ask you, though I'll let you sleep on the thought of 'em first. But I want you at Bow Street sharp and early in the morning. And make no mistake on it, if you're not there I'll have a warrant out against you. Is that plain enough?'

Seemingly it was, for he also divined that silence was the better part of wisdom and nodded without speaking. Then placing the money and poor trinkets, prayer book and rout card to carry away and lodge at Bow Street I finished, 'Now let's get out of this. There's something so damnation wicked in the air here that it makes even my blood run cold.'

TWO

I have set all this down with some particularity so that you shall know as much about the wicked devilment as I then did myself, and so to continue I was at Bow Street early next morning; that being Tuesday. Early as it was however our clerk, old Abel Makepenny, was even then scratching away at his papers with one eye cocked for me and an air of great events afoot; and no sooner had I appeared than he advised me in an agitated whisper that Mr A was already in his chamber and I was to present myself on the instant. This Mr A is our Chief Magistrate and head of the Bow Street Patrol—first founded by Mr Henry Fielding to put down the shocking misdemeanours of London—who receives complaints of crime and gives us our orders; and he is not a man to be trifled with as being of a damnation tetchy nature resultant on the gout, this arising from an over indulgence in port against all entreaties to take to Madeira. But a sagacious man otherwise in spite of an inordinate desire to have a handle to his name and be addressed as 'Sir Thomas' instead of plain 'mister'.

Today he was in no more than middling sarcastic mood, studying a letter on heavily important paper, and he looked up from it to observe, 'Well, good day to ye, Sturrock. It's fine and civil of you to be so early about. Or have you caught a hint of this a' ready? Bedamned, if they've notified you before me I'll have somebody's ears for it.'

Somewhat puzzled I replied, 'As to that, sir, I can't say before you tell me what it is. But I've caught more than a hint of a particular uncommon piece of devilment.' I was carrying Henriette d'Armande's writing case with me, and I placed it on the corner of his desk, adding, 'I've hopes that something here might help us in the matter.'

27

'What's that then?' he enquired though with no great interest, still thinking of his letter.

'One murder after another, sir,' I replied, 'at a certain kind of house off the Haymarket yesterday.'

I explained it briefly, but before I could finish he interrupted testily, 'God's sake, whores in the Haymarket; what's so uncommon about that? You've more important business now. You're summoned to Whitehall, my man. It seems Billy Pitt finds he can't conclude this little affair of Bonaparte without your advice and assistance.'

"Well, sir,' I said, 'I've served His Majesty, and I rate him higher than a mere Prime Minister.'

'Ye'll get a bit above yourself before you've done, Sturrock,' Mr A observed, shifting his gouty foot on its stool and cursing 'Was ever a man so plagued? Here.' He tossed the letter at me across his desk, and continued, 'You are requested and required to present yourself at the above mentioned office by eleven of the forenoon today. I am further requested and required to afford you such leave of absence as may be necessary for you to discharge such duties and instructions as may then be communicated to you. We are severally required, requested, and enjoined to observe the strictest secrecy and discretion as touching affairs of His Majesty's Government and the safety of this Realm. Begod,' he concluded, 'it seems we've hatched a swan in a brood of Bow Street ducks.'

Ducks, drakes, or swans, there was no mention of Mr Pitt nor any other of their Lordships of the Treasury in the clerical copper plate writing, being signed simply 'Yr obnt svnt, Charles Edward Grimble;' and judging by the fellow's tone he did not sound at all obedient or our servant either. Nor was I best pleased to be drawn away from the Haymarket matter but there seemed no help for it, and I said, 'It'll be spies or Frenchy agents, no doubt. The place is swarming with the rascals and we're bound to check their pranks if we can. Yet this Coventry Court affair's a wicked business. There's little doubt the old woman was done for to stop her describing the two men who came there, and it's my belief that Henriette d'Armande was poisoned. But how or by what means is a mystery.' I continued with some care, for when he had the gout on him Mr A was tetchy about being offered advice. 'If you could drop a hint to our Coroner to perform an anatomy on her it might tell us something.'

'What?' he demanded, 'that barrel of piss and port? Much good you'll get of him. True enough he's a surgeon of a sort, but he'll be full of huffs and puffs and ifs and maybes.' There was little love lost between our office and the Borough Coroner, Dr Badger, and Mr A shifted his aching foot and cursed afresh at the thought of him. 'You're a pertinacious rogue,' he grumbled, 'and you'd best be off about your own business. But I'll have Makepenny write a request. And I'll set Ludwell on to investigate.'

I was little better pleased by that, for once Ludwell got tramping about the Haymarket with his great shire horse feet there was no telling how many rabbits he'd start bolting to their burrows; though an estimable colleague otherwise. I resolved to say nothing of Mr Rodney Pottle yet, not least as I might have my own use for that gentleman, and replied instead, 'A capital notion, sir; Ludwell's the very man. And better still for being a first class horseman, as he's never tired of telling us.'

Mr A gazed at me suspiciously. 'What the devil d'ye mean by that?'

'The young woman had connections somewhere.' Opening her writing case I produced the Prayer Book and Assembly Rooms admission card. 'Mr Ludwell might even pick up something of them if you'd consider sending him to Bath. You'll note the card has a number on it, sir; and you'll know these things are sold by circulating libraries, the modish sort of ladies' shops, and suchlike. It shouldn't be beyond Mr Ludwell's wit to find out who purchased this. And the Prayer Book's a pretty thing. He might even discover where that came from.'

'Your new promotion's addled your wits, Sturrock,' Mr A observed. 'Send a man to Bath for the sake of a whore? Two days each way, and God knows how long idling about once he's there. It ain't worth it.'

'No, sir,' I agreed, 'maybe it's not. But it ain't so much the

29

matter of a common trot as a manner of murder we've never seen before. And I hope we may never see it again and not know what it is.'

The good gentleman made a rumbling sound not unlike the guns being run out on a man of war, took a breath before the broadside, and cursed yet more vividly as the excitement sent a fresh dart of gout through his burning foot. 'What?' he roared. 'You damned insolent rogue, would you teach me my duty? Be off about your business before you drive me to an apoplexy. Be off and leave me to thank God you'll be out of my sight for a bit.'

Not displeased by this outcome, for I could be sure by now that Mr Ludwell would be sent out of my way and might even discover something in Bath if Providence took him by the hand and led him to it, I returned to old Abel's office where by now Mr Rodney Pottle was seated on a bench waiting for me. Seen in daylight and recovered from that horrid spectacle last night he was a spriggish young rogue, and a damned sight more devil may care than any respectable lawyer who is up to his hocks in this kind of affair has any right to be. Abel was plainly at a loss with him, but before the fellow could say anything himself I started, 'By God, you're a fortunate man, Mr Pottle. The Magistrate was all for having you before the Court and committing you this very morning, but I talked him out of it.'

'And uncommon civil of you,' he retorted. 'But you'd have the devil of a job to commit me for anything, and well you know it.'

'Don't be too sure. Mr Abel Makepenny and me between us could swear a committal against the Archangel Gabriel if we put our minds to it,' I warned him, while Abel contrived to look as dark as a hanging judge himself; though a bit spoiled by dusting the snuff out from inside his nose with the feather of his quill. I continued, 'A mere articled apprentice'd be cat's meat; but I want a few words with you first, Mr Pottle, though I don't have time for many and not here.' I finished to the old gentleman, 'If Mr A should come enquiring, Abel, tell him I'm on my way to Whitehall at a trot,' and urged Pottle out of the

30

door to the street before he had time to find another pert answer.

Here Master Maggsy was also waiting, sitting on the steps and exchanging polite returns with other street arabs while surveying the passing traffic, and stirring him up too I led the way at a brisk pace through the morning crowds, round into Drury Lane and then to Will's Coffee House giving no pause for question or answer. This was pretty quiet, with the wenches still dusting and cleaning—for it is much affected by actors, who do not commonly show themselves much before midday— but it suited my purpose, and I found a corner settle and started, 'Now Mr Pottle.'

'I made sure you was going to lock him up,' Maggsy complained bitterly. 'I reckoned he was in the Common Lodging for certain and worth a shilling a time to me to bring in his dinner and supper. And what's more. . . .'

I cut him short, saying, 'There'll be no need of that; or not yet, so long as Mr Pottle knows what cards he's got and how many tricks I hold. Now,' I repeated, 'you say Henriette came running into you through the press by the Rotunda at Vauxhall as she might have been escaping from somebody. Did you see who it was?'

He shook his head. 'I was a damned sight more concerned with gazing at her.'

'You would be,' I observed. 'So what was her manner? Was it offended or afrighted? Or getting on for the vapours? You saw the look in her eyes last night. Was it anything similar?'

'I'd just as soon forget the look in her eyes.' He shifted uneasily on the settle. 'It was nothing like that, and not the vapours either; Henriette wasn't the vapouring kind. She was agitated, or so it seemed. To tell the truth when she cannoned into me I took it for a fresh trick of the trade.'

'What, do you know 'em all then?' Maggsy enquired with some interest. 'I'll wager you don't; Mr William Makepeace, the Practical Chimney Sweeper, used to declare there never was a man living as could.'

'So you brought her back to Coventry Court,' I said, silencing

31

the lewd little monster. 'And how often have you been with her since?'

'There was that time and a week gone today. Then I was away on affairs for Pottle Soskins and Pottle; in Bath. We appointed to meet again last night.'

'Begod, was you setting up to take a lease on her? So you went to Bath, did you?' I regarded him thoughtfully. 'Now then, did she ever give a hint of being in danger or that somebody might be after her? Did she ask you for help of any sort?'

He considered that and then shook his head again, but added, 'That last night, last Tuesday, I had a notion that she was going to ask for something.' He looked somewhat shame-faced. 'To be plain I fancied she was weighing me to see what I was worth. But she seemed to think better of it, and only begged me to come to her when I returned from Bath. Yesterday, as would be.'

'So ho,' I mused, reflecting on the note she had sent me in such haste on the day before, the Sunday. 'We're doing very well. You're plainly a man of experience, Mr Pottle. So would you fancy she was an old hand at the game; or pretty fresh to it?'

'God damn it, you're a hard case,' he started. 'Not as old as some. I've told you, she seemed a better sort than most.'

'And her tale was she came from Paris, in '93, from the Terror. It's not impossible, though she'd be a child at the time. And not a whore of her own choice? That's common enough too. But did she add any more? Of whom she came from France with; or of living with some family. Maybe in the country?'

The young gentleman was growing impatient. 'She spoke of the country when I said I must go to Bath. But be damned, I didn't ask questions. Why should I?'

'Then I'll answer some for you,' I told him kindly. 'I'd say she was most likely a governess in some fairish establishment. It's the mode to have your children learn French these days. I'd say she was in poor circumstances herself, but neat, orderly, and well thought of; and the lady of the house at least was kind in giving her articles of cast off clothing. The rest of it's a guess, maybe, but I'll say further that some other person in the place

32

might have presented her with something more; which the said lady would have reckoned too much kindness. It's not an uncommon thing. And less common still for a wench turned off without character or reference to come and try her luck in the Haymarket.'

'She could have gone to a screever to have him make her a testimonial,' Maggsy put in. 'Old Holy Moses can write one to melt the tripes of a moneylender.'

'She didn't know any screevers,' I told him. 'Nor the pretty ways of London; not yet.' I turned back to Mr Pottle for a few last questions, as my own time was running short now. 'Did she ever speak of Madame Rosamunda's?'

He gazed at me open mouthed. 'Never a word. That's the fancy shop in James Street, ain't it? I never tried that one myself, don't get a big enough allowance, but by all they say about it. . . .'

'By all they say,' I interrupted, 'it's no place for an articled apprentice of Pottle Soskins and Pottle.' I affected to consider him, for I could already see a way to make use of the young rascal and work faster than Mr Ludwell, and then said, 'I'm not by any means satisfied with you; but I might be if you made yourself useful. Can you get leave of absence from that respectable firm?'

He grinned at me cheerfully. 'I wouldn't be surprised. I ain't all that much of an articled apprentice.'

'The black sheep, are you?' I asked. 'And like to be blacker still if they ever hear of this lot. What was it you said your old father would do? Put a guinea in the bank and have you live on the interest? Well now, Mr Pottle, here are your instructions. First to go to Coventry Court and discover whether the man Tooley is back at that house yet. But take care not to frighten him or anybody else. You should let on to be a Frenchy; some *émigré* society or the other offering a reward for any information about the poor young lady. Drop a hint or two that you don't give a damn for the English law and you'll have 'em round you like wasps at a honey pot. After that you can go on to Madame Rosamunda's.' The whoring rogue lit up like a lantern at that, and I added sharply, 'From the outside.

Here you may affect to have a particular fancy for one of the ladies, and free with your money. Servants, flunkeys, hackney drivers, chairmen; anybody you can find. I want a list of Madame's clients.'

'Mr Sturrock,' he said, jumping up like a jack in the box, 'I'm already starting to it.'

Maggsy's face was as black as thunder, opening his big mouth for another pretty observation, but I stopped him before he could get it out, while Pottle was on his way to the door. 'Mr Pottle,' I asked, 'did you and Henriette d'Armande talk in English or French?'

'A bit of each,' he answered easily enough. 'Why d'you ask?'

'It's no great matter. But you speak French then?'

'Pretty well,' he agreed. 'My mother's French; of the family Latour, the Paris notaries.'

I looked at him with fresh interest. 'And up to their eyes in the Revolution no doubt? There was a fine gaggle of lawyers behind that mischief.'

'Not the Latours,' he replied shortly. 'The Pottles and Soskins had business connections with the Latours for years before the Revolution. They were Royalists; and lost their heads for it.'

'And most unfortunate,' I observed. 'Well then, Mr Pottle, we'll look to see you at the Brown Bear by nine o'clock tonight to hear what you've discovered.'

'Ever at your service, Mr Sturrock,' he returned, tipping his beaver over his eyes and going off as jaunty as a cockerel.

'Uppish, ain't he?' Maggsy enquired in a rage. 'And what're you at, might I ask? Good enough for low company, am I, but cast off when it comes to a bit of class and a fancy knocking shop in the Haymarket? What d'you fancy he can discover that I can't? Why, God's Whiskers, he ain't even respectable, he ain't got a notion in his head above trots and rollicking; he's very near as bad as you are. Though a comical cove otherwise,' he added generously, with the air of a man prepared to see all aspects.

'Master Maggsy,' I told the child, 'you're a contumacious wretch. Has it escaped your notice that there's swift and sudden death lurking close about Mademoiselle Henriette d'Armande?

Mr. Rodney Pottle's a philosophical experiment. We'll see what he makes of it, and then consider what to make of him; if he's still left to us. And if he's not we shall have a bit more to work on. But presently I've got bigger fish to fry.' I went on to tell him of the summons to Whitehall, and finished, 'Now whistle me a hackney, for I don't propose to approach this important office on foot like a mere artisan. It's a deep and secret business and I shall be some time about it, so you may meet me at Beale's Chop House on Charing Cross for our dinner; and while you're waiting, you yourself may go to the Seven Dials and in-struct Holy Moses that I'll have him also at the Brown Bear tonight.'

I shall explain this canting, canonical old rascal when we come to him, as for now we have more important matters to get on with. So to make it short having paid off my hackney in Whitehall—not without the usual discussion as to fare, man-ners, and parentage with its surly rogue of a driver—I presented myself at this famous office in good time, and was there admit-ted to a long corridor with penitential benches placed along its walls. Here there was a sort of whispering silence broken only by important footsteps now and again, a fellow in a frock coat and a look as if he had a dog's dinner gone bad just under his nose on guard at a pair of double doors, and a dozen to a score of others waiting; they were of conditions from snuff and ink to the military and even foppish, some clutching documents and portfolios, two or three clasping rolls of paper to their chests, and another sleeping as sound as if he had been waiting for a week. Here I cooled my backside by better than an hour while the doorman called one name after another and I restrained my rising choler as best I could, until at last he announced "Mr. Churrock?" and opened the double doors with an expression on his chaps as if the dog's dinner was getting worse every minute.

I was now in a sort of antechamber with several clerks and a smallish fellow having an old wig askew over one ear, and like to nothing in the world so much as a little brown gun dog gone anxious, flapping its ears and trotting up and down between a rabbit hole and a bitch. 'Mr Lubbock, is it?' he asked, consulting a paper and then answering himself. 'No, my God, it ain't, it's Mr Sturrock; well would you believe that? Beautiful weather for the season, ain't it, Mr Stubbock? But my word you're late. It won't do; no by God it won't. We're devils for punctuality and order here, Mr. Burrock; precise and on the dot, that's gov'ment business.' So muttering, while I clutched at what remained of my wits, he galloped to another pair of doors and whispered, 'Mr Spurrock, sir.'

This was a bigger chamber, with tall windows looking out over the Horse Guards Parade to St James's Park, another clerk scribbling for dear life in a corner, and a thin brownish figure standing with his back to me at the windows and watching a troop of volunteer militia on the parade ground. But it was the clerk who took my attention; looking up at me over his papers, shaking his head, and sending a message of entreaty from his eyes. On my part I stood gazing at him in ever more surprise; for it was none other than our would be reporter of *The Gentleman's Magazine*. In short, Mr Popham Snadge.

This, I reflected, might well be an interesting matter before it was done, but I did not speak and the other gentleman turned from the window to survey me; a face like a hatchet carelessly sharpened on a rough grindstone, but more than a touch of the fop about his coat, breeches and lace neck cloth; even affecting a powdered wig in spite of Mr Pitt's war tax on hair powder. He announced, 'By Ged, if them spavin hocks out there are the best we can do we're lost before we start. If they ever see a squadron of French cavalry they'll fall over their own arses,' he continued and then demanded, 'Sturrock, is it? Be demned, sir, you're late. And no demnition excuses, we've no time for 'em. Don't tell me it's the cursed London traffic, for I hear that tale ten times a day. I'll warn you we expect smart work in this service.'

'Quite so, sir,' I agreed, 'I've been observing that for the last hour or more.'

This seemed to give him pause, but when he got his breath back he said, 'Well, demmit, have a seat will you and let's get about it. I can give ye ten minutes.'

'I'm obliged, sir,' I replied politely. 'So if we'd started an hour since we'd have got our business done by now. I presume I'm to wait on Mr Pitt; or some other gentleman of the Treasury?'

A singular silence fell in the chamber broken only by a muffled snort from the clerical Mr Snadge, while the gentleman I took to be Mr Grimble studied me with a curious look. 'Ye'll be surprised,' he answered at last, 'but Mr Pitt feels bound to deny himself that pleasure. He's got a few trifling affairs to see to. Not a lot, but they run away with the time. Come now, Mr Sturrock, let's have done with cock fighting. You've been recommended to us as a rogue, but a resourceful rogue; you're said to be skilled at your trade and to have a wide knowledge of the rascals and villains of London.'

'I'm just as obliged for that testimonial,' I retorted, feeling my neckcloth starting to tighten. 'I'll admit an uncommon knowledge of the rascals and villains, though so far I've had little experience of government gentlemen.'

'I said let's have done with cock fighting.' But there was the beginnings of a grin about his hatchet face. 'Tell me, Mr Sturrock, what do you know of the *émigrés* here?'

'That there's still a damned sight too many of 'em, for all of Bonaparte's edict that they may return to France under an amnesty.'

He took out an elegant French enamelled snuff box and gave himself a pinch, but did not offer it to me. 'Are you aware that some of 'em have been advised that if they remain in England and make themselves useful to Boney it'll be to their advantage when they do go back at last?'

'It's a matter of simple commonsense to suppose that.'

'And do any of these villains of yours consort with *émigrés*?'

I reflected on this for a minute. 'Not as I've ever observed. You'll understand they're of different classes.'

'Aye. But would they if it were made worth their while?'

'Sir,' I said, 'there's nothing in the nature of a villain to prevent him being a true patriotic Englishman. But on the other hand neither is there anything to say he's bound to be. I could show you a score of rascals who would do anything from murder upwards for a sovereign or two.'

Mr Grimble put his snuff box away carefully and asked, 'Ye're aware that we've got our own agents over there?'

'We'd be fools if we hadn't,' I answered shortly.

'And we're not fools.' He pursed up his lips and added, 'Or at least some of us ain't. But I'll come straight to the nub of the matter, Mr Sturrock. We've a suspicion that one of our men may be running with the fox and hunting with the hounds. And we've word from another that whether he's in it or not the Frenchies are in correspondence with their people over here to effect some conspiracy.'

'Now we're talking, sir,' I told him briskly. 'Do we know the nature of it?'

'God demmit, man,' he enquired with the utmost courtesy, 'if we did d'ye think we'd need you? Cut the pack and that's trumps; fire raising and destructions, explosions, assassination, or abduction. D'ye recollect how they whisked Duc d'Enghien away from Baden in March? That rascal Fouché said that was worse than a crime, it was a blunder; but it was a demnition well played trick nonetheless and we wouldn't put it past 'em to try the same one again. Pitt, Canning, Castlereagh, anybody could be murdered or taken. If it was Pitt with the way his Government stands now Fox'd be at Downing Street in a matter of hours; and that'd suit Boney's hand nicely.'

I was in some doubt about this myself as it is in the nature of politicians and government officials to fancy that the sun shines out of their arses and the enemy can't bear the dazzle, but I said nothing while Mr Grimble continued, 'Or there's the Navy. It can't be Nelson for he's at sea, but Barham in the Admiralty or Lord St Vincent could be easy targets. Our fellow at Boulogne tells us that Boney says give him command of the Channel for eight hours and he'll crack us like a rotten nut; and they're the two who're denying it to him.'

He nodded his wig at the window, where the volunteer militia were tumbling over their muskets on the parade. 'That lot out there and others like 'em, and all the country ladies and gentle-men, was expecting the invasion last year and imagine Boney missed his chance; but we know better inside. He's a demned lot more dangerous now than he was then, and might well try to play his cards in the next month or two.'

'So this conspiracy might just as well be some plot to pave the way for him,' I observed.

'It might be anything,' he said testily. 'Ged help us, ain't you got that in your noddle yet? Here, look at that.' Putting his hand within a drawer under the desk he drew something out and tossed it to me.

It was a biggish coin or medal, and a pretty thing. On one side was the head of Napoleon, already crowned with a laurel wreath, on the other a figure of Hercules slaying a sea monster, and the inscription round it read, *"Descente en Angleterre, frappé à Londres en 1804"*. ' "Invasion of England, struck in London",' Mr Grimble kindly translated for my ignorance. 'Struck secretly in Paris a few weeks since,' he added. 'One of our fellows picked it up and brought it over.'

'The damned impudence of the rogue,' I breathed. 'Well, sir, let's set about clipping his wings. You say one of your men runs with the fox and hunts with the hounds.'

'Suspicion only,' Mr Grimble said. 'And we don't know where he is; he's dropped out of sight, either by accident or design. The only man as could tell you much is in Boulogne studying Bonaparte's dispositions. When he gets back, or if he gets back, I'll have him come to you secretly.'

'And when might that be?' I enquired.

'Demmit, man, how do I know?' he demanded. 'When he can do so without risk to his neck. As for the double chaser, if he is, we know him as Edward. What he looks like I'm demned if I know for I've never seen him; but I'm told he's a youngish fellow, half French himself yet hates the whole boiling of 'em like poison. Some tale of Mother Guillotine again very likely.'

'It don't help much,' I mused. 'Half French ain't common but I've heard of it before. Yet I must have somewhere to start, sir.'

'I've told you,' he answered, 'we've no more ourselves but hints. All I can add are two letters which might mean much or little. See what you make of 'em.'

He now produced two papers from his drawer; one fresh and clean but the other stained with water and what looked like a few drops of blood, having no address or superscription, the few lines written on it blurred and smudged, and in French; which again Mr Grimble did me the kindness of translating though I could make it out well enough for myself. ' "My dear Henriette",' he said, ' "Mama is most displeased by your continued silence. Cousin Jean will be with you in a few days more and she desires you to tell him everything of your lover. Our family fortunes continue to improve and will improve further, but how can you hope to share in them if you remain impenitent? We pray you to reflect on this and to speak everything to Jean with the love you should still have in your heart for him. In spite of all your ever affectionate brother, Maximilien".'

The name Henriette gave me food for thought, but I said nothing and turned to the other paper. This seemed to be a copy and was in English, dated the fifteenth day of July and addressed from Paris to a Gervase Markham Esqre at Mill End, by Medmenham. It read, 'Sir; I fear that I must be the means of sad tidings for you; *viz* that your esteemed friend and fellow scientist, Dr Joseph Priestley, passed away in February of this year in Philadelphia, to a higher condition. I am so tardy with the news as I have but lately received it myself, being brought to me by the eminent physician, botanist and traveller, Dr Wilford Caldwell; whereon I use this letter also to bring the doctor to your attention. Dr Caldwell has certain business in London and proposes further to permit himself the privilege of waiting on you. To this end he purposes to sail from St Petersburgh by a ship which we have sure word is leaving to reach London, God willing, between the first and the third of the month next. I shall request Dr Caldwell to present my compliments in person, and also some account of late experiments with Mr Robert Fulton. Presently however, permit me to subscribe myself your svnt, Robert R. Livingston.'

'So ho,' I mused. 'As you say, sir, they might mean much or little. How and when did you come by them?'

Mr Grimble was plainly displeased about something and took a fresh pinch of snuff before answering. 'From a Frenchy; coming ashore with smugglers on Romney Marshes. There was a skirmish with some volunteer militia; demned fools thought it was the invasion, so they pretend. The Frenchy was shot dead but the smugglers escaped or were helped to escape in the darkness. And I fancy them demned fencibles shared out the contraband between 'em. That was. . . .' He paused and addressed the only other person in the chamber; the innocent seeming clerk whom I knew as Mr Popham Snadge. 'Be demned, when was it, Merritt?'

Mr Snadge—or Merritt—looked up from his papers, catching my eye again; but still I said nothing, and he answered, 'The night of July twenty-second, sir.'

I gazed at Mr Grimble in astonishment. 'Better than three weeks ago?'

He was yet more displeased. 'There's a regular traffic of letters in and out; it can't be stopped. These seemed to be but two more, and harmless enough. But for the word from our fellow over there about this conspiracy they might never have been thought of again. And we only had his message on Sunday night.'

'When you concluded the letters might have some part of it after all? Very wise, sir,' I said, reflecting that with a British Government and officials like this Bonaparte did not need an army. 'So we've lost three weeks. And one plainly has not reached the woman Henriette; but what of the other? This seems to be a copy.'

'Demmit man, of course it's a copy,' he retorted. 'The letter itself was passed on to Markham privately; with no word of how it was discovered. It was a cursed delicate matter. The fellow's got influence and Robert Livingston's the American Ambassador to Paris.'

'Delicate indeed,' I observed. 'Let's have it plain, sir. You're not hinting that the American Ambassador in Paris is concerned in this conspiracy?'

The very thought near enough gave Mr Grimble a stroke. 'The Americans are neutral,' he cried. 'They've got a man here at St James's. Ged's sake be careful of your tongue; in government service you learn never to say anything.'

I studied the man with some care. 'Then why do you show me

this letter?'

Still agitated he said, 'Lookee, Sturrock, leave Livingston out of it. The mere idea of diplomatic questions makes my blood run cold. Consider the others instead. *Item*; Dr Joseph Priestley was a sympathiser for the Frenchy revolution. The fellow got his house burned down for it as far back as '91 and took himself off to America. *Item*; so was Markham and very likely still is. Moreover he's a close acquaintance of the Duchess of Bedford, who in turn's a professed Bonapartist and never slow to say so. *Item*; Robert Fulton fadged up some notion of a submarine boat and explosive torpedoes which he tried to sell to Bonaparte. True enough Boney wouldn't have 'em and Fulton's been over here since offering his crackpots to the Admiralty; who likewise refused, thank Ged. The devil only knows what war'd come to if we got up to mischievous pranks and tricks like that.'

'And as I understand this Mr Robert Fulton is also an American?' Mr Grimble nodded, and I continued, 'There's no doubt we've a fine barrel of herrings to look into here. What more is known of Mr Gervase Markham?'

'Justice of the Peace,' Mr Grimble answered, 'and demnition wide connections. Substantial fortune and estates, and calls himself a natural philosopher; which in the common tongue means stenches and bangs. We've information that he's lately been fiddling with this new fulminate of mercury and proposes it for explosions. Demned dangerous stuff.' He took out a fob watch to consult it and demanded, 'Now then, d'you want any more? You've had above ten minutes.'

'I'm obliged for your patience,' I told him. 'But there's a question or two; and certain arrangements.' He looked somewhat amazed at that but I continued, 'First, what is the nature of the warning you've had from your agent in France? And is there harm in telling me his name?'

'Haven't I told you we don't have any information?' he demanded. He turned to Mr Snadge-or-Merritt again. 'What's our man's name, Merritt?'

'Mackenzie, sir,' the clerk replied, this time without looking at me.

'That's right,' Mr Grimble said. 'Mackenzie. Well then, all we're sure of is that Boney is to review the *Grande Armée* at Boulogne on August fifteenth. It's to be an extra fantastical affair even for Boney, and Mackenzie's caught a whisper that he proposes some special spectacular *coup* to crown the occasion.'

'August fifteenth? And we've already lost three weeks,' I reminded him. I mused over that for a minute, reflecting on the fate of England if we had many like Mr Grimble in the seats of authority, and then continued, 'There's one more matter, sir. You say you've another man who might be running with the fox and hunting with the hounds, yet you've never seen him yourself. That's an oddity, ain't it?'

'Oh, be henged,' he protested, 'not in this demned trade. From what I see of it the whole thing's an oddity. We don't catch sight of our men for months at a stretch. All we get is messages as and when they can send 'em.'

'And no doubt by way of smugglers again. Begod, they must be doing a thriving business if nobody else is. Then there's only one last question,' I finished. 'Who is Dr Wilford Caldwell?'

'Demned if I know,' he answered. 'I never heard of the man before.'

I offered up a silent prayer to Providence but said mildly enough, 'Very well, sir, we'll do our best. As Mr Addison observes somewhere, " 'Tis not in mortals to command success, but we'll do more, we'll deserve it." And for that I shall require certain necessities. In short, sir, authority to hold a fast light carriage or chaise and horses on call day or night, funds to cover any sudden emergency, and approval to engage a strong, trusty and resourceful groom.'

Be damned, if Robert Fulton had exploded one of his infernal submarines in that chamber itself it couldn't have had more effect. It took Mr Grimble very near a minute to get his breath back before he enquired, 'You wouldn't fancy a ship of the line as well, and a frigate or two for scouting; or maybe a detachment of cavalry and an open draft on the Bank of England?'

'Not at this minute,' I answered. 'And by all I hear of the

43

state of the Bank a draft of any sort wouldn't be a lot of use to anybody. But I'm bound to have these simple needs or we're hog tied before we've started.' Mr Grimble's expostulations rose to a canticle until I said in the end, 'Sir; at the most we've four or five days and we don't know how far or fast we may have to travel. If anything was to happen to some important gentleman for want of a chaise and horses there'd be more than diplomatic questions asked. And what the newsprints would say about it I don't like to think.'

I shall not weary you with the scurryings to and fro, the conferences, head scratchings, mutterings and obstructions; such antics are the common lot of these pot bound government officials. In the end I had my way and got myself several and various written authorities, an arrangement for somewhat meagre funds, approval to engage a suitable groom—as I had my eye on a likely young fellow—and a chaise and cattle. I was not dissatisfied, for I had nursed an ambition of several years past to have a carriage and man of my own; and I was damned if I proposed to relinquish them either when this present emergency was done with. Such trifles are easily forgotten by government servants who don't even know their own agents.

THREE

So making a final arrangement to be admitted to Mr Grimble in future without the formality of cooling my backside for an hour or more, I took my leave at last; and the gentleman himself seemed strangely thankful to be shot of me. I was in no great hurry but made my way down the corridor with my cane under my arm, my beaver tilted, the air of a man with considerable business on hand, and a benevolent manner to the other unfortunates still waiting. It was pretty certain who would follow me; and neither was I disappointed, for I had scarcely reached the outer lobby before there came the sound of hurrying footsteps behind and a voice calling softly, 'Mr Sturrock, sir; a moment if you please.'

'Why Mr Snadge,' I said, 'here's a surprise now.'

'You'll not split on me?' he demanded anxiously.

'I don't see any reason to,' I told him. 'Not yet. But what are you most? Merritt or Snadge; journalist or clerk?'

'Why, Merritt,' he answered. "Cloudesley Merritt. Whoever heard of a name like Popham Snadge? It's a fine invention though, ain't it? As to the rest I'm a would-be journalist. Have you any notion what the pay's like in government service? A man's got to make his way in the world.'

'God help you if that's the road you choose,' I observed. 'You'll finish up living on snuff in Grub Street.'

'But you'll not split?' he insisted, yet more anxious.

'Not as long as you make yourself useful. How much was Mr Grimble not telling me?'

'Pretty well as much as he understands himself; and that ain't a lot about anything. Mr Sturrock,' the fellow added, 'I don't have a great deal of time. I only got out to attend to the calls of nature.'

'I didn't know government clerks had any. Mr Snadge, who took that letter down to Mr Gervase Markham at Medmenham?'

He looked over his shoulder at the whey faced doorman. 'I did. Was instructed to ride down there hard, and back in the day; hand it in at the lodge, ask no questions and answer none. The place was locked and shut up like the Bank of England; and the biggest, surliest dog of a gate keeper you ever saw in your life.'

'How long ago was this?'

'A day or two after we had it here. Near enough three weeks.'

'Maybe it's no great matter,' I said. 'But why don't Mr Grimble know his own agents?'

'Grimble?' he repeated. 'Grimble's a jackass with the wind and don't know an agent from a sow's arse. He hasn't been in that position much above a month. He's properly a secretary to the Board of Control under patronage of my Lord Castlereagh; but hopes to climb higher.'

'No doubt he will,' I observed. 'He's the stuff that governments are made of. Don't let me keep you from your offices, Mr Snadge. But if you want to persuade me yet more not to split you can see me most nights after nine at the Brown Bear. And where can I find you?'

'I eat my dinners at Beale's.' He seemed about to ask something more, but stopped short and only added, as if half to himself, 'It's no matter for now; I must get back to my quill driving.'

'So ho,' I murmured, standing to watch him hurry back along the corridor before turning out into the clatter and carriage wheels of Whitehall. This place is commonly called The Cockpit by the vulgar; and as I made my way towards the chop house at Charing Cross I reflected that it was no great wonder.

Here Master Maggsy was awaiting me; but already half way to a fight with a crossing sweeper boy who was jeering at his yellow coat and blue pantaloons after the fashion of all these disrespectful little wretches. Maggsy himself was not behindhand in his observations, but my appearance very quickly put an end to their poetics for even more than his love of bloodshed and disaster he has an inordinate affection for his belly.

46

It was a dimmish, brownish place seemingly much affected by government clerks—a muttering, secretive and snuff coloured gang, gazing at any stranger as if he might be at least a Frenchy —and for my part Mr Snadge was welcome to it. The shoulder of salmon was indifferent being all of three days out of the water, and the mutton chops fit for little more than making boot soles. Yet I shall acknowledge that the claret was very moderate; and none of the tale so often told these days, that there is a shortage of it owing to the war.

Here I pondered for a while on certain aspects concerning Henriette d'Armande and told Master Maggsy as much as I thought was good for him to know, and he likewise considered it in turn while mopping up the gravy on his plate. He has an affectation of profound thought now and again, and he said at last, 'If you ask me they're aiming to blow up the House of Parliament. Holy Moses was telling me once how there was another cove named Guy Fawkes who tried that some while back, only they catched him before he could do any good. D'you reckon they'll pull it off this time? God's Whiskers, I'd admire to see that.'

'A most improper observation,' I told him, 'and lacking in respect for a noble institution. Now pay attention and listen to your instructions. I want you to go to Lincoln's Inn and there discover all you can about the law firm Pottle Soskins and Pottle; and in particular Mr Rodney Pottle. There's a tavern or two close by where you'll find lower clerks and messengers, but be careful how you go about it; I don't want nobody to take fright.'

'What?' Maggsy demanded. 'D'you reckon he's a rum un then?' He shook his head wisely. 'That Popham Snadge might be if you like, but not Pottle. True enough he's a right roaring doxy hound, like I said before, but a very proper cove otherwise and uncommon free with his money. Which is more'n you can say for some people I know.'

'We can't tell what's rum and what's French brandy yet,' I answered. 'So be off to find out. And when you've done that you may return to our chambers to give yourself an hour or so at your lessons; and then meet me at the Bear with Mr Pottle and Holy Moses by nine o'clock. For myself I've other business.'

'And you don't need to say what it is neither,' he announced in a sudden rage. 'It's that *émigrée* fireship of yours again, ain't it? You can't keep off the rollicks, can you? Ain't you got enough on hand a'ready what with blowing up the House of Parliament and assackinating Mr Pitt, to say nothing of kidnapping His Majesty and a few other larks? Besides, it ain't your day for her; you're just as like to find another coney there taking a ride.'

'Master Maggsy,' I warned him softly, 'mind your manners.' Out of too much kindness I allow the dreadful child more leeway than is good for him, but not even he may presume too far. The truth is that he was plainly jealous of a light attachment I had for a certain captivating creature with whom I was presently making a deep study of the French language and several other matters; one, Anne-Louise Cléry and the prettiest, most provoking chit you ever saw in your life. The very thought of her was enough to throw him into a sulk, and for her part she could not put up with the sight of Maggsy.

It was an unfortunate domestic situation but the Art and Science of Detection must continue, and I said sternly, 'Set about your own affairs, boy, and leave me to mine. Even such an addle wit as you must see that Mademoiselle Anne-Louise might very well tell us something about Henriette d'Armande.' He grunted sceptically and somewhat coarsely and I added, 'But if it pleases you any better I shall go to Lady Dorothea Dashwood's first to ask a favour concerning her man, Jagger. We're to set up with our own post chaise and horses paid for by the government and we shall need a good groom who's capable of anything.'

No normal child could resist such a prospect, and he brightened at once; the more so as this Jagger is a sporting young rascal always game for a wager, a race or a mill, and not above seeing that the odds come down on the right side. A long sight better than hiring some surly rogue of a post boy—as most of them are—and on the several occasions when he has worked for me in the past he and Maggsy have been as thick as thieves.

So with that promise and sixpence to spend about the taverns for his enquiries the child went on his way more hopefully, while I myself engaged a hackney to carry me to the commodious and modern residence of Lady Dorothea in Hanover Square.

I have already written at some length of my lady several times elsewhere and as she has no great part in this narrative I shall not repeat much of it here. Described by some, in my opinion unjustly, as having a face like a horse's hinder parts, His Royal Highness the Prince of Wales cannot abide her; in short she is a very proper and respectable woman, much given to philosophy, Whiggishness and the damned nonsensical notions of Monsieur Jean Jacques Rousseau about equality. But coming from a good naval family and the landed nobility these are mere female whimishness and perversity, and nothing like the antics of certain other great ladies who are forever screeching their silly heads off in praise of Bonaparte. Moreover she also shows the most perfect kindliness and courtesy for me; and how I succeeded to that privileged regard is another story.

Her afternoon soirée of scribblers and encyclopaedists was just breaking up, and I lingered with this learned gaggle in the drawing-room for a minute or two before getting close enough to present my compliments, but then the matter was soon concluded. As you will know all of these great houses have such a swarm of butlers, servants, coachmen, grooms and stable lads eating their heads off in idleness that one more or less makes no matter, so when my lady enquired of my present business and I advised her that I was engaged about state matters she herself offered to place Jagger at my orders. It was a nice arrangement, for the household would continue to pay his wages and I should secure his services free while presenting Mr Grimble with a reasonable account for them; so by remitting a fair half of this perquisite to Jagger and perhaps even a bit to Maggsy everybody would be satisfied. It is always wise to consider such small diplomacies when dealing with the government.

That concluded with a dish of tea, a further exchange of compliments, and my request for the man to present himself at the earliest tomorrow's morning I took my leave and made my way back at leisure to Soho Square, where Anne-Louise has her lodgings on the south side in Bateman's Buildings; as I have my own chambers at the more modish north end above Mrs Spilsbury's well known dispensary for marital disorders, disappointments and surprises. The pretty creature's circumstances are becomingly modest yet, but they will not remain so if I am any judge, for Anne-Louise will go far if she lives long enough.

Neither has she risen to the mode of a page boy, black or otherwise, or even a private maid so there is some discretion to be observed in announcing yourself, and I ascended the stairs to scratch on her door with my own particular signal as decency demands. It was answered by a sharp scuffle from within and Anne-Louise's voice demanding, 'Oo iz it?'

'Your loving Sturrock, my duckling,' I replied.

I heard the mutter of a man's voice, but the wench herself cried, 'It is not your occasion. Go away.'

'No, my love, I will not,' I answered. 'But I'll wait a minute. You may compose yourself.'

'Compose you to the devil,' she screeched back to the accompaniment of further muttering, and I was curious enough to get my eye down to the keyhole; not as one of Master Maggsy's vulgar tricks, but because there was no need of such strange dramatics. It was a matter of course that she should entertain other visitors, for no lady can expect to advance herself very far by giving French lessons to one gentleman alone.

I could see nothing however as the key was in the lock, but heard fresh muttering and a hurried movement, and then had bare time to step back and straighten up before the door was flung open and my lady appeared. It was like a scene from Drury Lane, when the Godlings start to toss down the orange skins and nut shells on the stage. A further door in the apartment just closed with a slam and my pretty poppet herself confronting me in a Directory chemise which revealed more than it hid of her many and tempting charms. Not above medium height and slender with it, a pair of long hips that will earn her a fortune anywhere, a waist no more than a double handful, tits and shoulders as would become a small Venus, above the entire confection a squarish face, saucy nose and greenish blue eyes, and the whole topped off with a fiery, russet red disordered mop; and natural fiery russet red throughout, as I can testify. In short a tasty trollop.

There is no prettier sight than such a creature attired in little or nothing and a right imperial rage. Nature herself might have devised the female form for such passions, bosoms heaving, arms and legs akimbo, shoulders and eyes flashing and ringlets flying; but an end of it when she draws off one of her sandals and starts to belabour you with the heel. I am of a nicest gentility with the ladies, but there is reason in all things and some of her observations on my unexpected appearance would have made Maggsy blush. I was forced to restrain the wench and cast her on the sofa, where what little there was of her chemise somehow was torn off and she kicked, fought, scratched, clawed, bit and cursed like a wild cat. 'Come now, my dove,' I said, getting a half Nelson on her, 'what the devil's this about? Master Maggsy calls you The Fireship; and, by God, fireship it is.'

'Pig, devil, hog, Satan,' she screeched. 'Do not speak of that monster to me. He is also a pig and a devil; and it is not your day for a French lesson.'

'Come, my rosy tease,' I coaxed her. 'What's a day or so between you and me? Begod you look like a dish for a prince.'

'You are not a prince,' she observed. 'You are a *cochon*; also you have the *gentil* of a wild bull.'

I am a man of profound patience but enough is enough; no little whore shall say I lack the genteels. I planted a sharp slap on her pretty backside and demanded, 'Be damned, you hussy, what is this game? Disappointed of some other gallant, are you? God's sake what's the matter with me? I'm as good as any and better than most. Come now,' I said, 'let's have an end of it.'

'I am not of a mood,' she retorted. 'Pray let me be.'

It was a pretty teasing piece of play acting, and I sat with one arm round her waist and the other hand on her behind to steady her while surveying the further door; which led as I knew into a second chamber and out again to another flight of stairs. The chit had set up these fine dramatics to distract me while the other fellow made his escape; and no need of it, for I am a reasonable man. There was a mystery here, but no great account and I let it rest; I had other fish to fry and said cunningly, 'Well there's a pity. But don't fret yourself, I'll go instead to wait on Mademoiselle Henriette d'Armande.'

The passion and panting stopped at a stroke. She twisted herself up and sat flushed and pouting, gazing at me with her ringlets tumbling bewitchingly down about her shoulders. 'You will go to which?'

'To Mademoiselle Henriette,' I repeated. 'They tell me she's of an accommodating nature. And sweeter tempered than you.'

'Henriette d'Armande,' Anne-Louise observed, 'is a mare. Or more correctly she is a sow. Her bosoms are like saddle bags and she has a big belly. Her bottoms are of a leathery nature and thin. She must always keep her legs open, for when she closes them her knees knock together; she is of a sallowish colour all over, and she is at least, at the very least, twenty-five years old.' The dear creature shuddered extravagantly and closed her eyes, clearly considering what more she could add to this enchanting catalogue. 'Also her hair is like brass wire, but she has none on her head and so is forced to wear a wig. Which continually falls off,' she added thoughtfully.

'Begod,' I said, 'she sounds like a fit playmate for my Master Maggsy. We'll have 'em both in Bartholomew Fair for a pair of monsters. So you know the lady, do you?'

She lifted one shoulder and gave me a bigger pout than ever. 'She is not among my friends.'

I ran a shrewd tickle up and down her naked back, a trick which never failed to fetch a lively response. 'I'd heard that she was one of Madame Rosamunda's beauties, but left that establishment. They're laying wagers on the reason for it in the coffee houses. Madame's is a fine position for an ambitious young lady.'

Anne-Louise gave a laugh which might have stopped a four-in-hand. 'Laying wagers on Henriette d'Armande? Do not make me spit. And Madame Rosamunda's is not so fine as you may think,' she added darkly. 'For me I would not be seen there veiled in a coal sack, though I have been asked; oh, many, many times. It is not respectable; and Madame Rosamunda herself is a sow of the devil.' She did another elaborate shudder.

'By all accounts it's not Madame Rosamunda the gentlemen go to view. I wonder, did Henriette d'Armande fall out with one of 'em? As might have been an *émigré*?'

'The poor *émigrés* do not go to Madame Rosamunda's,' Anne-Louise answered coldly. 'They do not afford it. Jeremee,' she continued, 'if you determine to talk of this creature I shall either put on my clothes, my thickest and nastiest pelisse, or beat you over the head with my slipper. Perhaps both.'

'Come, my love,' I protested, 'that'd be a punishment too cruel. You're a fiery little Venus. But are you kinder to the *émigrés* yourself?'

'It is not the *politesse* to ask a lady what other gentlemen she entertains,' she reminded me, colder still.

'No, my pretty wanton, it ain't,' I agreed. 'But the truth is I want you all for my own and I'm jealous of the fellows. As jealous of all of 'em as you are of Henriette d'Armande.'

The chit pushed herself away from me, her hands flat against my chest and arms straight, head atilt and eyes sparkling green lightnings, her fiery mop of hair more unruly than ever and tumbling down over her tits in the most bewitching way imaginable; had she not spoiled it by fetching me an open handed clout across the jaw which might have felled a waggoner. 'Jealous, is it?' she screamed, using several observations with which I shall not sully these pages. 'Let me say, you great brutal, thrusting, *vaurien*, I would not be jealous of Henriette d'Armande were she mistress to a dozen great lords; no, not even a hundred. She is a cheat and an impostor. I am a French aristocrat and she is a servant, a mere children's *institutrice*, and moreover she has not been here more than three or four little months.'

'Hold your leaders, my lamb,' I said, getting a fresh half Nelson wherever I could find a grip as she drew breath for a further panegyric. 'You'll excite yourself in a minute.' I am always nice to know when I have pressed my questions far enough with the ladies, and by now I had most of what I was after.

It was a touching reconciliation and after that little more was said; or little more which concerns this tale unless I want that

53

publisher fixing me with his cold eye again. We set about our proper business, and with my pretty tartar having quite changed her mood I learned several additions to my command of the French language; and if, as the creature pretends, she was brought up in a convent in Paris they give the girls a damned fine education there. But all too soon it was time to rearrange myself, take my leave of the now languid little beauty with several loving farewells and other tokens of affection, and return to sterner duty.

All in all I was not displeased, for three things were now pretty plain. One, that Anne-Louise herself so far knew nothing of Henriette d'Armande's murder and, unless the sweet trollop was smarter about dissimulation than I took her for, little more about anything which might have led to it. Next, that my own clever deduction about that poor woman's past was near enough correct; and third, that she had not been long on the Haymarket round and seemed, whether by ill fortune or attention, to have got herself very quickly into some company she had been better off without. No doubt you will perceive certain other matters, as I did myself, and pondering on these, on that letter she had never received owing to Mr Grimble, and on a design which I could already see starting to shape itself, I made my way to the Brown Bear through the thunderous, oppressive night with fresh storm clouds lowering once more in the sky.

Maggsy, Mr Pottle and Holy Moses were already awaiting me there, sitting close together at a settle in the crowded smoke, candle reek and babel. By the look of Pottle he was vastly enjoying himself, roaring laughter and encouragement at Nan the serving wench as she tipped a jug of ale over the head of some rogue who had just half pulled her bodice down; a pretty scene but not uncommon in the Bear. Likewise by the look of the other two Mr Pottle was again being free with the money which he seemed to have too much of, for Master Maggsy was sitting with a pint of claret before him—a liquor which I never allow the child as it makes him impudent—while Holy Moses was lifting his canonical smile and rosy snout from a pot of gin.

I have promised to explain this Holy Moses in his place, and to be brief he is a canting old sinner and one time parson who fell from grace over some misdemeanour which I have never exactly fathomed. However deep he may be in gin and repentance, mostly on Fridays, you can never get the full tale out of him; but I fancy it was not unconnected with a lady in his younger years who took a yearning for a touch of the holies and got too much of it to do her good, thus causing some discomfort to Moses as her father was squire of the village and had the living in his gift. Whatever the truth of it, the sanctimonious rascal has been a notable screever in Earlham Street these many years past and is much respected by the criminal fraternity, who often have need of his services. I know enough about the rogue to get him on the Rochester hulks at least, if not a trip to Botany Bay, but I keep him by me part from the kindness of my heart, and part as tutor to Maggsy in reading, writing, and the gentilities; moreover there is little goes on in the stews, from Seven Dials to Greenhill's Rents and the Adelphi Arches, that he don't know or can't find out.

He is as full of sound and wind as an empty hogshead, forever spouting Latin, and he was well at it now as I pushed through the press, raising his voice above the clatter, laughter, curses and Nan's screeches to proclaim to Pottle, 'I profess myself a friend and champion of the poor. *Non ignara mali miseris succurrere disco*; "Not ignorant of ill myself do I learn to aid the wretched"; Virgil. And would you believe it, sir, I perceive that carried away by our most pleasant discourse I have finished all this gin.'

'And quite enough for now, Moses,' I said, coming up to them unexpectedly. 'We'll have some sense out of you first before you get to the sorrowfuls.'

'Why, Mr Sturrock,' Pottle cried out as lively as a fighting cock, 'here's well met. Be damned this is a rare place; as good as the pantomime, I wouldn't ha' missed it for a gold watch as big as a wagon wheel. A most salubrious haven and I'm obliged to you for bringing me here. What'll you take now?'

'You haven't seen the tenth of it yet,' I promised. 'And if you wear a gold watch of any size keep your hands on it. You may call up a pint of claret if you please. But no more gin for him or you'll have him wiping his eyes on your neckcloth.' The old humbug rolled his eyeballs up to Heaven as if beseeching the Almighty to grant me forgiveness, and seating myself where I could survey the rest of the ugly crew present—what you could see of them in that dim and cloudy light—I said, 'We're not here for the elegant company, Mr Pottle.'

'My oath we ain't,' Maggsy observed, while Pottle hammered with his mug on the table to call the wench. 'I got something damnation oddity about him,' he added under his breath, 'for all his free and easy ways; and what's more there's a couple of coves I don't like the look of colloguing with Sweaty Joe's gang and casting glances this way; I don't much like the look of that neither. Any of them'd fillet you for a pastime; and me too if they got the chance.'

I nodded to show that I took the message, watching Mr Pottle tip several sovereigns out of his purse to find a few coins to pay Nan, reflecting that the fellow was near enough drunk or reckless, and asking just as softly, 'Who are they?'

'Dunno,' Maggsy answered out of the corner of his mouth. 'I never see 'em before.' He jerked his head sideways at Pottle. 'They come in hard after him, and ain't the same sort as this lot; frieze coats and squash hats and gaiters all right, but like as if they ain't used to such rags. I wisht we was well out of here.'

'Keep 'em under observation,' I told him and went on louder to Pottle, 'Put that purse away; there's a score of rogues in here who'd cut your throat to get their fingers on it.' The wench herself was gazing at the money as she pushed my claret across the board at me, her eyes very near as far out of her head as her tits were from her bodice, and I looked up at her with my kindest smile—which Maggsy declares is enough to frighten a brewer's drayman—to add, 'Nan, my dear, Mr Pottle's under my especial care and he's wanted by Bow Street. Be a good girl now, if you can, and go and tell your master that Sweaty Joe's gang are up to something. Tell him if they start any mischief I know a dozen ways to get him into Newgate.'

Holy Moses let out an expiring squeal at that, for he knows the tricks as well as I do. 'God have mercy on us,' he cried. 'Mr Sturrock, I'll beg you to excuse me; I've a most pestilential watery rumbling in my bowels and must go to relieve myself.'

'You'll stay here,' I told him, and went on to Pottle, 'You might see more of a pantomime than you fancy in a minute, so we'll talk fast. Did you find the man Tooley in Coventry Court?'

The damned fool still seemed to fancy it was some kind of frolic. 'Never a smell,' he answered cheerfully. 'Save that he was seen in a beer house talking close to two others, strangers to the place, a bit before the rain started last night. Then the three of them went off together, and never a sight of him since.'

'So we've lost him. But it's no great matter. What of Henriette d'Armande?'

He shook his head. 'Little more there. Seems she hadn't been long enough about to be much remarked. But there's a young lad at the livery stables, a country fellow lately tramped to London to try his luck, who fancies that he's seen her before. In Chippenham, he says for what that means; some several months back.'

'Chippenham,' I repeated. 'That's close by Bath.' I mused about this for a minute, watching our landlord One Eyed Jack push through to Sweaty Joe's little lambs in a smoky haze at the other end of the room. 'I can tell you more about the woman myself,' I said, 'though her past don't matter all that much. It's Madame Rosamunda's genteel establishment we must look to now. What did you have of that?'

The silly fellow looked somewhat crestfallen and shook his head again. 'Not all that much, though it seemed I was in luck at first go. I found a hackney man in the Cock yard, opposite James Street, who claimed himself brother to one of the flunkeys in the house but the rogue was an impostor. Be hanged to it, he took a sovereign from me. Told me tales about curious entertainments and gaming for uncommon stakes, but then grew surly when I pressed him for more. We very near came to blows.'

'He took you for a countryman; as well he might,' I observed unfavourably. 'Begod if you don't know the nature of hackney drivers and chairmen by now you'll never learn. And to put money down before you get your information is the act of a simpleton.'

I twisted round to get a fresh look at Sweaty Joe's rascals, but there was another crowd standing in the way now and Maggsy muttered, 'Damned if I can catch sight either. There was a bit of an argify with Jack but he's moved on and left 'em to it; some of 'em broke off to come to the other tables, and the rest're dicing now so far as I can make out.'

'Are the strangers still there?' I asked.

'One's gone behind this minute as if to piss. T'other's there against the door with his back to you; like he might be waiting for more to come. I reckon we'd best get out of this quick.'

'All in good time,' I promised. 'But we'll see what these fellows look like first.'

Maggsy cursed briefly. 'You don't need to wait, I can tell you. That'n's got a black eye patch; and he's a right rare dandy with a triping knife if you ask me.'

'Why what's this then?' asked Mr Pottle innocently.

I studied the fellow at the door before replying. He was standing there with one hand on the lintel stooping to peer out into the alleyway. A well shaped hand with clean fingernails for all the dirt elsewhere on it, but the old three cornered chairman's hat, hair tied in a queue with twine, and dun coloured frieze coat were all commonplace enough. He couldn't have chosen better to go unnoticed pretty well anywhere. For a minute I debated whether to accost him myself and open the business, but then concluded it was better strategy to wait; to start a fight in the Brown Bear is no light matter, and I still wanted time to question Holy Moses and give Pottle fresh instructions. 'We don't know yet,' I told him. 'Maybe that pantomime you're looking for. If it comes to mischief your tankard there makes a handy weapon. Hold it by the handle and strike at the nose between the eyes with the bottom of it, for that discommodes the rascals most.'

He gaped at me with his mouth open like a whore's front door, while Master Maggsy cursed again and thriftily finished up his own pot in readiness for the battle. Moses let out another unhappy sound midway between a fart and the dying moan of

58

a sick heifer, starting to slide under the table but nonetheless reaching out absently to take a long draught of my claret on the way.

For myself I continued firmly, 'Now, Mr Pottle, you've not done all that well today, but you may try again tomorrow. Do you know Beale's Chop House at Charing Cross? It's much used by government officials, and I want you to go there before dinner and find out all you can about a certain clerk, one Mr Cloudesley Merritt. It shouldn't be beyond you, for the waiters at these places are always ready to talk if you show 'em a shilling or so. Have a word or two with Mr Merritt himself if you like. You may tell him that you've heard he has ambitions to be a writer and you might give him a leg up. But I don't want my name mentioned; is that understood? You ain't much use in a law firm if you can't tell a good tale.'

'Be damned,' he breathed in some admiration, 'you're a cool un.'

'I'm not without experience. After that,' I went on, 'I want you back to the Haymarket. I want to know if Henriette d'Armande was seen on the afternoon of the day she died. Where she was seen; and, above all, who with. You should try the coffee houses; and in particular the Prince of Orange, as ladies are admitted there. And then you may return here at about this time tomorrow night to report.'

'So long as we ain't all scragged, gutted and hung out to dry by this time tomorrow night,' Maggsy muttered. 'You're alooking for trouble again. I say let's get out of this.'

But I was not finished yet. I dragged Moses back to the settle by the scruff of his coat and continued, 'Now for you.'

Even then the old Pharisee could not stop canting; he must always get the Latin off his chest like wind from the bowels. ' "Non amo te, Sabidi, nec possum dicere quare;" ' he announced spitefully, ' "Hoc tantum possum dicere, non amo te." "I do not love thee, Sabidius, nor can I say why; this only can I say, I do not love thee." Martial.'

'And here's a nice time to think of that,' I observed. 'Talk quick and short, Moses. Have you heard of any villains getting in business with the émigrés?'

'As God will be my judge,' he protested tearfully, 'and will I hope be merciful, I have not.'

'So find out,' I told him. 'There's a plot hatching and I want to know what it is. Find me any hint you can.' He started to protest afresh, but I went on, 'And there's a man called Tooley, bulldog or guard at a whore house in Coventry Court; of no great account, but he'll very likely go to ground in the Dials or the Arches. I also want any word of him you may hear.'

Then Maggsy grunted, 'God's Weskit, here it comes.'

The fellow by the door turned suddenly on One Eyed Jack and flung him out to the alley. A rascal unseen bawled, 'God damn your eyes, that's my double six,' and as if at a signal most of the lights went out. In the stinking darkness there was only a smoky lantern over by the barrels and the candle left burning on our own table, but enough to see six or eight or more shadowy rogues falling on us in a body. In an instant it was pandemonium, stools and pots flying, struggling figures fighting to get out and others falling over 'em, Nan screeching fit to raise the devil above the chorus of yells and curses, the sound of pewter on bone and crash of tables going over; One Eyed Jack roaring like a bull somewhat ill tempered as he fought his way back in again, pitiful wails from Holy Moses flat on his face under foot, and over all the melodious accents of Master Maggsy. In short, a very pretty scene.

But I had no time to reflect on it for I was busy myself. Maggsy I caught a glimpse of crowning one villain with his pewter, Mr Pottle manfully hammering another's head against the wall and spoiling the plaster, while I snuffed out our last candle by thrusting it impetuously down the gullet of one more who was trying to throttle me; he must have chewed off a good finger length of it before he reeled back choking and screaming. Then in the glimmer of the last remaining lantern and a whirl of Bedlamite shadows I perceived the fellow with the eye patch; and perceived also a glint of steel, a little dagger or dirk in his hand. Mr Pottle was now turning with a snarl to find a fresh victim and whether it was aimed for me or him seemed uncertain, but I struck shrewd and hard with the iron candlestick and turned the weapon aside to catch the next rascal a

60

glancing cut on his neck.

He fell back more discommoded by Mr Pottle's tankard flattening his snout than the dagger, for the thing was a mere toy; but I had no eyes for that either as I wanted this other gentleman, and would have had him had not that excitable wretch Maggsy suddenly tossed over the table with a further wicked screech. This falling on Holy Moses—who was still trying to crawl away between our kicking feet—the pestilential parson let out a fresh howl and clutched at my knees, so fetching me over also just as I got a hand on the man's neckcloth to steady him for a quietener with my candlestick. There was never anything so vexing. I went down with a crash which very near broke my ribs, the rogue tore himself free, and I heard no more than an improper observation in French and my own hearty English prayers as I strove to break away from that damned importunate weeping canonical.

Pushing myself up I trod on his ear a bit heavily, and with a fresh shriek he disengaged his loverlike clasp, but it was already too late. My man was at the door flinging aside two others there fighting to escape and shouldering by One Eyed Jack, who was laying about him to sobering effect with a bottle in each hand while bellowing for lights. By the time I won out to the alley myself there were two or three private brawls in progress and a few bystanders joining in to be sociable, the sound of watchmen's rattles at a safe distance, but no sign of my villain except a pair of brief shadows which vanished into the night at the end by Bow Street.

I returned to a scene of carnage lit by Nan bringing in fresh candles and adding her own lewd remarks to illumine it still further; tables and stools overturned, tankards on the floor, and pools of liquor in the sawdust. Some few rascals were creeping out of their hiding places on all fours, Mr Pottle looking more than a little surprised and mopping his face, and Holy Moses on his knees weeping and praying; the fellow who had taken the little scratch on his neck dabbing at the dribble of blood with his fingers, Maggsy thoughtfully tipping the remains of a pot over another who was just coming to; and One Eyed Jack still weighting his bottles by the neck, breathing heavy and cursing. All in all a pretty commonplace mill, vexed as I was to have the man I wanted escape, but Jack was ill humoured about it. 'No, by God, Mr Sturrock,' he cried, 'a joke's a joke and I'll not deny anybody his bit of fun but you go too far; by God you do. I wisht you'd take your custom somewhere else.'

'You should keep your little lambs in better order,' I told him, turning sharp on the man with the cut neck, slapping him hard against the wall and adding, 'We'll have a word or two from you. What was that about? And who were the fellows that set you on to it?'

'Go easy, master,' he begged. ' 'Twarn't no more than a jape. And none of us never see the coves before, that I'll swear. They offered a crown piece between us to ruffle you; on account they said you was rolling a doxy of theirs and aimed to spoil your rides for a bit. There warn't no harm meant.'

'No harm meant?' wept Holy Moses. 'And might have killed me while about it? Is this gratitude, Jabez Stott? *Nomen amicitia est, nomen inane fides*; "Friendship is but a name, constancy an empty title"; Ovid.'

I looked back at him. 'So you know this rascal do you?'

He rolled his eyes up to Heaven again. 'I have shown him many a kindness. And even more to his poor unfortunate woman.'

Maggsy let out an evil snicker at that, but I asked, 'So ho? Then you shall show him another. You may go bail for his good behaviour, Moses.' The old bladder of Latin knew what I was after, for this rascal might well confide to him more than he would ever tell me. He started to protest tearfully, but I said, 'Be off now. And keep Stott in sight, Moses, or it might be worse for both of you.'

'You'd best all be off, by God,' One Eyed Jack cut in. 'I've had my belly full of you lot tonight.' He looked at Mr Pottle none too kindly. 'And you're very near as bad as Mr Sturrock.'

'I can use my dukes if I must,' Pottle confessed. 'Be damned, it beats cock fighting. They say make your will before you sup from home these days, but never did I see the like of this.'

'A Bow Street pantomime,' I told him. 'But I mean to know who Harlequin is and which of us was meant for Pantaloon.'

FOUR .

Leaving Mr Pottle to his own devices in Long Acre Maggsy and I made our way back to Soho Square keeping a sharp eye around and behind us; which is common prudence at any time. But there was no other sign of any worse rogues than usual about in the nightly traffic, and, save for Master Maggsy's observations and a few short words by St Giles Church with a pair of tipsy young militiamen who fancied they had discovered easy sport, we reached the peaceful seclusion of our chambers without further incident. Here at last I was at leisure to reflect on several matters over a glass or two of Madeira and a pipe, to lay certain fresh plans, and to discuss the late affray with Maggsy; for the little monster has a pair of eyes in his head as sharp as a starling's.

'I reckon they was after Pottle,' he announced, 'but it might just as well have been you. Just as I snouted one of Sweaty Joe's lot I see you knock that eye patch villain's pig sticker aside, but I thought "God's Whiskers, he'll have Sturrock in a minute" and chucked the table at him quick.'

'And that's how we lost the fellow,' I said. 'What became of the dagger, I wonder?'

'Ain't never thankful for nothing are you?' he enquired. 'He must've carried the sticker off with him, as I looked about for it after but couldn't catch sight of it nowhere. I'd ha' liked that for myself; particular genteel I thought that was.'

'Then thank God you didn't find it; you're quite genteel enough with only your natural talents. But we're left with nothing,' I mused. 'Save only to ask if it's me they were after how do they know so soon that I'm in the hunt? Or if it's Pottle was it only because he's been asking round about Henriette d'Armande? What did you discover in Lincoln's Inn?'

'Not a lot,' he admitted. I shall omit his various adventures with a gate keeper, a porter, and a coachman, and took another glass of Madeira myself while he was recounting them, but at last he continued, 'In the end I catched sight of a kind of boy coming out of Pottle Soskin's entrance, and him I tripped arse over tip and then offered to fight him for it or pay for a pint of beer instead whichever he liked best. So he chose the beer, and I let on I'd got a sister who was coming into a bucket of money when our uncle died, which wouldn't be long as he was drowning himself in gin, and she'd got a bun shoved in her oven at Vauxhall Gardens from some lawyer or t'other by the name of Poskins or Sottle, or something like that, as she wasn't just sure on account of being more concerned with holding her bonnet on and not stopping to ask. Particular genteel it was, like you're always saying, and in the end I damn near had him weeping on my shoulder. I likewise let on as I more than sus-pectioned that Poskins'd served that same fancy to one or two others in the Assembly Rooms at Bath.'

I considered this entrancing vision of the goings on at Vaux-hall and in the Assembly Rooms, and the lewd wretch con-tinued, 'It was word of Bath that done it, for this lad cried out, "That'll be Master Rodney Pottle for sure, as he's ever and again going off to Bath and he's well known to be a right royal roaring rollicking wencher".'

'Maggsy,' I told him softly, 'we know that much.'

'So we do,' he agreed in affected mock surprise. 'But what you don't know is that Mr Rodney Pottle's pretty near as often off to France.'

'So ho,' I observed. 'Are you sure of that?'

'According to this boy. A nasty prying little rascal if you ask me, forever with his snitcher in other folk's affairs and his lug at the keyholes. He says Mr Rodney Pottle's not long back from over the water, and with his own ears he heard old Pottle say to old Soskin that Mr Rodney'd never make a lawyer but he knowed more ways of getting letters in and out of France than a parson knows of dodging the Devil.'

'It's another thing that might mean much or little,' I mused. 'And if Mr Pottle don't meet with some small mishap first we

64

shall have to ask him. But for now we'll sleep on it; we've a long day ahead tomorrow.'

I am not a man to let mere affairs of state disturb my sleep —more especially after a loving occasion with Anne-Louise, a general mill, and a bottle of Madeira—and I slept sound to rise early, stir Maggsy out of his closet, and await the arrival of my new man, Jagger.

He turned up sharp at eight o'clock, grinning all over his face at the prospect of some livelier mischief than idling with the servant wenches of Hanover Square and as pleased as Punch when I gave him his instructions and authorities; namely to procure on long hire a smart, light chaise in spanking condition and horses to match, next to arrange for stabling in the nearest mews, and then to meet me at the Bow Street Office with the equipage ready to move off not later than ten o'clock. Telling him to drive the best bargain he could for the sake of the government, but to recollect that all of them were better off than he was and nobody could blame him if he contrived to pocket a bit of commission for himself, I despatched Maggsy with him and then set about my own preparations for waiting on a landed gentleman and philosopher. Finally arrayed with boots you could see your face in, my best tan pantaloons, coat only lately delivered from Mr Yorke of Piccadilly, and a neckcloth which I wear specially to Lady Dorothea's—and not forgetting my Wogdons, for no gentleman travels to the wilds of the country without his pistols primed and handy—I made my own way to Bow Street.

As he always was and no doubt always will be even in Heaven Abel Makepenny was still scratching and rustling at his papers and as I entered he peered up to gaze at my elegant attire in astonishment. 'Lord help us,' the good old gentleman enquired, 'where d'you think you're off to, Jer'my? You'll have Mr A in a tantrum if you ain't careful. He's snottish, and likewise the livers today. He was at the port again last night. You know he can't abide a man with a better coat than his own.'

'It's a coat for the occasion,' I said. 'I'm to wait on the gentry. And maybe you can tell me something of 'em Abel. What do you know of a Mr Gervase Markham of Medmenham?'

' 'Twon't be long before we have you affecting a quizzing glass and a Brighton drawl,' Abel complained. 'Gervase Markham Esquire?' he asked with interest, for he is a compendium of the nobility and landed quality and follows their fortunes, families and genealogies like a ferret follows rabbits. He flipped some snuff away from the end of his nose with his quill and then dusted out his right ear as well. 'Mr Gervase Markham? Oh dear me very well connected. Lemme see now; he's a member of the Royal Society and married to Lady Gwendoline Rampole as was, but that's a matter of politeness as she fancies Clarges Street and society better than Medmenham and philosophy; and on close terms with His Royal Highness's circle and Mr Fox. But very amicable with Mr Markham as I've heard. Then there's a brace of Members of Parliament in the family, also of the Fox persuasion.'

'Be damned,' I observed, 'that's no testimonial.'

In his agitation Abel damned near pushed his quill halfway through from one ear to the other. 'Be hanged, Jeremy,' he breathed, 'you don't show as nice respect as you should. You'd best be uncommon tender with that lot. They're all cousins in some sort or another to my Lords Rednal and Copton.'

'Begod it looks as if I need my best coat then,' I said. 'Is there any more?'

He started to add something, dusting at his nose again, but before he could get the quill out Mr A's voice was heard roaring from within; 'Is that Sturrock? Send the rascal through, will ye? Does he wait on me, or me on him?'

As Abel had warned me Mr A was not in the best of tempers. I was concerned to note an unhealthy flush about his countenance; his gouty foot was propped on a bigger cushion than usual, and he greeted me, 'Well, by God Mr Sturrock, sir, we're pleased and gratified to see you gracing our humble office. But ain't you been loitering somewhat, for you've had near enough twenty-four hours in government service and I see by *The Times* today that Bonaparte's still at large. I read that the invasion's expected to take place about Eastbourne. You'll have a lot to answer for if you don't put a stop to it.'

I let the amiable gentleman have his head for a while, though

I shall not repeat his witticisms here, for at their best they are nothing like as good as my own. But at length he seemed to have got some of the gout off his bowels, and as he paused for a minute I said firmly, 'Sir, I shall ask pardon of not reporting to you before this, but the matters disclosed by Mr Grimble was so grave and his instructions so peremptory that I set about them on the instant without thought to my own courtesies and inclinations; or even yours.'

He turned a yellow and bloodshot eye on me, but remained silent while I continued to recount my conference with Mr Grimble; though without mentioning Mr Cloudesley Merritt, or for that matter the man Pottle and my own adventures and arrangements, as I did not want to go on any longer than I must on mysteries and explanations. 'So there you have it, sir,' I concluded. 'Some conspiracy that's to come to a head on August fifteenth, when Bonaparte reviews his army at Boulogne; and very likely to throw us in confusion at one stroke. What it is we don't know yet, but nobody's forgot his rascally trick with the Duke of Enghien. The gentlemen of the government fear an assassination or abduction of some person or personages here; it could be a blow to signal the invasion itself.'

There was little more substance to the debate, though Mr A continued at some length on my modish style, on Mr Gervase Markham and his exalted connections, and on Mr Grimble and his agents which he did not seem to know. 'And here I am,' he concluded, 'with a dozen of port on it we shall beat Boney yet in spite of all our efforts. I always did say this damnation gov'-ment don't have a notion whether it's on its arse or its elbow.'

'And common to all of 'em if you ask me,' I agreed. 'But Mr Grimble's agents can't help us much. One who's in Boulogne is of little use; and another missing, if he ever existed at all, is even less. I fancy we shall have to show 'em what Bow Street can do. And August fifteenth,' I reminded him to cut the matter short, 'don't leave a lot of time for it.'

'Be damned, it leaves us but four days,' he announced as if the thought had struck him like a sudden poleaxe. 'What the devil are you waiting for, Sturrock? You'd best be off about your business, my man.'

'At my best speed, sir,' I assured him. 'But there's one thing first. The matter of Henriette d'Armande.'

A darker flush suffused his face again. 'Are you still on about that Haymarket whore? What the devil's she got to do with it?'

'Pretty well everything,' I said. 'Yesterday before I went to Whitehall it looked like a mere, common murder; though by some means unknown. Today it seems that the woman was up to her hocks in this business.' As quick as possible, for time was pressing, I went on to explain it to him and finished, 'In short, sir, she had either discovered this plot in the course of her trade, was party to it willing or unwilling, or was expected to give certain information to help it along; and was put away for turning fearful and threatening to split. We're seeking men with neither faces nor names,' I continued, 'and we don't know where to look. They may be lurking in the stews or mixing in the most elegant society, but one way or another some item we don't so far see about Henriette d'Armande will lead us to them.'

Mr A eased his aching foot and cursed, fingering a paper on the desk. 'If you ain't poking at a mare's nest. I hope you're not for your sake, Sturrock; for, as I said I would, I've set Ludwell on to that. I had him at Coventry Court yesterday, but he found little of note. He's on his way to Bath now, riding post.'

'No doubt he'll do very well there,' I observed politely. I refrained from adding that if I knew Master Ludwell he wouldn't hurry himself back from Bath either, and we must needs have this affair done with long before he could return to London. Ludwell was no matter and not worth wasting words on. Instead I asked, 'Touching our request to the coroner concerning this woman. Is there any word from him yet?'

Mr A took a hard breath. 'There's word enough, my man. Here, see for yourself.'

He tossed the paper at me; and it needed no second glance. It was headed, "The Coroner's Office", addressed to "The Chief Magistrate, Bow Street Court", and it said, "Sir; I am instructed by His Majesty's Coroner for this Borough, Dr Thomas Badger, to reply to your enquiry in the case re Henriette d'Armande, deceased. His Majesty's Coroner desires me to advise you that he sees no cause for an autopsical examination of the appertaining remains as there is no appearance of mistreatment sufficient to prove Fatal, and no indication of poisoning such as you propose. Taking into consideration the said woman's reported disorderly mode of life it is Dr Badger's considered opinion that death was due to some seizure or stroke incidental to her profession. In the case of the second woman, one Grope forename unknown, death was resultant on a severe wound in and consequent effusion of blood from the right side of the throat.

"Owing to the extreme temperature and heavy atmosphere presently prevailing, in the interests of public health and decency, the inquests on both of these remains were held today at eleven o'clock of the forenoon, when it was noted that none of your officers was present. For your information the verdicts were as follows; Henriette d'Armande, death in the course of Nature; the woman Grope, Murder by some Person or Persons Unknown. His Majesty's Coroner desires me to bring the second verdict to your attention and to intimate most respectfully that you shall instruct your officers in the proper discharge of their duties. Assuring you, sir, of our most profound deference at all times, your obnt svnt, etc. . . ."

Save only for a strange rumbling sound from Mr A there was a short silence before I announced, 'The man's a jackass.'

'He's a bladder of piss and port,' Mr A observed. 'But he's the coroner and a surgeon, and you ain't; you're a damned sight too smart for your own good. As I take it your whole precious case hangs on the notion that this whore was poisoned.'

'By some means unknown,' I added. 'But there's more in it than that.'

He leaned forward across the desk fetching a fresh wicked pang from his gout. 'I don't give a tinker's curse what more there is. Prove it, Sturrock. Make a fool of that windy gutted jobbernowl and it's worth a dozen of Madeira to you. Or, by God, if you don't I'll see you broke. And now get out before I fling my inkstand at ye.'

As you shall see it was an offer which was to have strange

and terrible consequences; but I said no more then as I am tender of the good gentleman's temper and health, and it looked as if he too might suffer from some stroke or seizure incidental to his profession. Nor was old Abel in much better case when I returned to the ante-chamber, for he considers it of importance to be well informed about what is going on in the office and had been listening with his ear to the door; I was forced to reassure him in a whisper that Mr A would not come to any harm if left alone for a bit before I could at last take my leave and go out to the front steps on the street to look for Master Maggsy and Jagger.

That fine fellow had done well for they were already waiting here with a near enough new post chaise and pretty good cattle; it was not of the class of any of Lady Dorothea's carriages, but by no means a turnout any gentleman need be ashamed of. He was grinning all over his face for his own smartness, with Maggsy standing importantly at the horses' heads consulting his gold watch—which the misguided Miss Lydia Palmer had presented him with,* and which I have never by no means been able to get away from the little toad—and cocking a snook at the several other urchins who were gathered around making the rude observations of their kind.

These I scattered with a touch or two of my cane, and then drawing on my gloves and settling my beaver added a few words of commendation to Jagger and continued, 'Now my lad, let's be on our way; to Medmenham. Keep the horses at it,' I instructed him, 'for it's a longish pull and we've no time to spare. We'll change 'em and take a pot of ale somewhere on the way.'

So once out of the traffic in Piccadilly and past the Hyde Park turnpike you are to see us clipping at a spanking pace through Kensington Village, and on to the wilder ruralities of Hammersmith. It was a good enough thoroughfare being the Bath Road, a fair width, dry and firm but not yet dusty; no hindrance or upsets from any damned roaring, racing stage coaches and their insolent drivers, and all in a fine holiday

* *The Wilful Lady*; my mysterious and diverting adventure with an American heiress, as headstrong as she was beautiful, which may still be obtained from the better sort of bookshops.

mood with Maggsy giving a cheer to every other carriage we passed, myself turning a philosophical reflection on the works of Nature, and Jagger carolling a song or two. Crossing the waste of Hounslow Heath he whipped up the horses yet faster and I looked to my pistols, for the place has an evil reputation; but highwaymen are no great danger in the forenoon and before long we were rattling gaily through the pretty little hamlet of Cranford and on west to Colnbrook, where there are several seats of the nobility to be glimpsed through the trees.

There was little incident save that just before Slough some young blood in a curricle and pair came high stepping from behind and took a try to drive us into the ditch for devilment; a challenge which Jagger was not slow to accept, and we finished by racing along wheel to wheel for a time with each of 'em using his whip, chickens squawking and flying, dogs barking, and myself roaring curses at all impartially. What the end of it might have been only God knows had not Maggsy let out a screech so wild and fearful that the other's spirited beasts tossed up their heads, snorted in terror, and bolted with him. The last we saw he was standing up, leaning back on the ribbons and yelling and hallooing like a madman; doubtless he came arse over tip somewhere, and a very proper end for the rascal. Not surprisingly after that our own cattle was blown, but on enquiry in Slough we learned that we could get a good change at an excellent and famous posting house at Salt Hill; the Windmill, six furlongs out of town. Here I admonished Jagger severely for his sporting instincts but nevertheless awarded him a quart of ale at my expense together with a pint of the same for Maggsy and a pot of claret for myself.

It was indifferent stuff, but I exchanged a few kindly words with the landlord; an amiable fellow though no doubt a rogue under his red weskit as most of them are, for when a man has passed only one year at a post house there is little left that he has not seen. Nevertheless he was civil enough, and more than ready to gossip, and on my asking our further road to Medmenham he enquired, 'What's on there I wonder? There's been several gentlemen to and fro that way lately.'

'There's a Mr Gervase Markham they visit,' I answered. 'Did

you notice was any of them foreigners?'

'We get all sorts,' he said indifferently. 'Was one a week or so back that the stable lads declared was a Frenchman. Did you say Mr Gervase Markham? We had another asking after his house but last night; and in a damnation lather. Horse very near foundered but wouldn't stop for more than change it, swallow a pot of ale, relieve himself and ride on for all it was early darkening with a thunderstorm brewing and he was warned of Maidenhead Thicket. Sure enough one more of my fellows swore he'd got a Frenchy shirt on.' He laughed comfortably and knocked the ashes from his pipe. 'The rogues go to bed with Frenchies on their poor wits since they all took up for Volunteers and playing soldiers with pitchforks.'

'They're doing their best after their fashion,' I observed, 'and good luck to 'em; we might have need of them yet. What's this about Maidenhead Thicket?'

'It's on your way to Medmenham. You bear off for Marlow at Maidenhead cross roads, and the thicket's just beyond. There's a gang of highwaymen said to be lurking about; they stopped a coach only on Saturday, cut the traces and bolted the horses, robbed a lady and gentleman of all they had.'

'They'll be wise not to try stopping me,' I told him. 'I'm carrying a brace of pistols by Wogdon that're more likely to stop them. And I don't ask the time of day before I use 'em either.'

'I see you're an experienced traveller,' he said, now listening with an ear cocked to the approaching blast of a horn and adding, 'That'll be the Bath Regent. She's a minute or two late.'

Hard on the signal the ostlers were already bringing out a fresh four in hand team and giving them a final whisk down, bystanders scattering like sparrows for their own safety and wenches appearing from the tap with jugs, pots, and platters; Jagger turning our own cattle about and Master Maggsy intimating in his genteel way that we were ready for the road by placing his fingers in his mouth and giving a splitting whistle. For an echo there was a louder blast still and the coach came roaring in with its guard winding his yard of tin like the last

72

trump, pulling up with a clatter and shower of sparks on the cobbles, passengers scrambling down to get a quick refreshment, the landlord hurrying off to oversee the change and collect the mails; and Maggsy stopping short in the act of another frightful whistle first to gaze at the coach like a terrier at a rat hole, then to saunter towards it with an air of most elaborate unconcern, and finally to scuttle back at a run to our own chaise where Jagger by now was showing signs of lively impatience.

He was inside before I climbed up myself. Without waiting for the word to give way Jagger wheeled out on the instant, going off with a jerk and a clatter and bawling, 'Get well clear of that bastard,' and we were a hundred yards gone before I had time to take in what Maggsy was screeching about. 'I said this lot's rum and gets rummer,' he yelled. 'Did you see that?'

'See what?' I demanded, calling on Providence and Jagger impartially to steady the horses.

'Mr Snadge,' he answered. 'Mr Popham Snadge. Inside passenger.'

'Snadge?' I repeated. 'Mr Cloudesley Merritt? Are you sure of that, boy?'

'I got a pair of peepers in my head, ain't I?' he demanded. 'I see him plain enough. He was just about to get down, seemed to catch sight of you, and ducked back; and damned near tripped that big fat woman arse over tits in his haste.'

'Now what the devil does this mean?' I asked. 'Did it look as if he was stopping there?'

'Dunno,' Maggsy replied, leaning out to look back and see if the coach was coming on, as it takes little more than a minute to change the teams.

'Much good that is,' I observed, considering what best to do. There was little in it either way for if Mr Merritt had stopped at Slough we had lost him by now, as we should lose him if he was travelling on further; while if like ourselves he was proposing to wait on Mr Markham he would be pretty certain to take up a mount or chaise from the nearest stage to Medmenham. That would be the Greyhound at Maidenhead and, my decision reached, I much surprised Jagger by ordering him to

73

stretch the horses yet more and get us to Maidenhead cross-roads in good time before the coach passed.

It was another sporting event for the rascal, and a damned rolling, racketing hell for leather dash he made of it until at last we reached the cross and pulled off the greater road to a lesser lane on the right. Here we stopped just past the corner and Maggsy leapt down, already primed with his instructions, to go off at a trot and find the inn. Then in another minute or so there was a thunder of hoofs, a tantara-tantivy on the horn, and the Regent came by with a flash of maroon, blue and gold, grey horses and glittering harness; a very pretty sight from a safe distance. I was content to wait and let our own animals take a breather while musing on what, if anything, this fresh turn might mean; but before long Maggsy came back at a jog, climbing up and crying jauntily to Jagger, 'Let 'em go, there, Thomas.'

'That's right,' he announced, as we moved off again, 'he's still there, sitting hard against the big fat woman, and she's still acussing him. Coach stopped for not above half a minute to set one cove down and I stuck my head in the door and says, "Why, what ho, Mr Snadge, what a wonder seeing you here; where's you bound for?" and he answers plain and straight, "Chippenham", gives a look at the big fat woman who's half smothering him, adds "Thank God when I get there", and continues, "It's an equal wonder seeing you. Where's Mr Sturrock off to then?" So I reply, "Dunno for sure, as he never tells me anything, but I wouldn't wonder if we're going fishing." And then he says, "I wouldn't wonder neither, so lookee Master Maggsy, just you tell Mr Sturrock that there's some uncommon big pike in that stretch of the river, and to watch his fingers, as they snap". What d'you make of that?'

'Not a lot,' I said, 'and no great matter, save you'll recollect that our other mysterious young gentleman, Mr Rodney Pottle, discovered a stable lad who said he thought he'd seen Henriette d'Armande before in Chippenham. I wonder is Mr Merritt going there as a government clerk or a would-be reporter for *The Gentleman's Magazine*? Or something else again? How did he seem when you accosted him? Surprised, guiltified or otherwise put out?'

'I dunno as he seemed put out or otherwise; but I dunno as he'd got much chance to seem like anything, not with that woman, all belly, tits and elbows asquashing at one side of him and a parson very near as fat aheaving and sighing at the other.' We were now passing through a more remote solitude with some pretty vistas of parkland here and there, but just as often long stretches of deep and gloomy woodland. It was no doubt the Maidenhead Thicket the Windmill landlord had warned me of, and while Jagger touched up the horses to a fresh canter Maggsy forgot Mr Merritt and his fat woman and leaned forward to peer fearfully to right and left. 'You have them barkers cocked and ready,' he added. 'It's a proper cut throat alley, this is, or I never see one.'

It was a reasonable precaution, for when highwaymen hunt in gangs or even pairs they are dangerous villains, but we passed through unchallenged and were soon crossing the River Thames to the pretty village of Marlow where I called a halt for our dinner. It was early yet, but I did not know what still lay before us and a wise man looks to his sustenance before venturing deeper into these outlandish country places. I have forgotten the name of the inn, but they gave us a nice dish of grayling— a simple country fish—followed by a very fair capon; then after that I sat over a pipe for a few minutes reflecting on Mr Rodney Pottle and Mr Cloudesley Merritt, and considering our next strategy, before giving the word for the road again. And I shall finish the rest of it by saying that following fresh instructions and one signpost after another we came at last to a scattered hamlet, a distant view of a church and a considerable mansion standing in its own grounds by the river, and a small tavern or beerhouse.

It was a decent enough place, with a red tiled floor, black timber and fairly clean plaster, the pewter well sanded and the bottle windows bright. The landlord was a monstrous rascal, bigger than I am myself, with corded arms, and fists like hams; by the look of his flattened nose and cauliflowered ear a practising or lately practising pugilist; and but seemingly genial with it. The only other person present was of a better order; a youngish fellow lounging against the bar, raw boned and weather-beaten, dressed in country clothes and wearing an expression of most profound ill temper but plainly a gentleman, though of the lesser sort. He also seemed to be of the sporting fraternity for he was gloomily examining a battered and splintered cricketing club or bat; leaning by him was a fowling piece, and sprawling on the tiles at his feet and guarding a game bag was two ugly looking liver coloured gun dogs with yellow eyes.

But seemingly his mind was only half on sporting matters, for as I stood in the doorway unnoticed for a minute with Maggsy close at my heels he was saying, 'You'll never do no good with that any more,' and then went on, 'but be hanged to cricket; cricket's no comfort to a man in love. I tell you, Trapp, Miss Geraldine'd have me quick enough were it not for that cursed brother of hers. Be damned to Markham and all his purse proud friends and their titles.'

The landlord gave a laugh at that and announced, 'There's a ready answer, Mr Ralph, and you're as plain with it as anybody; as many a wench hereabouts can testify. Rich or poor, high or low, they're all the same beneath their petticoats. Do your courting in the hay loft.' He broke off himself to look up at me, and added, 'Good day to you, sir.'

Before I could answer there was a strange and frightful sound like some giant slamming a great drum. The window rattled in its frame, the pewter jumped and clinked, and a flake of plaster fell from the ceiling; the young gentleman spilled his beer down his weskit and the landlord let out an observation which dumbfounded even Maggsy, while the dogs set up barking and howling and outside a crowd of rooks fled croaking from the elms. 'God's sake,' I demanded, sharply discouraging one of the dogs which now made a rush at me, 'what was that? You've some damned fine ducks here if you must needs shoot 'em with cannon.'

The landlord made another ripe observation. 'That was no cannon. That was Mr Gervase Markham.'

'Dropping a philosophical fart, was he?' Maggsy enquired politely.

'May he rot,' said Mr Ralph on a note of pious hope.

'Amen to that,' joined in Master Trapp. He listened for a minute as if waiting for another explosion and then continued, 'He's already blowed up the old boat house and lifted Bassett's mill clear out of the water; he's had half the tiles off Farmer Quince's cow byre and set Noggit's sow in farrow before her time, to say nothing of causing Meg Gabble to fall into a convulsive miscarriage. Not but what Meg's already got fourteen,' he finished with the air of a man striving to look on the brighter side, 'so one more nor less don't signify a lot.'

'He's frightened all the game,' continued the other, 'and exploded some damnation device in the river and killed all the fish. May he fry.'

'I'd admire to ha' seen any of that,' Maggsy announced, 'specially Noggit's sow and Meg Gabble.'

I silenced the creature and asked, 'Is the fellow a madman then? Don't you have any gentlemen or considerable land-owners who can restrain his antics? Can't they have a word or two with him, quiet and comfortable over half a dozen bottles of port?'

'I'd crown him with only one bottle for love,' the young man announced. 'And would too, if it warn't for Miss Geraldine.'

'Mr Gervase Markham is the considerable landowner,' Trapp said. 'Moreover there's the matter of the cricket field.'

Not for the first time when dealing with such country savages I felt my wits begin to spin, for they're like their horses; you can't tell which way they're going save by the twitching of their ears. 'Give me a pot of ale to steady me,' I ordered, and repeated, 'Cricket field? What of damnation does a cricket field have to do with it?'

He looked at me as I might have been a heathen Indian from one of the new South Sea Islands. 'Our event with the Hambleden men this coming Sunday. The first time in ten years we're set to trounce the rascals; save for a bit of ill luck as our stone-waller, Gipsy Tom's seen fit to up and die for no plain reason. Against that though their mighty hitter, the black-smith's been took with a stroke and Master Ralph here's contrived to lame their fast pitcher, the parson's son from Cambridge, by causing him to take a toss from his horse. Never

77

have we stood better. But Mr Gervase Markham owns the cricket field where we knows every furrow, bump, and tussock, and if we provoke him he's just as like to blow that up too.'

'Plainly an impetuous gentleman,' I observed. 'And what else does he get up to apart from explosions?'

Mr Ralph seemed to take a fresh turn for the worse and announced simply, 'Bullocks.'

I gazed at him narrowly, suspecting some such rudeness as you may hear among the commoner sort at Smithfield Market, and Master Maggsy screeched, 'God's Tripes. You want to watch it. He's a wicked tempered man is Sturrock, you want to watch it when you see his neck turn purple; he'll lay you cold as soon as look at you.'

I was not best pleased with the wretch for spitting out my name so carelessly, but the mischief was done, and silencing him once more I went on sternly, 'Come now, we'll have no unseemly language.'

'Unseemly be damned,' Mr Ralph retorted. 'I said bullocks and I mean bullocks.'

'I'll be obliged if you'll say what you do mean,' I told him in my softest and most terrible voice. 'And say it quick.'

'Purchased a bullock of Farmer Quince; d'ye follow that plain enough?' the fellow enquired incivilly. 'Well then thereafter he presented the carcase for an ox roast on the green by the church; as being the occasion of Miss Geraldine Markham's birthday last Saturday; or so he pretended.'

The ale was middling better than you might have expected, a well malted home brew, and I took a good draught of it to steady myself afresh before asking, 'What's wrong with that? It's a good old English custom.'

'Old English my arse,' Mr Ralph answered. 'First, it ain't in Markham's nature. Second, it warn't Miss Geraldine's birthday as I happen to be sure of. And last, nobody knows how the animal was slaughtered, for not a man as we've heard of was called in to the job.'

'No, Master Ralph,' Landlord Trapp argued. 'But it was a beautiful tender bit of beef; I never tasted sweeter. Folks was carrying off all they had a mind to take, sir,' he added to me.

'And I don't see the harm in it,' I said; though privately resolving that it was another matter to place under my Thinking Cap.

'Maybe he aimed to poison 'em all,' Maggsy suggested in his sweet way. 'God's Weskit, I'd admire to see that; corpusses all over the place akicking and screeching.'

None of us condescended to answer that though Mr Ralph gazed at the little monster with some interest. Instead the landlord asked of me, 'What is your interest in Mr Markham, sir?'

It was a nice question, as these country bumpkins are like the inhabitants of Seven Dials; whatever enmity they might have between themselves you can never tell how much they'll band together against the law. But I put on a mysterious smile. 'It's government business. A matter of the Income Tax; brought in again, as no doubt you know, by Mr Addington last year.'

I have played many parts in my time, but never a tax man before; neither was it all that well received, for they both edged away from me as if I had the yellow fever, and Mr Ralph announced, 'Be damned, I've a good mind to set the dogs on ye.' He let out a bellow of rude laughter. 'Did you hear the tale that's going the rounds at Reading? About a cursed great bull mastiff that bit one of your rogues? Uncommon sad and pathetic; for the dog it was that died.'

'We'll have less of the pleasantries,' I advised him sternly. 'I'm human enough myself.' Maggsy snickered at that, but I continued, 'I even enjoy a good sporting game of cricket when there's time for it. And what's more if I'm treated polite I might find a way to restrain some of Mr Gervase Markham's antics a bit.'

'Begod, I don't see how,' Trapp muttered.

'There's ways and means,' I promised. 'You play a nice full pitch to me, and I'll bat it back. To start with, what visitors has he been receiving of late?'

'A regular gaggle forever coming and going,' he grumbled. 'Frenchies and Americans and Dutchies and whatever else you fancy, so the servants say. But we see little of 'em here, for they all turn off just short of the inn and make for Markham's main lodge.'

'It's as I expected.' I nodded my head wisely. 'You haven't either of you heard of a Mr Cloudesley Merritt or Mr. Rodney Pottle?' They both looked blank at that, though it seemed Mr Ralph suspected they might be yet more beaux for his lady love. 'Or another visitor last night?' I continued. 'Latish on, and very likely enquiring the way.'

'So there was,' Trapp said. 'Sheltered here for a while in the midst of that thunderstorm, and took a quick bite of bread and cheese and pickled walnuts. Then asked how best to get into Mr Markham's grounds without going by the lodge. Offered half a sovereign to be told of it.' He looked sideways at Mr Ralph. 'I reckoned it'd be another one after Miss Geraldine.'

Mr Ralph exploded with a surprising love sick oath, and I warned the poor young fellow kindly against over exciting himself. Turning back to Trapp I asked, 'Is there some other entrance then? And did you tell the man?'

'Half a sovereign's half a sovereign, ain't it? However come by. He said he must go and leave again quick and quiet. So I told him there's a little wicket down opposite the back wall of the churchyard.'

'And was he English?'

Landlord Trapp scratched his head. 'Damned if I see what you be driving at, master. He spoke English plain enough.'

'It's no great matter,' I told the fellow; and did not ask for a description, for you rarely get anything that makes much sense out of such enquiries. I finished instead, 'Well, whichever way he went I'm bound to go by the lodge. So where is it?'

'Down back along fifty yards or so,' Trapp answered, 'and bear left towards the river.'

'And a damned ugly dog of a lodge keeper there,' Mr Ralph observed. 'I wouldn't wonder if you got a charge of small shot in your privates,' he added hopefully.

'If I do it'll be a vexatious occurrence for all concerned,' I promised.

But there seemed little more to be gained here, and I turned to urge Maggsy out to the lane again, where Jagger was waiting, and then went on to the child, 'Now then, you know what I want. You may go back in there to see what more you can pick up. I doubt there'll be much, though there's one Gipsy Tom who seems to have died for no good reason. After that find this wicket gate yourself and take a private look about the estate. Then come back to wait for me and Jagger here.'

'If one, t'other, or all three of us don't get blowed up first,' he complained, 'as might easy happen. If you ask me, this is a right rum lot.'

'I don't ask you,' I assured him; but for once in his life the wicked little monster spoke no less than the truth.

FIVE

The lodge was a little pagoda in the modish Chinese style—too fantastical and frippery for my taste, though much affected by His Royal Highness, the Prince of Wales—but fronted by considerable iron gates set in pillars each with some heraldic monster on top, as I have always considered a far more suitable adornment to any gentleman's estate. Behind them was a curving avenue of noble elms, and through this glimpses of an elegant park planted with stands of the handsome timbers now being imported from America; here a little temple, there what looked like an orangery with its own dwelling also surrounded by trees, and last the mansion itself standing on a terrace. In short every evidence of wealth and importance; and, surveying it for a minute, I reflected that if Mr Gervase Markham was as deep in this affair as all appearances seemed to suggest he was like to prove a prickly nut to crack, before at last saying to Jagger, 'Now, my lad, let 'em know we're here.'

This he did with a will, hallooing until out of the lodge appeared not a pretty little Chinese princess in silken robes, but as ugly a rogue as you'd wish never to meet on a dark night. Of shortish stature, but near enough as broad as he was high, as hairy as any wild Indian at Bartholomew Fair and much the same hue of copper, brawny arms dangling damned near to his knees and worked all over with tattooings, and a shambling, rolling gait; a rascal plainly born to be hanged. He surveyed us with no great favour from beyond the gates and demanded, 'What d'you want then?'

'Gen-leman to wait on Mr Gervase Markham,' Jagger announced. 'Look slippy now.'

'Ain't no gen'leman expected,' the rogue retorted, as surly as a hackney driver. 'Be off with you.'

'Why now, you walking bladder of piss and peas pudden,' says Jagger, as sweet as plum pie, 'do but come a bit closer and I'll have your beard out hair by hair, to say nothing of your cobblers after; if you've got any, which I much misdoubt.'

'You and who with you?' the rascal enquired, no less polite. 'Why, you runt, you bandy arsed, bean balled horse jockey, I've ate men twice the better of you for my breakfast and roared for more.'

'Is that so?' Jagger asked, as genteel as ever, 'and does that account for your constipulated look?'

Such exchanges are by no means uncommon between the lower sort and are often an expression of good will and esteem, as in the House of Commons, but fearing lest they should lead to wilder flights I judged it time to intervene. Dismounting and settling my beaver, flicking the dust from my coat with my gloves and slapping my pantaloons with my cane, I said, 'Come now, my man, let's have less of the courtesies. Take me to your master on the instant, and maybe it'll be worth a crown piece; for I've come a pestilential long way to meet the gentleman.' But neither a tax man nor a Bow Street Runner could expect to be admitted here, and I had my fresh tale prepared. 'You may present me as Dr Henry Summerlea, engineer of Philadelphia and Harvard University, Cambridge, Massachusetts, come to confer with Mr Markham on scientific matters.'

That fetched him up all standing and he muttered, 'I dunno as I must or no. Mr Markham's about his bangs and powerful sharp tempered with it if broke in at 'em. But I'll fetch Miss Geraldine.' On that he gave a pull to a most curious contraption set against the side of the lodge; a kind of wheel and lever, with wires running away from it over one little pulley to another set on short posts all up the drive. It looked as if we'd come to a house of many strange contrivances.

We did not have long to wait, for scarcely had the lodge keeper done scratching his head and then his belly before there appeared in the avenue what at first sight seemed to be a youngish fellow mounted on a rangy, evil tempered looking roan. Never was I so put about in my life, for on approaching the gates I perceived from the general endowments of the figure that it was a woman, or little more than a girl, and by no means ill looking; but most unseemly wearing a shirt and britches, dark hair cropped short, and—will you believe me ladies?—riding astride.

Not content with that, what must she do when she came up to the gates but cock one leg up like an impudent country urchin and slide down over her horse's neck without so much as troubling to dismount like a gentleman. Never have I beheld a scene so ungenteel, and my one thankfulness was that Master Maggsy was not here to view it, or for certain that lewd little monster would have made some observation which would have kept us out of Mr Markham's estate for ever; even as it was Jagger whispered something I shall not repeat. For myself I concealed my displeasure and remained silent while she entered into a short colloquy with her ugly Cerberus and then marched up to the gate to regard me from a pair of level and direct grey eyes; but an uncommon taking piece for all her outrageous manner. 'What is your business, sir?' she asked.

I was in some doubt how to address the hoyden, and made the best of it by lifting my beaver, doing a bow, and repeating 'Dr Henry Summerlea, young lady, of Harvard and Philadelphia; a natural philosopher not unknown in those circles, to wait on and pay my respects to Mr Gervase Markham.'

The grey eyes continued to regard me coolly; she enquired, 'To what end do you wish to wait on Mr Markham, Dr Summerlea?'

My choler was beginning to get the better of me, but I replied politely enough, 'Why to present certain scientific observations to him; also to enquire the present whereabouts of Mr Robert Fulton and what progress there is with his submersible ship.'

'Mr Robert Fulton,' she mused, 'and his submersible.' Then she smiled suddenly; and I should have been warned by it. She continued, 'My brother will be engaged to meet you, Dr Summerlea,' and nodded to her black avised custodian, who knuckled his forehead, to come forward with a great key while she added, 'Pray forgive our caution, sir, but Mr Markham's about a very particular experiment. Being a scientist yourself you'll under-

84

stand the need for care.' Swinging herself back on to her horse she finished over her shoulder, 'Please to follow me; it's to the end of the drive, where we're assembled on the terrace,' and was off like the wind raising spurts of gravel from the animal's hoofs.

As the gates opened for us Jagger saw fit to observe, 'That un'd never do for Hanover Square. Her'll have her arse spread like a pumpkin before long if her goes on riding like that.'

'I'd just as soon see a lady put her virtues to better uses myself,' I agreed. 'But I'll thank you to keep your mind on other matters, Jagger; we've serious business here.'

So calling the man to order we set off up the drive at a more sober pace, catching fresh glimpses of well tended gardens and stretches of grass like velvet, a prospect of the river and the little temple, some distance off the building I took to be an orangery with what looked like a dower house attached, and last the mansion itself. All in all a very respectable gentleman's country seat, built about the time of Queen Anne in nice rose brick, with well placed white windows, a commodious balustraded terrace, and wide flight of shallow steps up to it.

Jagger halted here with a flourish, and I got down to look up at the several gentlemen waiting above with that hoyden talking to one of them drawn a little apart; and turning another of her deceitful smiles back on me. There was a pretty plain air of something in preparation, but nothing for it but to doff my beaver and go on; though at the same time saying softly and quickly to Jagger, 'Take your horses back as far as the drive and stand by there. Don't let yourself be led off to the stables. Have my pistols ready, and keep an ear cocked in case I call for you.'

As I mounted the steps, not hurrying myself but looking uncommon pleased to be present with such company, I perceived that these were none of your common stink and snuff philosophers, but of the more amateur sort such as you often see at Lady Dorothea's salon. There were five of them standing about a long table or bench on which was arranged an array of jars, coils, wires, glass cylinders, brass and copper contraptions and strange electrical machines; while nearby was another attended by two footmen in livery coats and powdered wigs with a set out of flagons of wine and goblets. It was, as you might say, science with gentility; and the gentleman in conference with Miss Geraldine was the most elegant of all. His hair clubbed in the fashionable style, a fine lawn neckcloth and brocaded weskit, a blue coat with cut steel buttons, and pantaloons of an even better cut than my own; a bit above forty I judged, undeniably handsome and a fine take it or leave it style about him. He broke away from the wench and came to meet me crying, 'Well, Dr Summerlea, as my sister tells me, welcome to our modest circle; you do us too much honour, sir. We're in your debt to have you with us.'

Affecting a bluff and unaffected air, as is the manner of our late American colonials, I replied. 'No, but I'll not have it so, I dare say the honour is more correctly mine. Why, sir, when I left my good friends in Philadelphia these two months since they was all hell bent to press me to wait upon Mr Gervase Markham.'

'No, sir,' he insisted, 'I say the honour's ours. But let's cry quits on it.' Taking my arm in the friendliest fashion and drawing me in to the other gentlemen, he continued. 'We're a mixed college; each with his own furrow in the fields of knowledge. Here now is Monsieur Henri Leclerc, a most notable chemist of Grenoble; and here Mynheer van Maartens of Leyden, a worthy follower of the great Carolus Linnaeus in the science of botany; and Master Karl Hertz, a mathematical philosopher of Heidelberg. You shall come to know us all at supper, as I'll not permit you to leave us untimely. For now, sir, pray tell me how does my old friend Mr Oliver Evans do with his experiments on galvanism in Philadelphia?'

I had never before heard of Mr Oliver Evans from Adam, but not to be outdone I replied, 'Famously, sir. At his last demonstration Mr Evans had all beholders astounded and marvelling.'

'Aye,' Mr Markham agreed. 'I don't wonder at it. That would be at a soirée of the American Philosophical Society?'

The fellow was going too far and too fast, but I answered, 'Where else, sir? A body of most ingenious gentlemen.'

'Of which you are no doubt an illustrious member?' he enquired.

I much misliked the way this discussion was turning. It was time for both modesty and caution. 'Illustrious is a title to be conferred rather than assumed,' I said. 'I would not claim it.'

'But you have it thrust upon you.' He cast a curious look around the other gentlemen, including one more he had not yet presented to me, and allowed his gaze to rest for a moment on his sister; who was now half sitting on the balustrade swinging one unmaidenly leg and surveying the scene with a secret little smile on her lips, like a cat that's got at the cream. 'Come now, doctor,' he added, 'let's take a glass of wine. After that you shall give us your opinion on a most perplexing phenomenon we've observed today.'

Reflecting that I had fallen into deeper water than I bargained for, but resolved to swim it out, I moved with the others across to the second table where the flunkeys were dispensing goblets of Rhenish wine; poor thin gut sluice to a man who understands his claret, but no doubt suitable for scientists. With a ready invention I answered Mr Markham's interested questions about my late travels, and even took the considered chance of throwing in several observations about Paris, St Petersburg, and ships sailing from that great northern port as a bait. But except for a passing flash of interest in the eye of that gentleman to whom I had not yet been introduced there was no other rise to it, and while further continuing the civilities I turned my attention to the other gentlemen severally.

The German I dismissed, for he could not have been anything else; and although he bore a strange resemblance to the famous portrait of our late immortal Dr Samuel Johnson had but three or four words in our own tongue which he presented to me importantly one after the other, and then turned to a discourse in rolling Latin with the Dutchman. He too I concluded was no great matter, though doubtless profound on vegetables, and not unnaturally my main attention fell upon the Frenchy. A man of about the same age as Mr Markham and much the same manner; an aristocrat who had survived the Revolution I judged —or very likely a turncoat to the murdering side, as some of them were—of a similar distinction with his dress and a somewhat disdainful politeness in an English not unlike that of my own Anne-Louise; but not so pretty. We too exchanged several courtesies, but he was plainly more concerned with Miss Geraldine who had now also joined the party.

Mr Markham was still at my elbow going on about the electric force or galvanism or some such fantasticals but I answered him absently while continuing to watch the Frenchy. In spite of his insouciance—as Anne-Louise would say—there was a small but very plain uneasiness about him, not unlike some of the little lambs at the Brown Bear when they have been up to mischief and wonder how much I might know about it. The moment passed however, for giving one glance back at me over his shoulder he moved away with Miss Geraldine, while on this the last gentleman approached us; the deep set eyes with a certain quizzical glint about them, a craggy face tanned by stronger climates than ours, and wearing his own hair and a frock coat in the American style. I needed no telling who this must be. The water now was not only deep but like soon to become stormy as for certain it was none other than the Dr Wilford Caldwell, physician, botanist and traveller spoken of in the American ambassador to France's letter which Mr Grimble had shown me.

Nevertheless he started pleasantly enough. 'It's a particular privilege, Dr Summerlea. No doubt you're well acquainted with Mr Thomas Jefferson?'

The acquaintance of the President of America is one I cannot fairly claim, and I replied plainly, 'I do not have that honour, sir.'

'Do you not?" he enquired. 'You're unfortunate then, for Thomas is a great patron of scientists and often has them to visit at Monticello. But did I hear you speak of St Petersburg? You wouldn't by any chance have sailed from there on the *Lubeck*, which fetched up in London a week ago last Sunday?'

For what it seemed worth that was one item of information; but also a trap which I perceived before it was sprung. 'I fear I must disappoint you yet again, sir,' I said. 'I have been in England some several weeks.'

'Come, Caldwell,' Mr Markham joined in, 'we're fretting Dr Summerlea with too many questions. Let's set about our experiment again.' He cast another curious look at his hoyden sister while turning back to the other table with its mess of scientific apparatus, and then asked me, 'You'll be familiar with the properties of the Voltaic Pile and Franklin's Jars, sir?'

I am about as familiar with them as I am with honesty in Seven Dials, or virtue in Drury Lane but I answered, 'Tolerably so; though I protest I am no more than a mere engineer.'

'No, sir,' he smiled, fiddling with the contrivances there, 'you're too modest.' Modest or not I could make neither head nor tail of any of the contraptions and had no great wish to, for in my opinion such devil's playthings are best left alone by honest men. 'And I'll not presume to explain them to you,' he continued, 'but as you will know it has already been shown possible to pass the electric fluid along a wire for no less than two miles. We here have been trying whether by so doing we could also ignite an explosion.'

I restrained myself from announcing that it was a damned mischievous objective too, and observed instead, 'An ingenious project, sir; and more than successful judging by the reverberation a short while ago.'

'Not entirely so. There was a phenomenon we hadn't expected and which we've been discussing since.' He looked round at the others again and went on, 'And I fancy we need an engineer's knowledge here to explain it for us.'

'Sir,' I told him, 'I know little or nothing of explosions, save that they are frequently inconvenient.' But even a babe in arms or a government official could perceive that we might have here the heart and substance of this French conspiracy, and I demanded, 'Do you tell me that you can now cause such detonation at a distance without fuse, slow match or other agency?'

'We shall do,' Mr Markham asserted, 'when we've got it right.'

The mischief of it dumbfounded me. 'In short, sir, you could blow up a ship at a distance? A naval dockyard? Or even the Houses of Parliament if you were so minded?'

Dr Wilford Caldwell gave a laugh on that. 'Faith, Dr Summerlea, we know there's many of us just don't see eye to eye with our British friends on many things; but blowing up their Parliament on account of it's a thought extreme.'

'Take my word on it, Caldwell,' Mr Markham told him, 'there's many a gentleman sleeping there wouldn't be aware of the explosion. No, Dr Summerlea,' he added to me, 'the Houses of Parliament are a mite ambitious, and a ship offers problems of its own. But there's little doubt that when we've got my contrivance certain we could remove smaller buildings, or even bridges.'

'Then, sir,' I retorted, 'pray God it remains uncertain. For it seems like a project better left alone to me.'

'Be hanged, doctor,' he protested warmly, 'is that spoke like an engineer? What of the advancement of science, sir? Begod, you'll have us doubting your credentials in a minute. But I perceive what it is,' he cried. 'You're sceptical of it and too genteel to say so. Very well then, we shall prove the matter. D'you see that old willow tree there, leaning out across the river? I'll engage to blow it clear from the ground at a single stroke. Or rather you shall. What d'you say now? Are you game?'

There was a sudden silence among the others, save that the Frenchman whispered something to Miss Geraldine. I fancied I caught a brief look of concern from the American, as if about to declare that the jest might go too far. But if I can dare the rogues of Seven Dials I can dare a country philosopher any day of the week, and I answered, 'Why not, sir? I don't doubt my advancement of science is as good as yours.'

'Well said, sir,' he applauded deceitfully. 'So come now, first lay aside your gloves for there's something about leather which seems to retard the force. So,' he continued, 'next take a firm grip of this rod.' He demonstrated an appendage standing out of a sort of glass cylinder on the table, and then announced 'We have a very determined scientist here, gentlemen.' I should have been warned again by the fresh breathless silence, but not if His Majesty the King himself had commanded me would I have drawn back now. 'And last,' concluded our fine Mr Markham, 'keep an eye on the willow tree, but place your other fingers on the metal coating of the Franklin Jar.'

Be damned to the willow tree, for it was me that exploded. No sooner had I touched that cursed jar than I was seized with such convulsions as I cannot speak of. The devil and all his imps was in it. Such a cramping of the muscles, fiery constriction, stoppage of heart and breath, twisting of the bowels and locking of the jaws that I could not even bellow a curse before I was flung flat on my back helpless, with that wicked gang standing about me and laughing to crack their sides as I rolled there in a racking tingle.

Never was I so put down. But not for long. Be he scientist or not the man is a fool who plays such a trick on Jeremy Sturrock. With what dignity I might I got myself to my feet, dusting off my coat and britches, and then addressed them all severally and collectively. I spared them nothing despite all my respect for the country gentry; their past, their present and their future, their parentage and the geniture of their children, what they could do with themselves even with the utmost difficulty, and what they could do with their triple damned science.

'Gad,' cried the wench between ill mannered shrieks and hoots, 'here's a most undoctorial language. And I'll swear to it, most unphiladelphical.'

'As for you,' I retorted, 'I'll have you know that a hen in britches is an offence to God and man.'

'Now be damned,' roared Mr Markham between his own bellows, 'I'll not have you speak so. Shall I trounce him, Gerry? Shall I give the cursed impostor another lesson?'

Beside myself with rage I announced, 'Be damned to yourself, sir. Try to see if you can do it and we'll find who does the trouncing.'

I might have added more precise advice of what I'd do with the lot of 'em but for the presence of a lady; and also had not my good Jagger now come roaring up brandishing my Wogdons and in a very fair mood for battle himself. In an instant the sight of that mighty armament stopped the laughter. The flunkeys got themselves beneath their table with no effort, our learned philosophers was frozen as still as statues and the wench herself sat with her mouth open in the middle of a hoot cut short. Only Mr Markham and the American faced it out; and even they were struck with such astonishment that it near enough paid for my own discomfiture. I could still feel the horrid tingling and my limbs still shaking.

Mr Markham was the first to recover. 'What the devil's this?' he demanded. 'God's wounds,' he announced, 'they're cracked; it must be the highwaymen from Maidenhead run mad. Put those pistols down you Tom-fool,' he ordered Jagger, 'or you'll hang for it; I've a dozen men within call and you'll be overpowered in a minute.'

He took a step towards me and so far from putting them down my good fellow raised them; but I said, 'Let it be, Jagger,' and went on, 'Neither cracked nor highwaymen.' There was nothing for it now but to reveal myself, and I added, 'The Bow Street Patrol,' producing my baton and crown to prove the fact.

Mr Markham was yet more astonished. 'Bow Street?' he repeated. 'A mere damned thieftaker? Then why of God's name did ye not apply for admission, sirrah, as you should? Instead of this damned play acting imposture.'

I could scarcely answer that it was because I suspected him of some part in the French conspiracy and told him instead another plain truth. 'Because had I applied for admission it might well have been refused. Or at best I'd have been left cooling my heels in your servants' hall to await your pleasure.'

The hoyden went off into a fresh peal of laughter. 'He's not so far mistaken at that, Brother Gervase.' She surveyed me as cool as a melon. 'But if the fellow is a Bow Street Runner he's also a very idiot.'

'I'm bound to agree that's correct,' the American observed. 'Nobody but an idiot, sir, would handle a charged Franklin's Jar as innocent as you did. And as for Oliver Evans, with whom you claim acquaintance, Mr Evans has lately constructed a steam car in Philadelphia and knows no more of galvanism than it seems you do.'

I felt my neckcloth tightening and my weskit buttons strained, but said, 'Very well, sir, we'll have an end of the dramatics. If it pleases you I'll own myself at fault. But I'm here on a matter of the law, and my business admits no delay.'

Somewhat strangled in his voice Mr Markham called to the flunkeys, 'You there, be damned, get out from under that table and fill me a glass of wine. By God, I need it.' He considered me unfavourably. 'Well then, you Bow Street dunderhead, what is your business?'

I looked to Jagger and told him, 'That'll do then, Jagger; you may return to the chaise. We shall be leaving in a minute.' He was standing by the balustrade dangling the pistols and grinning all over his face; like any good servant he saw no harm in watching his betters being taken down a few pegs now and again and he turned away reluctantly. None of them made any move to stop him, and I continued, 'My business is murder, sir. The killing and murder of a woman, Henriette d'Armande, in London on Monday last.'

Save for wiping the Frenchy grin off Monsieur Leclerc of Grenoble's chaps the announcement had little effect that I could see and Mr Markham burst out, 'To hell with it, my man, what's that to do with me; or any of us? I never heard of the woman. Who is she?'

'In simple, sir, she was a whore. Apart from that her family and former life remain unknown, but it seems she was an *émigré*.' I paused for an instant for the effect and then finished, 'As to what does it have to do with you, sir, the poor woman spoke your name. On her last dying breath she murmured "Mr Gervase Markham, of Medmenham".'

As you will know this was not precisely true, but we are sometimes permitted such small stratagems in the Art and Science of Detection. You might call it a ranging shot though it was hard to say where it fell, for except in bringing up a flush of apoplectic colour in Mr Markham it produced no other effect; though the Frenchy turned his back to me and took a glass of wine from the flunkey with a certain over nice elaboration. It was Miss Geraldine who broke the fresh silence, giving another laugh and saying, 'La, Brother Gervase, are your pranks and pastimes in London treading at your heels now?'

He turned a glance on the immodest creature that should have struck her to a block of ice had she been capable of such sensibility, observed, 'Pray restrain your pertness, Miss,' and in the tone of one gentleman offering a compliment to another continued to me, 'God damn your eyes, you poxy Drury Lane rat, if you don't take yourself and your Newgate stink off my land this instant I'll set the stable men and dogs upon you.'

Just as genteel I answered, 'With infinite pleasure, sir, I'll not outstay my welcome. But I'll advise you that when I return it'll be with a warrant in my hand.'

Once again it brought a sudden stillness; the Dutchy and the German plainly did not know what to make of the scene, though Mr Markham's colour went to a darker shade of puce but before he could get a word out Monsieur Leclerc said something in his own language, added, 'A moment,' gave me a look up and down which should have spoiled my health and demanded, 'This woman; what is it? Henriette d'Armande? How did she die? Is it that you know?'

'She was poisoned,' I told him shortly.

That was a shot which did go home, though once more hard to tell where it struck. But before I could follow it with another and demand what else were they experimenting with here besides mischievous explosions, and why should Mr Markham purchase a young bullock only to give it to the poor villagers for an ox roast, Master Maggsy must needs make a dramatic appearance to take a hand in the game. Never was a man so unfortunate at a critical minute, for from round the corner of the terrace below us arose such an uproar of screeches and oaths as could only come from that sweet angel; and a spectacle I could well have done without. First two grinning stable lads and between them the ugly little monster kicking, fighting and cursing, while one held him by his left ear and the other marched him with an arm twisted up behind his back; following these two more rascals armed with dung forks and helping the unhappy child on with prods at his hinder parts; and bringing up the rear four or five more come to watch the fun, with Maggsy shrieking objurgations and observations at every step.

'God's Tripes, Sturrock,' he howled, perceiving me, 'see what you've let me in for now; they've very near got my arse in rib-hobs a'ready and they'll have my cobblers next.'

'That's enough,' I said sternly. 'Mind your manners in the presence of a lady, you wretch.' I looked at Master Markham, who I will wager had spent more time speechless that day than ever in his life before, but my chance had gone. What little advantage I had won was lost, for if he was dumbstruck for a minute the others was starting to laugh again. You cannot conduct a murder investigation in the middle of a Sadler's Wells farcical. All that remained now was to escape with what little dignity we had left to us, and before Mr Markham could start I said, 'My clerk, sir. A venturesome child; and must have rambled away from my chaise to get lost in your grounds.'

'Your clerk?' demanded Mr Markham, gazing down at the apparition in wonderment while Miss Geraldine went into new fits and peals.

'Found 'n peering and poking about the windows of the old orangery, your honour,' one of the rascals explained, knuckling his forelock.

'The laboratory?' Mr Markham asked.

There was a change in his voice which warned me of danger. I saw the Frenchy too stop his sniggers, and as quick as thought I cried, 'What you wretch, you've been prying, have you?' I turned back to Mr Markham, adding, 'If he's been in mischief, sir, I'll correct him. I'll teach him better manners.'

'We'll save you the trouble,' he said. 'My men shall see to it. Did the little mohock get inside?' he asked. 'Or steal anything?'

'No ways near it,' the fellow answered. 'We was too quick for'n.'

'That's something to be thankful for,' Mr Markham observed with a side glance at the Frenchman. 'We've already had one mishap too many.' He turned a Justice of the Peace look on Maggsy; and had they known that child as well as I do they would have been warned, for the stable boys were slackening their grip on him and he was hanging between like a drooping buttercup with the snivels. But all oblivious Mr Markham continued, 'You, Crabbe, fetch a good whippy riding switch. Whichever one of you fancies the job best may lay into him.'

Somewhat to my surprise the American intervened. 'Come now, Mr Markham, you'll not have the boy thrashed for a mere childish mischief?'

'Damned dangerous mischief,' Mr Markham retorted.

'Dangerous indeed,' I announced. 'The first of your men that touches him will have me to deal with. I'll put 'em all down one by one if I must.'

95

What the end of it might have been I do not care to think as I have a proper respect for the landed gentry on their own estates—besides we were heavily outnumbered—but Jagger was now coming back intent on battle, though thank God this time without the pistols, and Master Maggsy caught sight of him, saw his chance and seized it. With a further fearful screech he hacked out backwards like a gamecock at one fellow and on the instant swung a wicked blow into the other's lower belly. The first fell back bellowing in pain and clasping his shin, the second doubled over on his private parts with squeals like a ruptured pig, my sportive little rascal somehow tripped a third over flat on his face, seized his dung fork to threaten the rest of 'em while Jagger came roaring in to toss one more aside, and then broke clear away and made off as fast as his legs could carry him for the chaise.

It was all done quicker than the words themselves and there was only one way to end it now. You can often confound the gentry with an impudence as great as their own, and before Mr Markham could get another word out I doffed my beaver with the utmost politeness, said, 'I'll give you good day, gentlemen, and you, ma'am,' and turned to descend the steps. The coolness of it halted them all and the fellows below paused to stare at me, not quite knowing what to do, but I continued kindly, 'Now, my lads, let me pass.'

'No, by God,' Mr Markham started behind me.

For a minute it was touch and go. They were looking up to him for fresh orders, and ripe enough for mischief if set on to it, but then Miss Geraldine cried, 'Oh Lud, Gervase, have done. Faith, they're vastly diverting, a damned sight more diverting than your bangs and stinks but enough's enough; they grow tiresome. Let them be. They're nothing but a pair of clowns or Punch and Judy men.'

Upon that Mr Markham was kind enough to say, 'Well enough then; on your good offices, sister.' He must have made some sign to the men for they fell back, but he called, 'You there, sirrah; one moment more. What's your name?'

I turned again to face him, studying the fine company up there. The Dutchy and the German still spitting Latin in each

96

other's eyes with never a thought for anything else in the world, and Miss Geraldine hiding a yawn behind her fingers; Monsieur Leclerc, Dr Wilford Caldwell and Mr Markham all looking uncommon thoughtful. I fancied they had more than enough to be thoughtful about, and might have more yet before I was done with them, but as polite as ever I answered, 'Sturrock, sir; Jeremy Sturrock. And not unknown in certain quarters.'

'I'll not forget you,' he promised. 'I'll see you're even better known in certain others. Now get off my land before I change my mind and set the dogs loose.'

So in no great hurry, like a gentleman taking his afternoon stroll and daring the pack of them behind me, I returned to the chaise, where Master Maggsy was cursing, complaining, and easing his sore backside upon the leather. 'Jagger,' I commanded, 'take that grin off your face to start with, and then proceed up the drive brisk but sober; we'll not have it look as if we're retreating in disorder. And as for you,' I continued to Maggsy, 'you monkey brain, you turnip headed goose, how often must I tell you that in the whole Art and Science of Detection there's no crime like getting caught?'

Maggsy's reply surprised me not so much for what he said as for the manner of it. He was strangely subdued and so far from bursting into his common torrent of poetic curses he growled only, 'You want to go easy or I might wish an arse on you as sore as mine what with kicks and pitchforks and none of 'em any too gentle. Or I might reckon to keep my trap shut about what I seen, and where would you be then?'

'Where I am now,' I told him, not in the best of tempers myself. 'Beaten and bested; but not for long, by God. Providence loves to chasten us now and again, and it's a poor general who throws up a war on a single battle. One way and another that fine gang of villains have let out a lot more than they know of.'

'I keep atelling you, it's a rum lot this,' he continued to soliloquise, 'and too many corpusses about. Mr William Makepeace the Practical Chimney Sweeper always used to say one corpuss leads to another; particular them with staring eyes.'

'Be damned to Mr William Makepeace,' I announced. 'What

have you got in your thick head now?'

'Another corpuss too many,' he answered. 'But let's get out of here first. And when we do, have Thomas turn back to that beer house; it's called the Waggoners. I reckon they'll still be there. They didn't look the sort that'd hurry themselves about anything.'

'God help us,' I cried in exasperation and rage, 'who'll still be there?'

'A couple of grave diggers,' he said. 'I never see them come in pairs before neither. I wouldn't wonder if that ain't bad luck too.'

SIX

With that I had to be content, for along with all his other faults the little wretch can be uncommonly obstinate too when he pleases. But we were near enough to the gates by then, though even here we did not escape without further discussion as it seemed the surly rogue of a lodge keeper had got a notion from somewhere that I had promised him a crown piece. By now more than out of patience myself it was a heated matter for a minute until one of the stablemen came riding up on a hack, sent to see us well off the grounds, and we parted in the end with several expressions of esteem on both sides. Then at last I ordered Jagger to walk the horses quietly towards the tavern to give Maggsy time to tell his tale and demanded, 'Now what in damnation's this about a pair of grave diggers?'

'That Gipsy Tom,' he answered in the sulks. 'You said to go back in the Waggoners and ask about him, so this I done. Well then the landlord and Mr Ralph was colloguing about their cricket match and Miss Geraldine, and I says I dunno about Miss Geraldine, but I got a brother who strikes for the St Mary Le Bone men, likewise he's a mighty hitter or a dead stone waller whichever they fancies best; and he's got to come to Marlow on account of being left a fortune on Saturday, and if spoke to the right way and offered his beer he'd be just as like to come on here the Sunday and play for them as well.'

'I'm thankful it's not your bereaved sister this time,' I observed. 'With your touching romantics you'll grow up to be another poor damned scribbler and bane of publishers if you don't take care.'

'Got to tell 'em something, ain't you?' he enquired truculently. 'Well enough then; so they reckoned that was worth a pint of ale, and then I ask what's took off this Gipsy Tom anyhow?' He looked at me out of the corners of his eyes like an ill tempered pony. 'They says Gipsy Tom was found corpussed day before yesterday alying in the little temple on Mr Markham's land; they says furthermore as there warn't nothing to account for it save a gaze of most fearful dread, terror and despair on him and his eyes apopping like a bullock's cobblers; the same which they reckoned was uncommon, as Gipsy Tom warn't the fearfulling sort, being simple. And if you've forgot what that whore in Coventry Court looked like, I ain't,' he finished. 'Nor never likely to.'

'So ho,' I mused, reflecting on Mr Markham's observations that they'd already had one mishap too many, and that there was damned dangerous mischief in the orangery. 'The same appearance, was it? Continue, boy. What else was there?'

'Ain't that enough?' he enquired. 'If you asks me, it's ghosks. Like Mr William Makepeace used to say, things no mortual eye should look on or be struck dead. I reckoned it was ghosks in Coventry Court and I reckon it's ghosks here. So I says it was very likely ghosks done him,' he continued hurriedly catching the look in my eye, 'and they answers they dunno about that, but something done him for certain, and if I fancy to take myself off down along outside the graveyard wall I'll very likely find Niggle and Naggle aputting him under now.'

'God in Heaven, and all His mercy,' I cried. 'What the devil are Niggle and Naggle'

'I'm telling you, ain't I?' he screeched. 'The grave diggers. I go down the way the landlord says, where there's a wicket gate to the estate on one side of the lane and a bit of common land on the other, and the graveyard wall; as was plain having crosses and suchlike sticking up above it and likewise further off a church and two three cottages. Have you got that straight enough? Well then, there they was adigging for dear life this side of the wall and cussing wicked as the ground's so hard; and close by there was a bundle wrapped up in sacking on a hurdle. Likewise a fattish kind of parson, the beef and port wine sort and looking as if that's what he's got his mind on now, and in a hurry to get this lot over and done with. So I says to myself "This here's damnation rummy".'

100

'Rummy indeed,' I observed. 'They was burying outside the graveyard, you say? Was they being secret and cautious about it?'

'Never see nobody less secret. I draws behind a bush to watch and one says "Rackon her'll lie quiet now, Parson, so the flints don't stick in her arse; 'tis blasted flinty ground", and parson goes to have a look and says "That's deep enough, but we're bound to do the best we can for the poor soul. Unbaptised he might have been, but he were a damned good cricketer and we'll put him where he'll have a chance to stand up when the Last Trumpet blows; though it's only in the back row." With that he lifts up his book and his eyes, like Holy Moses does when he's in the gin, and mutters and mumbles and then says "Name of God the Father, God the Son, and in the hole he goes. So put him in, men, and cover him up tidy; and there'll be a half crown apiece for you from Squire Markham and a quart of ale at the Waggoners".'

By this time we had reached the tavern ourselves and with an air of triumph, as if he had specially arranged it by his own cleverness, Maggsy announced, 'And there they are; the self same pair.'

Sure enough sitting at a bench outside was a brace of gaffers, both still somewhat earth stained, and I called upon Jagger to hold the horses for another minute while I got down to have a word or two with these ancient rustics. They were as like as two peas; each with the same chin beard, button nose and uncommon cunning blue eyes—there never was a countryman that wasn't born cunning—each with his earth stained spade beside him, each blowing a whisp of smoke from a little bitten off pipe, and each clasping a quart pot in gnarled hands. All in all they was a picture to set Mr Thomas Gray off on a fresh elegy and I could have composed a philosophical reflection or two myself had I had the time, but being pressed for that commodity, and Jagger also a bit uneasy as we had a long ride ahead of us back to London, I greeted them simply, 'Good day to you, and a fine warm day it is for grave digging.'

They seemed to turn that over in their minds before one answered, 'I've knowed it warmer.'

His twin gave it further consideration and answered, 'Likewise knowed it colder.'

Perceiving that this profound discussion might well continue without end I said, 'Well, either way, warm or coldish, who was it you was putting under, outside the churchyard wall? Ain't that commonly the fate of suicides? What was it now? Some poor maid with an unwelcome bun in the oven and hanged herself to have an end of the trouble?'

The first pondered on that at length before observing, 'I never heard of a maid as hanged herself for a hot bun. Not about here.'

'I have then,' asserted the second. 'I recollect hearing a pedlar tell of one once.'

'Not about here,' his brother insisted pettishly. 'If maids about here hanged themselves on account of buns there wouldn't be one of 'em left abouncing in a twelve month. Proper little bakehouses all our maids be,' he announced proudly, and fell into a fit of wheezing and chuckling. He broke off to regard Master Maggsy unfavourably and then enquired, 'Ain't that the little toad as was standing there apissing when we was putting poor Gipsy Tom to bed? He were apissing on a hemlock plant and that's mortal bad luck.'

'Tain't near so bad as pissing on an henbane,' the other asserted. 'And after this day I racken catching coneys live is worse'n yet. I racken 'twas catching coneys live for Squire Markham were the end of Gipsy Tom.'

Feeling my breath starting to come short I demanded, 'What the devil do rabbits and Squire Markham have to do with it?'

They both blinked at me like a pair of egg bound owls caught in a thunderstorm, but Maggsy hissed at my elbow, 'Rabbits, is it? God's Whiskers, rabbits don't get ghosks, do they?'

'God help us, at least you keep out of this,' I begged him. 'If you join in it'll get more like Bedlam still.' It was fortunate for the balance of my wits that Landlord Trapp appeared at the door then, and I viewed him with some relief, adding, 'Well, you're one tender mercy Master Trapp. We might get some sense from you; if there's any to be had anywhere in this pestilential place, which I doubt.'

102

He considered that thoughtfully himself. 'There's a fair bit if you knows where to look. But you has to go round and under to get it out of Joshua and Jeremiah Boone. They'm the most cantankerous old scamps you ever see in your life; we calls one Niggle and t'other Naggle to tell 'em apart. Did you settle your business with Mr Markham then, sir?'

'After a fashion; though I wouldn't be surprised if there's more to come.' I viewed the two contumacious ancient rascals with increased dislike. 'And I suppose when you cry "Naggle" it's Niggle that answers? Now then, what's this tarradiddle about catching rabbits alive for Mr Markham?'

'Why that's simple enough,' Trapp answered. 'Any fool can catch coneys in a snare. Poor Gipsy Tom was clever to take 'em in his hands.'

'Don't you tell'n, Master Trapp,' either Niggle or Naggle bellowed in a sudden rage. 'You'm too rash and forward. Is it worth a shillin, master?' he asked cunningly.

'No, by God it ain't.' I offered up a silent prayer to my Maker, and went on, 'Now think careful, Master Trapp. There's a certain Frenchman, Monsieur Leclerc, lodging with Mr Markham.'

'And his valet,' Master Maggsy interjected. 'In the dower house, against the orangery.'

'In the dower house against the orangery,' I repeated. 'So was Gipsy Tom catching rabbits for Mr Markham before this Frenchy came here? Or only since?'

The fellow gazed at me with his mouth as wide as a parish bakehouse. 'Damned if I know. Tom's allus catched coneys with his hands; but only the last week or so took them to Mr Markham for a ha'penny apiece. God help us tax men don't count rabbits, do they? They'll be reckoning up a sow's tits next.'

'Tax man be damned,' I retorted. 'I wouldn't sink so low.'

There was no help for it and I told him plain and straight who I was, though not my business here. But he did not seem to fancy that a lot more, for he muttered, 'Bow Street, is it? Well then, we're respectable folk, master, and don't reckon a lot to thieftakers.'

'You can be as respectable as you like,' I told him, 'but you're bound to answer my questions, so let's have it, my man. Who was Gipsy Tom and why was he buried like that?'

'There's no secret about it,' the fellow retorted. 'He were a simple, poor soul, and a wandering man but settled here these six or eight years or more. Nobody knowed where he come from but he were a wonder with the animals and with herbs and physic and such. He lived in a little bothy as he'd built with his own hands down in the lower woods; and Mr Markham said he wasn't to be stoned, chased or otherwise tormented. Not as anybody'd be likely to for he were a stonewall wonder at cricket. Stand him up against the wickets and he'd remain there for a week if need be.'

He looked across at Maggsy and seemed about to start on something else, but I said hurriedly, 'Let's leave cricket out of it; we're all crazed enough as it is. Continue with this Gipsy Tom.'

'Aren't much to continue with,' he grumbled, but went on about him being discovered in the little temple by Mr Markham's gardeners, and then concluded, 'So there it was. The poor soul couldn't go in the churchyard on account of nobody knowing if he was a Christian or not, and likewise as a charge on the parish. So Parson Oates says to put'n as close as they could get him, and if they want a good stonewaller in Heaven he'll be there handy.'

'And Squire Markham paid for it,' I observed. 'Half a crown apiece to this pair of comicalities. It's a lot of money to put a pauper underground. What did he die of?'

The fellow did another bakehouse gaze. 'Be damned, how should I know? Shortage of breath most like.'

'Not so much impudence, my man,' I advised him. 'Wasn't there an inquest?'

'Inquest?' he echoed. 'God's sakes, you don't have a parish inquest on a poor soul like that. Mr Markham sent for Dr Sugarwhite from Marlow to come and look at him, and as we understand he reckoned it was a seizure of some sort. There's an end of it.'

'And a very handy end,' I said. 'But let it pass; it's no great

104

matter.'

Giving Maggsy a light touch with my cane to start him I turned back to the chaise where Jagger was by now in a fine fever of impatience, and Landlord Trapp called after us, 'Don't let that boy forget about his brother; to come down and strike for us against the Hambleden men. Not but what he's got the look of a flaming little liar about him to me.'

'He has and he is,' I agreed. 'But never fear, we'll send somebody. Though it may not be to play cricket,' I added softer. 'Let 'em go, my lad,' I told Jagger. 'And don't let 'em loiter; but when we come to Marlow stop at any place convenient and enquire where we might find one, Dr Sugarwhite.'

Jagger shook his head on it. 'As you say, Mr Sturrock; I'm game for anything. But time's running on and we've yet to change the hosses. It's a long pull back to London and it'll be full dark well afore we come to cross Hounslow Heath. If you fancies a brush with the highwaymen I don't mind, but I'd just as soon do without.'

'Be damned, Jagger,' I rallied him, 'I always took you for a rare good sportsman. What d'ye think I recruited you to my service for? But you've no need to fret. You won't see London or your bed tonight, neither will any of us. I've a notion we're more like to be disturbing somebody else's rest. So whip 'em up now; but no racing with coaches or similar events.'

The rascal never needs a second bidding and we went off at a fine clip, though tossed about like peas in a colander on the rough lane. But before long we turned on to the better road to Marlow, when I found leisure from cursing the reckless villain for his charioteering to demand of Master Maggsy, 'Now my sweet little angel, we'll have the rest of your adventures, and how you came to let yourself get caught.'

'The rabbits is it?' he asked. 'Did you ever see a rabbit as corpussed itself of fear and dread and something no mortual eyes should look upon?'

'I don't spend a lot of time gazing into rabbits' faces,' I told him, 'but I fancy that fear and dread come natural to most of 'em. I've a pretty fair notion what the rabbits and that young bullock are about, Master Maggsy, so start your report at the beginning as you've been taught.'

We may be spared his dramatic account of the fearsome dangers of snares, man-traps and gins he had braved to make his way by a back path through the park to a natural rendezvous which in his nature he would find by instinct; the stableyard. This being the place where you will hear most of the gossip of the household; though the lower servants' hall is better still if you can gain admission to it. 'Shinned over a wall to the muck-yard,' he said, 'and swear I wasn't seen at that. No end of a set out it was, up'ards of a dozen hosses, to reckon by the stabling, a town carriage and curricle, ladies' pony cart, and a hired chaise like ours; and four damned wicked ugly looking hunters with their heads out of the half doors.'

'We know what a gentleman's stables are like,' I said. 'What did you have, if anything?'

'Done very well,' he boasted. 'Doing it all for you again, I am. The stable lads was in the harness room, asitting round and clacketing, though I couldn't see 'em as I was hid under the window, but that was wide open and I ain't got big ears for nothing. Well then, they was going on mostly about that Frenchy you spoke of, Monsewer Leeclark, and they don't reckon him not at all. One of 'em says if that's a fair sort of the Froggy gentry he don't wonder they had a revinglution and chopped all their heads off, as this cove acts like he'd as soon spit in your eye as talk decent to you.' He paused to draw breath and then added, 'No more they don't reckon his valet neither.'

'Hold hard there,' I said. 'He's got a valet here, has he?'

'That's right; but not a lot like any valet they've ever seen before, as another observes that if Master William's a valet he's a cow's arse, it being well known that valets is stuck up snots but they reckon to ape the gentleman whereas this'n couldn't even look like a gentleman if he tried. Moreover there's some-thing rummy about him as it seems he come with Monsewer to start with but then went off again and only come back yesterday in an hired chaise; this same and hosses still being in the yard and according to instructions give to Mr Bramble, the head coachman, to be kept ready and waiting, as if Mon-

106

sewer gets a message he might have to leave at any time. Which the stablemen considers is likewise rummy.'

'Rummy indeed,' I mused. 'You didn't discover when Monsieur Leclerc and the valet first arrived?'

'Couldn't hardly poke my head up over the window sill and ask, could I?' he enquired pettishly. 'I only catched any of it in bits and drabs. Anyhow this Monsewer Leeclark and valet are lodged in the dower house. And there's an American and two foreigners in the mansion. Mr Bramble, the coachman, had it from the butler as this American was heard to say an uncommon wicked and improper thing over dinner the other day, as we should do better without a king here the same as France and America; and Mr Markham was heard to agree. The butler told Mr Bramble as it give him a turn. But there ain't no harm in the two foreigners, them being a pair of right roaring comicalities; they don't have a dozen words of English between 'em and booze themselves pissticated every night, and have to be pretty well carried to bed. Which same it seems Mr Markham ain't much behind at neither when in the mood for it.'

'It's common practice in gentlemen's houses,' I observed. 'Though I'd have thought philosophers might be above it. Did you hear anything of the man, Gipsy Tom? Or the other last night who wanted to get into the park unseen?'

'Ain't never satisfied are you?' He shifted his backside and cursed as Jagger whipped up the horses to a fresh trot and we lurched over a rut. 'Only thing about Gipsy Tom was they reckoned the dogs was abarking and howling over him last night. As far as I can make out he was laid in this orangery place. Then one of 'em announces that's all cobblers and cock as the dogs was only letting off at fox cubs and a vixen running the park; and another declares that's cobblers and cock as well because fox cubs don't run in a thunderstorm; and one more says the dogs was at it again later still, as he woke up in the middle of the night and heard 'em then.'

'You've done very well, Maggsy,' I told him generously. 'You might even come to earn your keep if you live long enough. Was there any more?'

'Not a lot. Hard on that one of them damned hunters starts

107

kicking and squealing, and somebody says "You'd best go to see what's up with Beauty, Capper," and I reckon it's time to take my arse in hand and get clear of this quick, which I done. Come out to a kind of vegetable garden, and there's a boy raking and scratting at the earth and I say "Here, if you let on you see me come over that wall I'll wring your bleeding neck with one hand and gut you with the other, and where's the orangery as I've got a very particular message for Miss Geraldine from Mr Ralph to give to her at the back of it". So he answers "Who'll gut who? That's it over beyond them trees, and you'd best dodge round through that archway in the hedge there," which likewise I done.'

He went on to a further graphic account of creeping through the ornamental bushes like a wild Indian, but at length continued, 'It's a biggish red brick place with great tall windows, and joined up to a fanciful little house with a kind of covered passage. Well then, I reckons to leave the house be as I don't fancy the sound of that valet somehow, so works round to the far end to have a snout through the glass. And what do I see there?'

'Oddities and contrivances,' I answered. 'Tables and benches, bottles and jars very like an apothecaries' shop. And rabbits.'

'God's Whiskers, there you go again,' he screeched in a rage. 'What of damnation do you set me on for if you know it all to start with?'

'You told me yourself, you ill tempered little monster,' I admonished him. 'It don't take much adding up anyhow. And if it's any solace to you, I'll say again you've done very well. But how did you come to get caught?'

'Cops a prod in the arse from a muck fork,' he said, short but somewhat mollified. 'And there's them stable men all about me together with that horrible garden boy acapering and jeering. I offered to wring that little bastard's neck, and if we ever goes back there I will; and crown him with an old horse shoe.'

'When we go back it'll be for bigger game than garden boys,' I promised. 'Was the rabbits alive or dead?'

'They was as dead as that whore. Five of 'em laid out on a table with their hair like hedgehogs, and grinning. You ever seen a rabbit grinning?' he demanded. I repeated that I rarely spent much time studying rabbits' expressions and he went on, 'Well these was, and I been reckoning it out. Rabbits don't die of seeing ghosks, or not as I've ever knowed. So no more did that whore. So I reckons further that what corpussed them rabbits corpussed her.'

'Maggsy,' I told him, 'you've got the beginnings of something starting to rattle in your noddle. Though what it is only God knows. Five rabbits at a ha'penny each,' I mused. 'So the poor devil died for tuppence ha'penny.'

But further philosophical reflections was cut short by our rattling into the busier streets of Marlow, Jagger exchanging a few politenesses with a surly rogue of a waggoner who was blocking our way, and then pulling up at the inn where we had taken our dinner to enquire how we might discover Dr Sugarwhite. This turned out to be the first good luck we had encountered that day, for the gentleman himself was already in the tap room and more than convivial.

The company was a dozen or so of farmers, horse dealers, chandlers and travellers, and from what I could make out they was generously toasting a fine bouncing son presented to him that very day by his amiable and industrious wife. A youngish fellow, and newly set up in practice I judged; very likely not much of a doctor yet, and compound of bone sawyer, physician, horse leech and tooth puller. Nevertheless my heart bled for the blow I was about to inflict upon him, for although some of my enemies and even Master Maggsy pretend that I am as empty of the bowels of compassion and kindness as any publisher, I still have my proper nice feelings on these happy occasions. But I must serve the law as best I can, and as soon as I could get edgeways on to the doctor I drew him aside and made myself known.

'Bow Street, is it?' he asked with a cheerful hiccup. 'Well you ain't after me, I hope; I ain't killed nobody yet, or not as far as I know.'

'But you attended a dead man a day or two back,' I reminded him. 'One known as Gipsy Tom.'

'Yesterday,' he said. 'What's that to do with you? He was

as dead as anybody I ever see.'

'What of? What did he die of, Dr Sugarwhite?'

'Damned if I know,' he confessed plainly. 'I set it down as a convulsion of the heart. The man had a grimace to his lips as sometimes comes with a sudden spasm.'

'There was no sign of wounding or other mistreatment?'

'Never a hint of it,' he answered, just as cheerful. 'Not unless you reckon a little cut on the ball of his left thumb as he might've got by trying the point of an oversharp knife. That wouldn't have harmed a baby. And talking of that wasn't I telling you that my wife's just pupped me as fine a colt as ever I've seen? Begod there's a woman as knows her business. Come and take a drink with us.'

'All in good time,' I promised. 'But for now I'd sooner withdraw somewhere to talk quiet for a minute. We've got a serious matter here.' He looked at me in astonishment and near enough told me to go and damn myself, but then warned by my manner led me to a little snug behind the tap. Before he could get another word out I started, 'Tell me this first. Who was present when you examined the body?'

'God's sake what're you after?' he demanded. 'Nobody but the groom Mr Gervase Markham sent to fetch me; and a gentleman I took to be a Frenchy. Then another who came in later; some kind of upper servant, I fancy. What's the pother, I say? The poor devil was of no great account.'

'So it seems,' I agreed, 'by the way he was disposed of. Are you regular physician to Mr Gervase Markham or any of his people?'

'Not commonly,' he confessed. 'Mr Markham has Botfish of Henley when he needs a doctor. A damned port and brandy butt in my opinion, but rides to hounds with Markham now and again.'

'And this time you was called in. You didn't reckon that was anything strange?'

'Confound it,' he cried, 'why should I? Botfish wouldn't ha' bothered himself. And Markham's Justice of the Peace, he couldn't have a corpse on his land without notifying somebody of it.'

110

'It's the notifying that frets me. That you didn't think it a matter to notify the coroner; for an inquest.'

'Inquest be damned,' he answered. 'I've told you there was no sign or mark about the fellow that called for an inquest.'

'Or none in your experience,' I said.

He flushed a deeper shade of red, made half a move as if he was about to present me with the tankard he still held in his hand, then looked back to where his merry companions were bawling lewd jests and announced, 'Be damned to this; I've got better company than you to keep.'

'You might keep worse,' I told him. 'Conspiring to conceal the cause of death's a felony.' There was no evidence that the poor young man had tried to conceal anything except his own simplicity, but this is another trick we are permitted, and red as he was one minute he turned pale the next. I continued, 'I'll do my best for you, Dr Sugarwhite. I'd dislike to distress your young wife who's just done you so proud. But let's have the answers short and quick. As I understand the body was discovered in the little temple in Mr Markham's grounds. Where did you examine it?'

'In that place they call the orangery. It's set up as a chemical and mechanical laboratory. Mr Markham's well known for it. Lookee now, let's have this plain. Was the fellow killed then? Murdered?'

'I don't think so. I'd say it was an accident. But there's been one more killing of a like nature that wasn't, and there might be more yet if we don't put a stop to it. Were you told the circumstances of the case?'

'Nothing save that he'd been discovered by one of the gardeners about nightfall the day before. By that time Mr Markham was already at supper with his guests and it was considered too late to send for me. The man was dead anyway.'

'So you've no means of saying precisely when he did die? Was anything said to the effect that he might have been poking and prying about in this laboratory?' Dr Sugarwhite shook his head on both counts, and I observed, 'By God you've been careless. For a young physician with his way to make you've been damnation careless. But I'll get you out of it if I can; so long

111

as you'll help me. This Frenchman present; did he say anything or make any observations while you was about this examination?'

'Not a lot,' the perplexed physician admitted. 'Mostly in his own language, and I don't understand the lingo. Only thing he said in English was something about a convulsion of the heart.'

'So he put the idea into your head?' I enquired.

'Be damned,' the doctor exploded, 'that's what it looked like.'

'No doubt,' I said. 'It seems there's a lot of medical mysteries we don't understand yet; though I mean to bottom this one. Now then, you say the Frenchman was talking in his own language, but you don't speak it. So who was he addressing himself to?'

'Why to the other one that came in; the servant.'

I was already starting to ponder on this servant or valet, and asked, 'Was he answering in the same?' This time Dr Sugarwhite nodded, and I pressed him, 'What was he like? Would you say he was a Frenchman himself?'

'Hanged if I know. How can you tell? I recollect though that I thought he looked a roughish fellow for a servant of that sort. Had a scar down the side of his face, heavily built, and an uncommon odd manner about him.'

'Some of the revolutionary rascals was roughish kind of fellows,' I told him. 'And many of 'em are still about. What d'you mean, an uncommon odd manner?'

'Oh be damned,' he cried, 'is there no end of this? It was supposed to be master and man, d'ye see? Well then it seemed more as if the boot was on t'other foot.'

But before I could make any further observations on this Master Maggsy came roaring in crying, 'Here, it's astarting to rain and Jagger wants to know what's about the horses if you're reckoning on any fresh travels and troubles tonight.'

'You may tell him to water and feed them, and give them a good rest,' I said. 'We shall be returning to Mill End, but we'll take our supper here first. What we're after tonight is best done in the dark. And you, sir,' I continued to the doctor, 'will meet us here at ten o'clock, together with two stout fellows who are not over squeamish and provided with spades and lanterns. You'll attend yourself with a suitable conveyance, as no doubt you've got a gig or chaise of some sort for your professional duties.'

'God help us,' he gasped. 'You don't mean to dig the man up?'

'I mean to dig him up,' I announced. 'And I want you present to swear to his identity.'

Maggsy himself started to screech out something, but the doctor forestalled him. 'No,' he announced. 'I'm damned if I'll do it; I'll have no part of this. Where the devil am I to get a pair of gravediggers from? And what may I tell my poor wife?'

'You may be more damned if you don't,' I advised him. 'We have here a terrible and secret poison that kills on a mere cut or scratch, and you let it slip under your nose. I'll see that man properly examined, Dr Sugarwhite, before it can kill others like him. Tell your wife you're called to another lying in; she'll be kind enough about it after her own happy deliverance.'

Even Master Maggsy was dumbfounded, as to stop any further discussion and uncertainties I hustled him away to the common room for our suppers. 'God's fire irons,' he muttered, 'this tops the lot, this does; this takes the top brick off the chimney. Mischief and fighting comes natural to you, you can't help 'em; but I never before thought to see you turn Resurrection Man.'

SEVEN

So you are to see us at this unhallowed place close upon midnight; a dark and mysterious crew under a light rain gusting on the wind, a weak crescent moon as pale as a ghost itself scudding through the clouds, and the flickering candlelight of lanterns wavering our own shadows over the mound of earth. Beyond us were the black trees, in front the glimmering tombstones in the churchyard; and we went about our strange work with never a sound but the scrape of spades, an occasional rude observation from our labouring fellows as they struck an extra big flint, Maggsy whispering and cursing under his breath, now and again an uneasy jingle from our horses, and over by the church one melancholious owl complaining to another.

It was a particular nice occasion for philosophical musing and I composed several improving reflections while damning those unwilling rogues for their slowness in getting the fellow up, and they answered me back no less heartily from the uncertain gloom of the narrow grave. But I was more concerned still that our rash and reckless doctor had extravagantly promised them no less than half a sovereign each for their trouble; neither was he any less impatient than myself, being somewhat nervous of the whole undertaking, and for the sixth or seventh time he whispered, 'Let's have it done with. You there, Jem, give Cobley a bit more room at the end; let's have it handsome now.'

'Handsome me arse,' one of them growled. 'What's handsome about this? And who said he wasn't all that deep. God blast it we've very near dug a clay pit a'ready.'

Even Jagger was not in the best of tempers, and Master Maggsy must needs distinguish himself. No sooner had one of the men muttered, 'Rackon we've got'n,' than he ventured too close to see what awful sight lay down there, let his clumsy feet

114

slip on the heap of soil and went rolling down into the grave too; where tangled with the labourers' spades and legs, floundering in the wet clay and sweeping over one of our lanterns, he now made the peaceful night echo with his yells and curses. His howls could have been heard a mile away and I had the wretch out quicker than he went in, silencing him with a hearty cuff, but the mischief was already done; there were other people abroad about unholy business that night for then Jagger, who was doing his best to calm our horses by the roadside, added his own voice to bawl, 'God's sakes, what's this? We'm spotted.'

'Silence there,' I whispered at him as we all stood set like stone at this fresh sound in the uneasy darkness.

In short carriage wheels and hoofs and lights coming from Mr Markham's lodge, rattling up at a reckless gallop and on us in a minute; yet plenty of time for whoever it was to perceive us there about the open grave. It was a swift confusion in the wan moonbeams and flickering candlelight. Our animals kicking and plunging with Jagger and the doctor striving to hold them, our gravediggers caught with the muddied body half out of the ground, and Master Maggsy bolting with a yell into the bushes; the strange chaise checking and lurching as its own horses shied at these ungodly sights, two fresh voices screeching out in French, and then the flame and explosion of first one pistol shot and then another. Be damned the second might well have had my left ear off had it been but an inch closer. As it was the flash very near blinded me and I went backwards on the heap of muck, pitched arse first into the hole myself and finished with my own arms about that stinking corpse while the other two cowardly rogues let fall their spades and fled hallooing for the doctor's trap.

What befell them I do not know, though I heard the physician's voice raised in expostulation, the gravediggers cursing him back, his horses clattering away snorting for terror, and Master Maggsy's laments rising from somewhere in the darkness. Adding my own observations to them, by no means sure whether my head or my neck was the worst broke, I clambered out of that noisome pit to perceive the doctor also picking himself up off the ground while adding his poems of

115

praise to mine, Jagger clinging to our frightened cattle and addressing them no less fervently. In the distance there was the rattle and clatter of two carriages retreating hell for leather; though which of the two was in front and which behind only God could tell.

Taking up my beaver I clapped it on my head and straightened my coat as best I could; there was little to be done with my pantaloons, but with order and authority restored I said to the doctor, 'So your two ruffians have bolted?'

'They've bolted,' he answered bitterly, 'and in my trap. By God, I wisht I'd never set eyes on you.'

He added several further strictures which he must have picked up in medical school. They were not worthy of an answer, and next taking our last remaining lantern I turned again to survey the corpse. As if reluctant to be disturbed he had fallen back into the grave with a fair portion of the soil on top of him, but that was no great matter if we were quick. I continued, 'Jagger, calm those horses and back them up. And you, Maggsy, you little whelp, come out there.'

The moon even had modestly hidden her face again at the doctor's expressions of regard, and from the fresh darkness came a stream of complaints, snivels and curses as Maggsy limped out of the shadows into the uncertain light of the candle. 'What a day,' he was announcing. 'God's Tripes, what a lovely bleeding day, and all for Sturrock. And to cap it all I must needs dive into a thorn bush. That old Niggle says it was bad luck to go pissing on an hemlock. I wisht somebody'd show me what an hemlock is so I needn't never do it again.'

'I'll show you what a sore backside is in a minute,' I threatened him. 'Get along the lane now, quick; keep watch by the lodge gates. And you two,' I added to the others, 'let's have that body out.'

With one accord and one voice though different tones they all howled, 'What?'

'No,' the doctor said. 'By God, no. You're stark, stare raving cracked. Any minute we shall have villagers on us in a bundle. I'm surprised they ain't here already after that rumpus. God damn it, you maniac, they'll scrag us for Resurrection Men.'

116

'I came for that corpse and I mean to have it,' I replied. 'If I know villagers anywhere they'll have their doors and shutters double bolted by now. If danger there is it'll come from the house, but work quick and we'll be away first. Maggsy, get up to that lodge I say, and if you see lights along the drive give one of your whistles. Set about it,' I roared, 'for I'm in no temper to be trifled with.'

The wretch limped off up the lane, still complaining, and the doctor added a few further remarks of his own, but seeing there was no help for it he and Jagger fell to with the spades, though equally unwilling. So unwilling indeed that they worked the faster, and after barely more than a stroke or two he grunted, 'Here he is, be damned to him; and to you.'

So lending a hand myself we dragged the poor horrid bundle out, and Jagger went off to steady the horses while we got him up, for by some mystery I do not understand these sensitive and wilful creatures became uneasy at the smell of death; and I can't say I much care for it myself. What with the fellow's weight and limpness and being slippery with wet clay or chalk, the rain now falling afresh, it was no light matter, and even while we were heaving and shoving and cursing at him Maggsy's horrible whistle came shrilling from up the road. It was followed a minute later by the child himself galloping as if Old Nick were on his heels, and roaring, 'A gang of 'em; forty or fifty or an hundred, lanterns and fowling pieces and that lodge keeper coming with a blunderbuss.'

With their footsteps and shouts already close on us we thrust the unwilling corpse into the chaise and scrambled after him, dragging Maggsy up by the scruff of his neck, crying to Jagger to give way, and going off with a rush and clatter. But already that rascally lodge keeper was yelling alongside brandishing his fearful weapon and had not Jagger lashed out with his whip, and Providence Himself touched off the trigger as the rogue stumbled, it might have been the end of all of us. He fell back tail over ears and the storm of shot, nails and stones flew above our heads; though not before the evil tempered rogue had seen and recognised me. An event which was to have dire consequences.

117

I have often before pointed out the danger of blunderbusses, and I never advise their use in any circumstances, but as it happened that one rendered us a special service. Lending fresh terror to our cattle in a twinkling we were away at a bolt, scattering some four or five fellows who were emerging from the wicket gate and far outdistancing those who were coming up behind from the lodge. As is always his habit Master Maggsy had exaggerated when he screamed of some fifty or a hundred; there was never more than a dozen at the most.

They fell behind in a rabble, and but one more shot came after us. Not the devil himself could have caught those animals as we rushed swaying and jolting into the night at a most reckless speed with Master Maggsy crouching on the footboard adding his own yells and imprecations, and that damnation corpse lurching from one to the other of us as if it desired nothing better than to lay itself lovingly in our arms. With every roll the doctor thrust it back pettishly against me while, not to be outdone, I returned the like compliment to him; it might have come to an altercation between us had we not been more concerned with saving what little breath we had against the pitching and jolting, and clutching everything we could get a finger on to prevent ourselves being tossed out.

The immortal Dr Samuel Johnson is said once to have observed that had he no other cares he would spend his life driving briskly in a post chaise with a pretty woman; he should have tried it on a rainy night with a corpse for passenger. How Jagger kept us on that dark road I shall never know; but even the wildest brutes must tire in the end, and by degrees their headlong gallop fell to a blown trot and finally to little more than an amble. Then I was free to make several fresh announcements and on concluding them to ask the physician, 'Tell me, sir, when those rascals of yours made off did they go before that other chaise or after?'

Still somewhat ill humoured he made several further remarks which are not fit to be set down, but I took the general drift of them to be that he neither knew nor cared and continued, 'It's a cock fighting certainty that the fellows in that chaise were Monsieur Leclerc and his valet. And if your men

118

went after they'll fancy we're in chase.' I reflected shortly on whether there was any hope that we might catch up with them, concluded there was little chance of it, and finished, 'It's another vexation, for God knows where we shall find the rogues now.'

In this I was mistaken, as you shall see, but there the matter ended then as we were by now approaching the first cottages of Marlow deep in darkness and innocent slumber—if anything in the countryside is innocent—and here the physician bawled to Jagger to stop and be damned to him, and then turned to address himself again to me. 'Mr Sturrock,' he enquired, 'might I be permitted one last heartfelt prayer? I hope to God I may never see your face again.'

'You can hope so for your own sake,' I retorted. 'But there's one face you must look at. I'll have the forms of law obeyed.'

Taking up our dark lantern, upon which Maggsy was now warming his hands, I opened the shutter and set to work to loosen the sacking about the corpse's head. It was no easy matter for they had trussed him up fit to wait for ten Days of Judgement but at last I accomplished it, drew the stuff aside to reveal the deathly countenance, and held up the lantern. On the instant Master Maggsy let out another screech which very nearly set the horses bolting again; and indeed the spectacle was by no means a picture for the Royal Academy, being of a pallid greenish hue and besmeared with clay, the eyes glazed but fixed in that stare of dread, and the lips drawn back in a strange grin. It damned near gave even me a turn but I announced, 'Dr Sugarwhite, I want your solemn oath and affidavit. Is this the man you was called upon to examine?'

'No,' he answered, turning paler himself. 'It ain't. By God, it ain't.'

'What?' I cried. 'Be careful what you say now. Look closer and be sure of it. Is this Gipsy Tom or not?'

'I've told you,' he asserted, 'it ain't.'

'But for God's sake, it must be,' I insisted. 'Are you out of your wits too, sir? D'you mean to tell me we've dug up the wrong corpse? Take a fresh look,' I urged him, holding the lantern closer. 'Let's be sure of it.'

'God rot your eyes,' he roared, 'I am sure of it. It ain't.'

'Come, sir,' I said roundly, 'let's have a bit of sense. If it ain't our man, who is it?'

'I'm damned if I know,' he announced. 'Nor don't care. I never set eyes on him before and he's another I hope never to again. Now will you put me down, I say, before I run as mad as you are and do a mischief?'

There was nothing else for it for he was plainly put out. The poor bewildered fellow leapt down to vanish into the darkness, though long after he was out of sight he could still be heard cursing. Nor was I any better pleased myself, and hardly less perplexed. 'We've got a pretty tangle now,' I mused. 'But I've a fair notion of who this fellow must be. There was some damnation mischievous tricks at Mill End last night, Master Maggsy.'

'God's sake, cover him up,' the child demanded. 'He's enough to give a butt of gin the grues. There's some damnation mischievous tricks tonight as well, and copping the wrong corpus tops the lot. So what d'you reckon to do now? Take him back to put him under again and start to look for the right'n I wouldn't be surprised. Well I'll tell you straight you can do without me as I've had my bellyful of resurrectioning for ever.'

'Hold your witless noise,' I commanded him. 'We've got the fellow and we'll keep him; he'll very likely do as well as Gipsy Tom, or even better. We'll drive on; but you get up here on the seat and hold him from falling against me at every turn.'

'I'll be damned if I will,' he screeched. 'I've had my bellyful of corpusses too and partic'lar that'n.'

'You brainless ape,' I admonished him, 'recollect what Mr William Shakespeare says: "The sleeping and the dead are but as pictures; 'tis the eye of childhood that fears a painted devil".'

'And sod Mr William Shakespeare likewise,' he retorted. 'It's plain Mr William Shakespeare never catched sight of this cove or he'd have changed his mind quick.'

With one thing and another I was fast losing patience, but nothing would persuade the obstinate child to do as he was told, and Jagger himself was becoming unaccountably surly. In the end we laid the fellow down athwart the footboard to rest our feet on him; he dangled over a bit on either side, but nothing out of the way as there was no other traffic on the lanes.

120

So we went on at a funeral pace through the silent village and over the river to come at last to Maidenhead Thicket, where with the trees meeting overhead and close about on either side the darkness was profound. There was nothing to be seen but the wet and glistening rumps of our weary horses in the glow of the lamps, and Jagger counselled, 'You have them pistols cocked; I daresn't force the pace and we'm sitting ducks here.'

I needed no second bidding and we crept on keeping a keen eye to right and left, and ears alert. But there was never a sound above the drip of the rain, the jingle of our harness and Maggsy's snores, and after what seemed an endless crawl through this Stygian gloom I was just about thinking that we must be past the worst of it by now when without any warning our nearside animal shied and snorted, Jagger let out a fresh ill-tempered curse, and we stopped with a jerk. The events of this unlucky day had not done with us yet, and I had my pistols up on the instant, demanding, 'What's now?'

'Be damned if I know,' Jagger said. 'And damned if I like it neither. It's another chaise; half arse over. Holy Jesus,' he added on a yet higher note of alarm, 'there's a cove ahanging out.'

It needed no deep thought to perceive what this was. One wheel half in the ditch, the horses gone, the empty shaft and loose traces slewed across the road, a dark figure lying motionless with one arm dangling, and blood still dripping from the footboard. We had found Monsieur Leclerc quicker than I thought we might, though in no shape to tell us much. It was yet another vexation, and I said to Jagger, 'Hold a minute,' getting down in a hurry, waking Maggsy, and ordering him to bring the dark lantern and quick about it.

'God help us,' Jagger cried, 'you ain't going to hang about here?'

'I'm bound to,' I told him. 'Here, take the pistols. If you see or hear anything don't wait to wish the rogues good day.'

To be plain there was little danger. Highwaymen rarely linger once they've got their pickings, but still it was an uneasy business not knowing who might be watching from the mysterious darkness all around and I wasted no time about the matter.

There was small need to. Whatever mischief Monsieur Leclerc had been engaged on he'd gone to his reckoning for it now. A ball had struck him below the left shoulder and must have killed him pretty well on the instant; but not before some defiance of his own, for there was a little double barrelled French carriage pistol lying discharged by his hand. It is not always a wise plan to fire on highwaymen when they attack in a gang of two or three or more; at best you can hardly hope to steady more than one of the rascals, and that will often render the other blackguards murderous when otherwise they would be content with mere robbery.*

For the rest there was nothing to discover; neither valise, baggage, nor even portfolio or letter case. The villains had stripped the chaise of everything and even turned out the Frenchman's pockets, as I made certain of by going through them myself; but again finding no more than a folded paper which they had either overlooked or reckoned of no value. From the single glance I gave it in the light of my lantern it seemed to be a map or plan of some kind, though I had no leisure to consider it then and stowed it away in my own pocket for safety, before next turning to search for the valet or servant who should have been driving that chaise. In spite of all prayers, entreaties and curses I went both ways on the road and even some distance into the sodden darkness of the trees. To make it short there was no sign of him, and only when I was satisfied that he was not lying somewhere close by did I yield to Maggsy's fresh imprecations and give the word to set off once more.

There was fresh food for thought in this mysterious and vanished servant, though much disturbed by Maggsy's complaints; but thank God he soon dropped off to mutterings, grunts and at last snores, and left me to my reflections in peace. Before long then we came to Maidenhead cross and turned off for London on the wider road, where also the watery moon appeared again and gave Jagger a bit more light to coax what little more he could out of our jaded animals. It was a wearisome drag, for they were in no better shape than we were our-

* For inexperienced travellers this advice alone is worth the price of the book.

selves, but at length we came back without further incident to the Windmill at Salt Hill, where we must at any cost change the poor beasts if we were to travel much further this night.

This proved easier said than done for the place was as dark as the tomb, bolted and shuttered up, and it took the devil's own tattoo of hammering and hallooing before a window opened above us; and only then to toss down the contents of a chamber pot with a sleepy voice offering certain advice to match the contents of that humble vessel. By now however I was in no mood for trifling and roared back, 'On the business of His Majesty the King. Do you fancy being murdered in your beds, you damned fools? The French have landed.'

'Eh?' the fellow enquired sleepily. 'What's that then? I don't see no beacons.'

'You wouldn't see even a torch if it were set to your arse,' I barked back at him in fine military style. 'They're coming up the river in barges.'

'And adropping in balloons,'' Maggsy screeched, freshly awakened but as quick witted as ever.

On that also ever kindly Providence saw fit to lend His Hand. There was a flicker of pinkish lightning and a low rumble of thunder. 'Don't you hear the cannon, you blockhead?' I demanded. 'Stir yourself man; I must have fresh horses to carry the alarm.'

'God A'mighty,' he cried falling back, bawling and shouting within, fetching up a growing chorus of women's shrieks and wails and lights in the windows. In another minute the doors were unbarred and men tumbling out, some having coats over their night shirts, others with them half tucked into their britches, but all full of questions and one recklessly brandishing a cutlass. Maggsy and Jagger were already unharnessing our spent horses, giving some uncommon fantastical answers, while I marched up and down like a major roaring for fresh animals and announcing that we had here a French spy, the rascal, dead and trussed up, being carried to see what papers he had about him, and come what might we must get him to Windsor at the sharpest. I was so carried away by the dramatics that I even tossed the landlord half a sovereign above his livery charges;

but demanded a good pot of rum apiece to me and my men for it.

How it all ended I do not know, for we were off once more pretty well as quick or quicker than it takes to tell; but we left a pleasurable excitement behind in these good people's quiet country lives. Nevertheless I made a note to myself that if occasions called me back to Medmenham it might be well to travel by another road the next time. For the rest the journey was uneventful; Master Maggsy for a little while cackling in his wicked way over the stratagem before dropping off to his snores again, myself musing and nodding, and Jagger carrying us safely through the night. I spared him a kindly thought now and again; though it is the natural way of things that man must work while master sleeps.

I was awakened by the chaise stopping and the good fellow announcing, 'We'm at Tyburn turnpike, so what now?'

'Then we'll not be long; you shall soon have a good fire and your breakfast,' I answered to encourage him, for he seemed to be in an ill humour. 'Head straight down Oxford Street and make for West Smithfield,' I added, getting out my purse to pay the toll.

'Might I be so bold as to ask what you're at this time?' he enquired with a quaver in his voice. 'You and your corpse?'

'Why to be sure, my lad,' I told him generously, 'we're going to St Bart's Hospital. When we get close by enquire your way and find Well Yard.'

It was then near on five o'clock and not yet light, but the early labouring classes were already abroad and the streets noisy with drays, dung carts and waggons going and coming from the markets; to which Master Maggsy added the clamour of his own fresh complaints as he woke with the sound of our wheels on cobble stones to announce that his belly was as empty as a drum. Promising him also that he should have his breakfast before long we edged our way through the thickening traffic and the press of cattle and drovers in Smithfield, working round the back of the hospital to a certain tavern which I shall ask your permission to leave nameless. To be short it is where the regular Resurrection Men ply their trade; where also lodge

124

several apprentice medicos and in particular one Bob Snaffle, a wicked young devil, but acute, enquiring and inquisitive in his trade. He will live to become a fashionable surgeon if he escapes the gallows that long.

The mistress of the place was Mother Gregg, a biggish woman of middle age who worked in the hospital herself on occasion, and one who knew which questions to ask and what not to answer; if I was known to her as Sturrock of Bow Street she never said so, and I never saw any reason to tell her. She was already astir, for people start the day early in these parts, and I said, 'Bob Snaffle, ma'am. Tell him I've got a delivery for him; and you may add that it's his old friend Jeremy and in a particular hurry. And after that if you can find some vittles and hot water and the necessities we shall bless you, for we've had a long hard night.'

'You look as if ye've been delving in a clay pit,' she observed. 'There ain't nobody after you, is there?'

'Never a soul,' I assured her. 'It was all done quiet and decent, and a fair distance out.'

She regarded Maggsy thoughtfully for a minute but then said, 'I'll see. Bob ain't expecting a delivery so far as I know and he's got company. He might say be damned to ye, but I'll ask.'

So she went off leaving us to warm ourselves by the fire in the common room until at last Bob came clumping and grumbling down the stairs; a lanky rascal with a face not unlike a skull himself, a long lock of black hair hanging over one eye, yawning prodigiously, still buttoning himself up, and announcing, 'God dammit, to call me at this hour; if it's Sturrock it's mischief,' then standing to survey us up and down and finish, 'God's Blood, you're a fine collection of mudlarks. What the devil's this then? You ain't gone into the resurrection trade, have you, Jeremy?'

'Not as a regular thing,' I answered, reflecting that I'd like to observe this young rip in ten years time at some lady's bedside with a gold watch in his hand. 'It's a special case. Uncommon out of the way and a rare favour to you, Bob.'

'Be damned,' he argued, 'I know your slim tricks, Sturrock. Your rare favours've got teeth in their tails. What're you after?'

125

'Poison,' I told him. 'Something you've never seen before, and I'll lay a wager few other people have either. But damned wicked stuff whatever it is.' This roused his interest, and I continued, 'It's outside in my chaise, trussed up nice and neat, and my man'll drive it round where you want it delivered. So be a good fellow and let's be shot of it. Then I'll tell you the tale after breakfast.'

So to make a short issue of smaller matters, he consented to show Jagger where to take our prize, we attended to our needs, and then sat down to as fine a saddle bag steak apiece as ever I recollect. Mr Snaffle declaring that he had a tender stomach and did not much care to discuss such business over a light breakfast little more was said but general politenesses until we all drew back contented, the table was cleared, and Jagger and Maggsy sent off to look to the horses and clean the chaise in the tavern yard. I was thankful enough for the respite myself, but when Snaffle at last produced a bag of tobacco and we lit our pipes I continued, 'I want an examination of every inch of that body, Bob, inside and out. I want a particular note of the appearance of the face and eyes, and a small wound or cut that I'll take my oath you'll find on it somewhere. I'll thank you to have it all set down as a report, signed by yourself and one or two of your professors if you can get 'em to it. I'm after the plain conclusion. Poison.'

He blew a whiff from his pipe. 'You don't want much, do you? Which one?'

'Now, be damned,' I answered, 'if I knew that I wouldn't be asking, would I? You shall hear it all.' So starting with Henriette d'Armande's note I went on from that all through to our adventures last night—though drawing a light veil over my own misfortunes at Mr Markham's ungodly seance—while Bob made various exclamations, let his pipe go out several times, and in general expressed a lively interest. 'There you have it,' I finished. 'A double barrelled mystery. The French plot for one and this poison for the other. But thanks to our windy blockhead of a coroner the woman's underground now, and no use to us. We had dire need of another body, and there it was, provided handy. Moreover I've a dozen of Pickering and Clarke's Madeira promised if I can make a fool of that butt of piss and port and prove how she died.'

He gazed at me in admiration. 'Begod, Sturrock, you're the only rogue I know of who'd turn Resurrection Man for a dozen of Madeira. And to cap it all you get the wrong corpse. God's Teeth that's rich.'

'Be damned to the Madeira,' I said. 'Though I mean to have it. And as for the wrong corpse I'm pretty sure this fellow's a bigger prize than the other poor devil. If there's certain matters come together as I fancy they will he might lead me to the heart of the business.'

'Aye,' Bob agreed, filling his pipe again and gazing thoughtfully into the fire, not all that concerned with which corpse was which but reflecting on his own mysteries. 'You reckon this stuff was tried on the animals, rabbits and a bullock; which Mr Markham then presented to the villagers. What for? To find out if it'd do for them in turn? That's a bit tall ain't it?'

'It's a damned sight too tall,' I confessed. 'Even for Mr Gervase Markham that's too chill blooded; there'd be some tasty questions asked if a Justice of the Peace presented his parishioners with an ox and it killed the lot of 'em. He'd get his house burned down, for these countrymen are savage rascals. No, Bob; he gave 'em that animal for the simplest of all reasons. To get rid of the carcase in the easiest way and to explain why he'd purchased a bullock to start with. Curse it, as I'm certain sure the beast was poisoned that's what perplexes me most.'

'Does it?' he asked mysteriously. 'It don't me. It makes the matter clearer; defines the observable indications, as we say in the trade. I've a notion I know what it is you're after; or leastways I've heard of it.'

'Then, God dammit, why didn't you say so at once?' I cried.

'Don't rush your fences,' he answered. 'It may be a mere traveller's tale. But we had a visiting professor a while back; a rare good sport, uncommon fond of a pot or two and a pipe, and one time a physician with the East India Company. I recollect him telling us of a poison used by the Indians of the South Americas on their arrows. It was reputed to bring down the biggest game, yet leave the meat unharmed and fit for eating.'

'Then we've got it,' I announced; but pondered on this for a minute and added, 'Did you say the South Americas? Begod, this thickens the plot more yet. It's ticklish enough with a gentleman like Mr Gervase Markham in it up to his gullet, but an American concerned as well makes it worse. Tell me one more thing, Bob, did you ever hear also of a Dr Wilford Caldwell; physician, botanist and traveller?'

'Dr Wilford Caldwell?' He shook his head. 'I can't say I have. Who's he then?'

'I mean to find out,' I mused. 'And what he's up to. Save I've a suspicion growing on me that the gentlemen in Whitehall are waiting for me to pull some damnation hot chestnuts out of the fire for 'em. But we'll see who gets his fingers burned the most. For now, Bob, have that professor of yours examine the body too and add his observations to your report. We're doing handsome.'

The young rascal grinned at me. 'Not so handsome as you think. He took up an appointment in Bombay some several months ago.'

I considered that in further silence and then said, 'Be damned to it. Yet we're getting on by degrees, as lawyers go to Heaven. You've given me a notion where to ask my next questions. And there's one more matter with this corpse you've got. I want every stitch of his clothing considered and every little thing you find aboard him preserved, whatever it may be. In short I must find out whether he was a Frenchy or a good, honest Englishman. And I must find out quick, for time's at my heels. I'll have your answers tonight over a pot of claret at the Brown Bear; but not too late, as I've other business on hand. I mean to pay a call on Madame Rosamunda's genteel establishment. I've no doubt you've heard of the lady.'

He let out a whistle and considered me speculatively. 'I've heard of her right enough, though she's out of my class and pocket. D'ye need company on the job? See now, Sturrock, if I do you a favour with this cadaver what's to stop you doing me one? I could fancy a bit of entertainment better than the

128

Smithfield blowens.'

'It'll bear thinking of,' I answered with some care. 'We'll see how we go, if it happens you discover anything of interest for me.' There is never any harm in offering a bait and Master Bob might even be useful in case of disagreement; or if matters turned out sociable the young rascal could very likely set a whore talking as fast and free as anybody. I said, 'Bring your best frock coat; and don't come stinking of the anatomy rooms. The ladies don't like it.'

.

EIGHT

I was late at Bow Street this morning, as on leaving Mother Gregg's hospitable tavern we returned first to Soho Square for Jagger once more to procure fresh horses in case of sudden need, and to repair our dress; in spite of all our efforts we still carried a mud and graveyard air about us. By then, when I presented myself Abel was in his common state of agitation and Mr A already sitting in the Court so could not see me; a merciful dispensation which saved further time and trouble. But Mr Pottle was waiting, seated on the penitential bench with a look about him as if he was barely recovered from an uncommon thick night, though otherwise in no way put out by the dark looks Abel was casting right and left while he scratched and rustled with his quills and papers. I announced, 'You're well met, Mr Pottle.'

'Begod so are you,' he replied heartily. 'We waited till close on twelve for you last night, me and that old canonical humbug. He was weeping tears of gin on my shoulder with his back teeth awash before we'd done. We concluded you'd met with a mischief.'

'An affecting scene,' I observed. 'And why should you conclude that?'

'There's mischief enough about,' he answered. 'That fellow Jabez Stott, who was wounded in the mill t'other day, took and died of it not an hour later. Be hanged, it's like the plague.'

'What's that?' cried Abel, 'the plague?' He peered unfavourably at Mr Pottle. 'Bepox me, he's a plague if ever there was one. Been chattering me head off this last twenty minutes. Have him out of here, Jeremy.'

I needed no second bidding, for the last was news I wished to consider; though not all that surprising. But I had another duty before that, and as is always my habit I might also strike down several birds with one stone. I said, 'So I will, Abel, but there's a report for Mr A first, a matter I had no time to attend to myself,' and went on to tell him of the chaise left in Maidenhead Thicket. 'It might well be looked after by the magistrate and constables of Maidenhead,' I finished and then, closely observing Mr Pottle, added, 'For your own records, and from certain information received, the name of the gentleman killed and murdered is Monsieur Henri Leclerc of Grenoble.'

The shot found its range and for an instant Pottle's careless air of quizzical humour stiffened. It was come and gone in a flash, and too little to hang a man on, though he would have some sharp questions to answer before I was done with him. I was satisfied enough for now, and leaving Abel dusting out his nose with his quill, exclaiming and scribbling, I hurried Pottle out to the street before the good old gentleman could keep me longer for further enquiries. Here Maggsy and Jagger were waiting with the chaise, and instructing them to follow us round to Will's Coffee House I led the way there myself at a brisk pace. Conversation is pretty well impossible in the morning clamour of Drury Lane and not until we reached our haven of quiet—with Master Maggsy pushing in like a thruster and plainly hoping for another breakfast—did I start with Pottle, 'Now then, what's this about Jabez Stott?'

There was little more he could tell me. Holy Moses, he said, had already been in tears, terror, Latin, and the gin repentants. It takes a firm hand to get any sense out of the old rascal in that state, but seemingly on leaving the Brown Bear Stott had declared for entering a further tavern in the Long Acre. Moses himself had hailed this as an excellent notion, in particular as Stott appeared to be flush with money and more than half ready to make a pretty fair night of it. But before long Moses observed that the fellow had become pale, sweating and trembling like a man in an ague, and had then further declared that he had a sudden fever come on him and could not swallow his drink. Thereupon they had set out again towards Seven Dials, where Stott had fallen to the ground and was dead even before Holy Moses had time to offer up a prayer for his soul.

'No doubt a prayer like a rabbit bolting,' I said.

'No doubt,' Pottle agreed, and then continued, 'but in between the tears and gin it's plain that fellow was struck the
same way as Henriette d'Armande. Lookee now, Mr Sturrock,
what the devil is it? D'ye know?'

'Don't you?' I asked.

'I'll be damned if I do. Nor don't like it neither.'

For once I fancied he was telling the truth. It was another
perplexity, and I tried a fresh tack. 'What's of greater moment,
Mr Pottle, is whether that dagger was meant for me or you.'

'For me?' he cried. 'Why the devil should it be meant for
me?'

'That's another thing I don't know. I'm half persuaded you
might tell me.' But he was not giving anything away; he contrived even to seem bewildered and a bit simple. It's a trick I
use myself now and again and I did not press the matter; I
went on, 'I've said several times before, there's sudden death
hangs about that poor woman, and it still hangs about her
though she is in her grave. What did you discover of her today,
if anything?'

He grinned at me as lively as a cricket again. 'She frequented
two coffee houses in the Haymarket. But I had the best of it,
as you said, at the Prince of Orange.'

'Commonly used by actors,' I mused. 'And what was the best
of it, Mr Pottle?'

'An ancient server named Samuel who had a particular fancy
for her even though he must be close on ninety and can scarcely
cling to his coffee pots. He says he's seen a gentleman awaiting
her there on several occasions for the last two weeks or more;
and not in the way of the profession either as their colloquies
were always more like business matters and conducted in
French.'

'Did he ever overhear anything?' I asked.

'He did not. He don't follow the language, and they always
fell silent when he got too close. But he says the young lady
appeared pleased enough to see this gentleman the first meetings, but then seemed to turn against him. He says he knows

132

enough French to understand the word "Non" when he hears it.'

'Mr Pottle,' I said, 'you're not telling me anything I couldn't guess at myself. Did your server describe this man?'

'Pretty fair. He's as inquisitive as an old billy goat. Between thirty and forty, sallow, dark, sharp eyed and sharp featured, a little pointed beard and his own hair, of gentlemanly appearance and masterful manner.'

I reflected on that for a minute, though I have small faith in such descriptions. Save for the little beard it might have been Monsieur Leclerc himself, but I would not have taken a six-penny wager on it. 'You still don't tell me much,' I observed.

In no way put out Mr Pottle continued, 'That was up to last Friday. On Friday it very near came to a quarrel and Henriette pretty well ran out of the place. Then on Saturday there was another fellow appeared with our first gentleman. Well enough dressed but of a commoner sort. Roundish red face, shaggy hair, and a scar down the left cheek.'

I perceived Master Maggsy prick his ears up like a terrier at this, and interrupted, 'Hold there. You're sure of the scar?'

'That's what old billy goat Samuel declares. And furthermore that mademoiselle was dumbstruck at the sight of the fellow. As haughty as a lady, Samuel says. This time there was even fewer words exchanged, but he swears she demanded in English, "What are you doing here, William?", gave the fellow a single look up and across, and then walked out once more.'

'So ho,' Maggsy announced, aping my own manner on such curious disclosures, 'and likewise not half so ho. If that ain't Monsewer's valet I'm Napoleon Bonaparte.'

'We can't say yet,' I told him. 'How often have I instructed you not to run ahead of your observations. Is that all?' I asked Pottle. 'That was the Saturday. And on Sunday she came to look for me at St Giles' Church, but not discovering me then sent a note; which by ill luck I did not receive until Monday night. It's what she was doing on Monday I'm after.'

'She went to see a Mr Sims.'

'Mr Sims,' I repeated. 'Is that Sims the actors' agent at the Harp Tavern in Russell Street? How did you find out this?'

'Didn't I say she frequented two coffee houses? There seemed no more to be had from the Orange and I went back to the first. There by good fortune I came upon another lady I know.'

'You know 'em all, don't you?' Maggsy observed, torn between envy and admiration.

'A few here and there,' Mr Pottle admitted modestly. 'This one calls herself Lucille; a splendid creature, a regular Juno and good natured with it, though about as much in her head as a kitten. But by God you should see her stripped.'

'You may spare us your raptures,' I advised him. 'We don't have time for 'em. Pray come to business.'

'It's simple enough. Lucille was with Henriette d'Armande on the Monday, just before three of the afternoon. Lucille's a soul they all confide in, and she says Henriette was much agitated. She told Lucille that she was being pressed too close by some person she now knew was not William but Jean-Pierre, and she meant to have no part of his business. Accordingly she purposed to wait on Mr Sims to find out what he could do for her. What d'ye make of that? It's a devilish fine conundrum, ain't it?'

'We might make much or little of it,' I said. 'And William we may know. But who's Jean-Pierre?'

'Now here's the oddity,' Mr Pottle answered. 'Lucille's commonly as expansive as she's generous in bed. She'll talk a baker's dozen on a cuddle and a few fair words, but no sooner had I asked that myself than she was off in a fluster. Declared she'd a military gentleman waiting on her, that madame would be tantrums if she was late for rehearsal, made a dozen other excuses, and rose like a hen pheasant from cover.'

I considered him reflectively, but mused, 'Then we must let it pass for now. Did you call on Mr Sims?'

'Not to any purpose. I went to the Harp Tavern but they told me he finished his day's business by three o'clock and wouldn't see nobody more after that. I concluded you'd talk best to him.'

'And so I will. You've done very well, Mr Pottle. Now I asked you also to find a Mr Cloudesley Merritt at Beale's Chop House. Did you do as well there?'

'Never got near it,' he confessed. 'Was up and down the

Haymarket till near on five o'clock, and you said to go to Beale's for an early dinner.'

'It's no matter,' I told him kindly. 'You can't do everything. And today I've something better for you, if you're still game.'

'Game for anything,' he asserted. 'Begod it's better than stewing in Pottle Soskins and Pottle's back office.'

'It's fortunate they give you so much leeway,' I observed. 'But no doubt that's their affair, and yours. I'll tell you what I'm after next in a minute. First I want you to look at this.'

I produced the paper discovered with the unfortunate Monsieur Leclerc last night. This I had already examined while setting myself to rights not long since at Soho Square, and I shall now describe it here. It was a neatly draughted plan or map of some small coastal town. To the left there was a long finger which ended in a kind of island, and inside of that a narrow inlet just as long; next a further squarish area of land, and inside of this again what were clearly the streets lined in facing a bay or the opening of a river. It had no name or other writing on it, but here and there were letters and numbers marked with precise care; on the island there was a cross surrounded by a circle; and on the front street which faced to the bay there was a strong black square, again encircled, which could only represent some particular building. And I had the worst forebodings of what it must be; as I was all too well aware that today was the thirteenth of August.

Once again I watched Mr Pottle closely as he studied it; and once again I perceived that instant of sudden sharpness about him. It was come and gone in a flicker, and when he looked up at me he was as cheerful, guileless and simple as ever. 'Even I can see it's a plan,' he announced. 'But what of it?'

'Where is it?' I asked. 'Do you know?'

He shook his head. 'Damned if I do. I ain't a geographer.' But then his look turned keener again. 'Nor all that much of a fool either. See here, Mr Sturrock, there's more to this affair than the murder of a poor whore. This is what you said at the Brown Bear t'other night. This is the French conspiracy, ain't it?'

'That's right,' I agreed. 'You've hit it like a shoe nail. But

135

there's no time to tell you more about it now, for we must all be about our business; and about it damnation fast.' He started on a fresh question, but I repeated, 'We've no time. I'll say only this; recollect what happened to the Duke of Enghien in March of this year and you'll understand what that map means. So now let's set about it. Are you a fair horseman, Mr Pottle?'

'Pretty moderate,' he admitted. 'I'm forever trying to get the guv'nor to buy me into the Light Brigade. But he's devilish stiff.'

'Then you shall try your horsemanship now. I want you to ride hard to Maidenhead. There you will make certain enquiries at the livery inns; the most likely being the Greyhound. You're seeking news of a friend of yours who hired a horse or chaise early today; he might also have made a complaint of being stopped by highwaymen, though I think that unlikely. He would not wait to be delayed by constables and magistrates. I wish to know where he was making for and in particular if he was heading back to London. If you hear nothing of him work further afield towards Maidenhead Thicket to discover whether a second body or a wounded man has been discovered. As for his description, you already have it. It was given you by your billy goat Samuel at the Prince of Orange; the roughish fellow with a scar down his cheek.'

'It's a job after my own heart,' Mr Pottle announced. 'I'm as good as on my way.'

'You may report to me at the Bear tonight,' I told him. 'Or if I'm not present at Bow Street tomorrow. But don't delay. Mr Pottle; time's treading too close on our heels.'

He went off as spritely as a fighting cock, while I gazed after him and Maggsy announced darkly, 'He's a rum un. A right rattling, roaring whoremonger but a rum un nonetheless. What's a regular Juno?'

'A woman of widespread advantages,' I said.

'And can't be too widespread for Mr Pottle neither if you ask me,' he muttered reflectively. 'What I accounts rum is he says this Looseel says madame'll be tantrums if she's late, and that can't but mean Madame Rosamunda; so if he knows Looseel he must know of madame as well, yet t'other night he

136

declared he couldn't find out nothing about that lot.'

'A confusion second only to your ugliness,' I observed, 'but the slip did not escape my notice. Neither did it that he took so long in the Haymarket over enquiries which needed only an hour or so at most. Or that he spoke of the French conspiracy when I have never mentioned more than a general plot to him.'

'It's telling up, ain't it?' the sentimental child asked gloomily. 'Do you aim to let 'em corpuss him like the others or just hang him? I dunno as I should reckon that much. Mr William Makepeace the Practical Chimney Sweeper used to say it gives you a kind of holy feeling to watch a pal of yours adangling at Newgate and reflect that it ain't your neck, but I dunno as I should fancy to see the strangler hanging on to Mr Pottle's knees to finish him off.'

'We may see worse if we don't make haste,' I answered. 'Have done with your homespun philosophising, you little ghoul, and listen to your own instructions. For a treat you may take Jagger and the chaise about them.' That fetched a whoop of delight, though tempered with some suspicion, as I thought it would. 'First to Coventry Court, where you'll discover whether the man Tooley has yet appeared again. Next to Beale's Chop House on Charing Cross. There you may use your evil wits as you please, but what I want is whether Mr Rodney Pottle is known there, whether he is known to Mr Cloudesley Merritt or Mr Merrit to him, and whether the last is back from Chippenham yet. Though he's been travelling damnation fast if he is. And last to our good old friend Captain Isaac Bolton at the Prospect of Whitby in Wapping.'

I gave him certain further instructions as to what he was to do and what to ask in that mysterious village of seamen, but as by now you will perceive for yourself what these must have been I shall not repeat them here. So sending the child off with a generous half crown for expenses, as cock-a-hoop as he was wicked at the thought of riding round London like a lord all day, I set out on my own business; in simple a short walk to Russell Street, out of Covent Garden, to find Mr Sims at the Harp Tavern.

The Harp is a respectable house much frequented by members of the Thespian profession, where they recount their past glories, their present resting, and future hopes. The tap and common room are much decorated with playbills, broadsheets and the like and lie to the right, while Mr Sim's lodgings and office are above; these approached by a mysterious passage, a dark little winding staircase to a half landing, and then more stairs up to a closet where the supplicants wait. It was early yet for Mr Sims' trade, for actors do not like to stir themselves much before midday, but on desiring his clerk to acquaint him of my urgent and immediate business, he consented to receive me at once. I was well known to the gentleman as being an informed critic of the drama, of regular attendance at Drury Lane, on more than nodding terms with Mr Sheridan himself, and he greeted me, 'Why Mr Sturrock, here's a pleasure I didn't look for. Don't tell me you've got tired of the law and thinking of going on the boards yourself.'

'Not yet, Mr Sims,' I assured him. 'Though to be sure in my trade I'm called upon to play many parts.'

He was a smallish, fattish man, of benevolence tempered with caution and, like all these agents, with an air of being particular pleased to see you but hoping to God you wouldn't stay too long, or worse still ask him for something. 'Just as well,' he replied, shaking his head. 'Things are bad; damme, I've never known 'em worse. Managements at their wits' end, costs going up and audiences down, and God's sake look at the plays. There ain't a play on in London that I'd take my horse to see.'

We exchanged several more such civilities, and then seeing that Mr Sims was just as anxious for me to come to business as I was myself I said, 'One Henriette d'Armande as I understand waited upon you two or three days back.'

'Henriette d'Armande,' he mused, turning over a page or two of his ledger and then gazing at me from under his eyebrows. 'Is she in any sort of trouble? I'll be plain, Mr Sturrock, I thought she might be.'

'As to what she's in now,' I replied, 'only a parson could tell you; and he might not be all that certain. But I'm bound to push certain enquiries, Mr Sims, and I'm persuaded you might help me with 'em. Did you know the young woman?'

138

'Never see her in my life before my clerk, Lancelot, ushered her in that afternoon; and wasn't best pleased as it was close on three. But she was an uncommon taking piece, and I've ever been a fool for the ladies. Not to make a long story of it, as I've no doubt you've got as much to do as I have, she announced that she was seeking an engagement, no matter how small, and most particular not in Town. That was sufficiently surprising for most of 'em scorn the provinces.'

'In short she wanted to get out of London?'

'And in a hurry,' he agreed, 'for she pretty well implored me when I said I'd do what I could, but there was nothing starting just now. She next enquired was there any openings in America, no matter what as she was particular adaptable. I advised her that she'd do best to consult Mr Miller of Henrietta Street if she was set on America; though she wouldn't find it easy to get accommodated if she wasn't experienced in the dramatic art.'

'Mr Sims,' I asked, 'did you know she was a whore?'

'It ain't a question we discuss in this office. The word she used was "adaptable".'

As so often with Maggsy Mr Sims was telling me nothing I could not have surmised for myself. But in the Art and Science of Detection you must make sure of all things; and moreover I had been curiously moved by the poor soul from the start. It seemed a last kindness to her to put a few more questions, and I asked, 'Was that the end of it?'

'Save what happened on the stairs. She took herself off, and be damned not a minute later there was such a commotion as you never heard. Young Lancelot ran out with me hard after him, and there she was half down the stairs, against the wall dabbing at her arm with a kerchief and screaming that she was murdered. "Confound it, ma'am" say I, "if you're murdered you're uncommon lively with it". And sure enough when we came to look there was nothing but a little cut or scratch on her wrist.'

'They might just as well have cut her throat,' I said. 'But was more concerned to make it seem like natural death. What were her exact words?'

He pondered on that. ' "They mean to kill me", or some-

139

thing of the sort. Lookee, Mr Sturrock, I didn't account it much. I reckoned she'd scratched herself with her shawl pin and was making the most of it. As I recollect she went on about Jean-Pierre and some fellow William, and declared that one, t'other or which was waiting on the stairs, caught her wrist, stabbed her, and made off.'

'And while you were talking there he got clear away,' I observed. 'Was she screeching murder in English or French?'

'Why in English,' he cried, growing impatient. 'Is there much more of this?'

'Not a lot,' I promised. 'But people in extreme agitation commonly speak their native and natural tongue. I'm obliged to you, Mr Sims. You've revealed something I'd only half considered before. Tell me now did she say anything, no matter how little, about some plot or conspiracy she'd got wind of; or was pressed to take part in?'

'She babbled something of the sort. Said what it was she did not fully know, but it'd be a fearful mischief; and there was others beside this Jean-Pierre in it, but he was the ringleader. God bless you, Mr Sturrock, you've no notion of the tales some of 'em will tell to gain attention. I answered that I get a fresh plot every day put on my desk, and sometimes several; so she should go away and write it all down and send it to Mr Sheridan, and maybe he'd put it on at Drury Lane for her.'

'Very witty, Mr Sims,' I told him. 'Most uncommonly witty. And what then?'

'Why she turned as haughty as a duchess. Announced if nobody wanted to know of it she must look to herself. But would I do her one kindness at least; to advise her of some respectable theatrical lodgings where there'd be a lot of people about as she was now afraid for her life to stay where she was.'

'Nobody wanted to know of it,' I mused. 'And so it must have seemed to the poor soul, for she'd already written me a letter which I had not received. Was there anything more?'

'Be damned, that was already enough,' Mr Sims retorted. 'I told her she'd find several lodging houses about Bloomsbury Market, and wished her good day. I'll tell you plain, Mr Sturrock, what with wasting time and advice, getting no fee for it,

140

and wanting my dinner I'd had my fill of Henriette d'Armande by then.'

'And I hope it was a good dinner,' I said, taking my leave. 'For the invasion and the fate of Britain might well hang on it.'

I hastened my steps next towards Seven Dials to find Holy Moses; and today, the thirteenth of August, the spectacle of the thronging thoroughfares, the ladies of better quality now appearing, the soldiers, street criers and vendors, carriages, wagons and horses, and perhaps even some honest men, all passed my notice for I had weightier matters on my mind, and could even fancy that the clamour and clatter of London itself was the footsteps of Fate close at my heels. I can turn a nice touch of the poetics now and again; and so also could that Latin belching scribe when I discovered him in his hovel. He was busily scratching for some pretty saucy trull, while the wench herself with her bodice undone in the sultry heat was half perched on his knees, her tits wrapped around his ears, and tickling his bald pate with a quill as he protested, squealed, cackled and scribbled. A most affecting scene for a canonical of his age, and a damned difficult way of writing our noble English language; though I have read books which might have been so composed.

Having despatched the trollop with a light touch of my cane to her rump, and warned the old rascal that he was dissipating his profits in such excesses, I demanded to know quickly what he had discovered for me; but I had best make short work of it here or I shall have that publisher reckoning up his quires of paper on his fingers. In brief it was little or nothing. Turning up his eyes to Heaven he declared on a flood of prayers and protests that none of his parishioners in Seven Dials knew or had heard of the man Tooley from Coventry Court; neither did any of them have to do with the émigrés, being all true loyal Englishmen and even with some talk of forming their own ragged militia. As for the dreadful death of Jabez Stott he could not add much to what Mr Pottle had already told me; except that on Stott's last dying breath, thickened and mumbled as if his very tongue and lips were paralysed, he had muttered something about a Monsieur Hirson—which Moses pointed out sounded like French—who had lately come to lodgings some-where by Covent Garden from Wapping.

I perceived a ray of light here, and could only hope to God that Maggsy might see more from old Captain Isaac. But Moses could add nothing to it, though I told him plainly of the awful issues at stake. Even he blenched under his flush of gin at that; and ordering him strictly that as he loved His Majesty the King if he discovered anything fresh, no matter how small, he was to come to the Brown Bear tonight, I hurried off on my next errand. That to the corner of Broad Street to find a hackney, and then to desire the surly dog of a driver and his flea bitten horse to get through the traffic anyhow and take me to Mr Hatchard's bookshop at 104 Piccadilly.

As all the world knows Hatchard's is a most proper and genteel establishment, and I had a double reason for my call. One to make sure what that map represented, though I was already pretty certain of it; and the other the chance of finding out something more of Dr Wilford Caldwell. This I shall confess was slender, but as I keep well up with my London news I was hopeful of it; and in the outcome, as you shall see, Providence was smiling on me today as yesterday at Medmenham. He had frowned. I can only conclude that He had just perceived the danger Himself.

I shall make brief work here also. I first requested a book of maps of the southern coast of England; and within a minute or two more it was proved beyond doubt that my worst fears were well founded. In short Monsieur Leclerc's paper was a plan of the town of Weymouth; where His Majesty the King and the Queen were presently taking the pleasures of the sea with their family, after His Majesty's latest illness, like any simple country gentlefolk. The map of Dorset, in which this pretty little town is situate, did not show such large detail as Monsieur Leclerc's plan, but it needed no great perspicacity to read what the signs and marks must mean. The cross within the circle on Portland Island was the beacon, the numbers could be taken to refer to military posts, and the letters per-haps to the placement of French agents; the road facing the bay was the Esplanade, while the building marked heavily in black

142

could only be His Majesty's residence, Gloucester Lodge. I stood there in thought, pondering on how many copies of this mischievous chart might be in dangerous hands, until I perceived Mr Hatchard's shop assistant regarding me curiously; then I announced, 'I fear it's not what I'm looking for; though perhaps you may find another book to interest me. Do you have Dr Wilford Caldwell's latest work?'

The young man was somewhat nonplussed. 'I was not aware of any such volume; though of course Dr Caldwell is well known.'

So here was something. I continued, ' "Studies in the Botany of the South Americas", and most highly thought of in Philadelphia. But no matter. Pray tell me instead, does not the new Horticultural Society meet here; and would not Dr Caldwell be a corresponding member?'

That was a shot at random, but it fetched down a fine plump bird; for the young man himself was an enthusiast of the horticultural science. In a perfect spate of information I learned that there was to be a meeting of the society tomorrow, and even that the doctor himself was to read a paper; and then it became an easy matter with a slight ingenious tale of myself also attending a botanical conference—but placed mysteriously in Edinburgh—to extract Dr Caldwell's London address. That he had returned or was expected to return to Town was a further useful discovery, and in a few minutes more I was rattling off again to Mrs Dobie's particular lodgings for learned gentlemen in Queen Street, by the British Museum.

Here it looked at first as if the new smile of Providence might be tempered with another frown. The good woman was not all that forthcoming, but by dint of a fresh invention—this time of having travelled from India to consult with the doctor—she at length unbent to inform me that he had arrived from his ship in the early part of the month, had gone to the country last Friday, and might be expected back in these lodgings this evening. By now getting on like a house afire with the discreet lady I next made so bold as to ask after my illustrious friend Professor Leclerc of Grenoble and any of his colleagues; but on this she took a fresh touch of the chills and announced

143

that she had never heard of the person or persons, and did not hope to do so as she was not partial to the French. A very proper sentiment with which I heartily agreed; though did not say so.

Mrs Dobie could offer no more, and anxious but not dissatisfied I repaired next to Mr Hackett's eating house at the bottom end of Oxford Street, by Stevenson's Brewery, where I studied the day's newsprints while refreshing myself with a light dinner; a brace of woodcock fresh from the country, an excellent rare cut of sirloin of beef, and an uncommonly tasty blue Dorset cheese. The claret was indifferent, but I made shift and sat at leisure over a pipe while reflecting on the reports; all of them full of Bonaparte's review of his *Grande Armée* at Boulogne on the fifteenth. *The True Briton* asking why our frigates should not bombard the rascal while he was about it; *The Times* demanding thunderously was the government, which seemed to be aware of so little, aware at least of the danger of some blow or *coup de main*; and *The London Packet* advising simply the militia should cease its social activities and stand to arms.

There was nothing which threw much fresh light on our matter, and after some reflection as to whether I should hurry at once to Mr Grimble to acquaint him with what I had discovered already or whether to wait a few hours more, what profits to be gained by one or what dangers risked by the other, I concluded to continue with my own plans. My case, as we say in the Art and Science of Detection, was yet far from complete, and tomorrow forenoon would still give us time to take what action we must. In short a call upon my pretty, teasing little trollop Anne-Louise was much to be preferred to the corridors of Whitehall, and being Thursday it was an afternoon I was expected to pay my respects. But it is no gentleman who will dally on a doxy with his king's safety in the balance, and I meant to include certain sterner duties with our more tender pleasures.

I discovered her reclining on a day bed toying at a fancy bit of needlework, hair done *a la Grecque* with one coppery curl falling on her shoulder, gilt sandals, and her favourite Directory

144

chemise which fell to her points, promises, and mouldings as wanton as the little romper herself. 'Jeremee!' she cooed holding out her hand for me to kiss, 'Jeremee, you are late, Goddam; I have been all *inquiétude*.' She gave a wriggle which fetched one shoulder out of the little there was of her bodice and pouted at me sideways over it. 'Why are you so late? What is this dreadful things you are enquiring in now?'

'Why, my love,' I asked, settling beside her and helping the chemise down a bit further, 'What have you been hearing? Tales from some of your pretty playmates?'

'It does not matter.' She pouted at me afresh. 'And you are a great roaring impatient pig. You will spoil my gown,' she screeched, 'which I have assumed special to please you. It is a great trouble to place it on with such care only to tear it off in an instant.' All the same she wrapped herself around me as conformable as a pretty kitten hiding its claws for a minute, kicking the rag off with a pretty, naughty leg, gazing up at me with eyes of blue innocence and even somehow contriving a blush. She very near took the lobe of my left ear off with her teeth, and then whispered, 'Jeremee, I am afraid for you.'

'Are you, begod?' I asked, fondling the curve of her round little rump and debating whether to give a hearty smack on that most inviting anatomy to induce her to tell the truth. 'I wonder why? You'd do well, my rosy Venus, to be more afraid for yourself.'

The minx drew herself away, twisting round to sit on her haunches and present a fair view of all she'd got; and that was plenty. She lifted her arms, loosed off the fillet round her hair, shook her head to tumble the russet tresses down over her shoulders and tits, and enquired, 'How do you choose it best, Jeremee? Put up, or like so? Myself I consider it is prettee so, but concealing.'

'You're all pretty, you rogue,' I told her, 'and what you conceal don't need a lot of looking for.'

'I am all love for you, my Jeremee,' she protested, and to prove the matter flung her arms about my neck, very near smothering me in her hair, shed a maidenly tear on my shoulder, took another bite, and wept, 'You have nothing for me today but talk and talk and talk and words.'

'Then we'll have done with 'em,' I announced, falling to in a clinch; and a rollicking bout it was, seconds out of the ring, no breaking from the close work nor ears for the timesman's bell, and to hell with the referee. I shall not particularise for fear of my publisher, but it was a lively encounter with honours even, each side giving as good as received until we hauled off for truce, a breather, and several further expressions of esteem before returning to a longer engagement at leisure with fresh squeals, squeaks, murmurs and whispers. The passionate creature was as eager as a cat with the cream, and in no great hurry to have done with it, but at last even she cried quits to lie back purring, and I demanded, 'Well my little game chick, would you call that nothing but talk and words?'

'Indeed, my Jeremee,' she sighed. 'You're a very proper man.'

'That's right,' I agreed, clasping her tight with one arm round her backside and the other on her heart, 'I'm commonly reckoned a model of propriety. But tell me while I think about it, my rosy Cyprian, are you acquainted with a certain Monsieur Jean-Pierre; the second name as yet unknown?'

As instruction in the Art and Science of Detection you should always seek to question a naughty wench in her naked skin if possible, for pretty little liar as she may be her natural frailty will always give her away; in particular at a tender and unguarded occasion. So it proved now. Under my loving hand her heart gave one great thump and then for a minute raced nineteen to the dozen as if it would come up out of her throat. But the slut soon recovered herself; she fetched me a smack that rattled my teeth, kicking and fighting like a wildcat and adding a number of expressions of affection before I stifled her outcries and said, 'Come now, take care or you'll irritate yourself.'

She made several further observations of what she would do if I vexed her further, the least of which would have been a fatal impediment to any further loving exchanges, then pushed herself free to sit back on her haunches again and screeched, 'You are a vile monster. To ask a stupid question at such moment. Have you no *sensibilité*? I do not know why I have

146

such *tendresse* for you; and I do not have it now, not any longer. I hope the committee may take you. I hope Jean-Pierre. . . .'

The little fool stopped short, and I asked soft, 'What about Jean-Pierre, my duckling?' When the conversation takes a turn like that a gentleman should reach for his britches quick. I lost no time about it and continued, 'Let's have it now. Is he here?'

'He is not, Jeremee,' she cried. 'I swear to you.'

Tucking in my shirt tails fast I flung back the other door in the room. Beyond it lay a bedchamber, a further door, and outside that again a passage. So much was true enough; there was nobody here. By this time quite out of patience I turned again to the silly little slut, now lying face down on the day bed and sobbing like a prayer meeting with her naked backside and shoulders heaving; but her head turned to peer at me with one eye through the tangle of her hair, still fancying she could cozen me. 'Jeremee,' she wailed, 'you are a monster; but I love you.'

There was only one way to have an end to these dramatics. I fetched her a slap upon the arse that would have bolted a dray horse, snatched her to her feet before she could get the half of a shriek out, and shook her by the shoulders till her teeth rattled. I do not commonly mishandle ladies in this fashion, but she was fighting back at me with all her talons and it took another open hander—though placed considerately where it would not spoil her beauty, at least when she had her clothes on—before I could calm her enough to listen to me. Then I said, 'Take notice, you addle witted bitch. There's a hanging in this; there's several hangings. And, God help me, I've a fondness for you also; it'd grieve me to see you standing with a six foot drop under your feet and a rope about your neck. So let's have the truth of it.'

She stopped on a hiccup, with her mouth wide, though still as artful as a vixen; yet her eyes went past me to the mantelpiece. It was laden with feminine knick-knacks, but from that single glance I perceived there was something more there and with one hand none too gentle in her hair I dragged her across to look for myself. 'What?' I demanded; and then stopped. It was plain enough; and of all places the thing was resting in a fanciful porcelain cornucopia held aloft by a silly, simpering cupid; a little dagger, seemingly no more than a toy.

I said, 'God Almighty' and flung the woman back at the sofa, adding, "Get your shift on,' while taking up the weapon to examine it. It was very simple. As sharp as a needle, a lozenge shaped blade, a little groove down each side, and in this groove and smeared over the point a dark substance not unlike treacle. There was little doubt of what it must be.

I turned back to the creature, now with her poor pretty rag clutched up to her tits as if to hide her naughtiness, gazing at me wide eyed and tears rolling down her cheeks. 'Jeremee,' she wailed, 'I would not have done it. I swear I would not.'

My own feelings were too profound for rage. 'You'll swear something before you've done. You were to use this on me?'

'I was to make a quarrel,' she wept. 'And then to make you a little stab with it. Only a very little one.'

'God help you,' I told her, 'I'd have strangled you. But I should've been another natural death, and no questions asked. Do you know what killed Henriette d'Armande?' She shook her head, and for once I believed the slut, but pressed, 'Did you know she was dead?'

'Only but yesterday. Then it was Antoine Hirson said it. He brought me that; that thing. Jeremee, I swear again I would not have done it.'

'We'll get to that in a minute. There was a man here when I came unexpected on Tuesday, and you were not entertaining him; not as your pretty entertainment goes. Who was it?'

'That also was Antoine Hirson. He ordered I must tell him if you were asking of Henriette, but not to answer anything of her myself.'

'So if I didn't enquire they could reckon I'd no suspicion she was murdered. Tell me this now. Did you guess she was not French at all, but English?'

The pathetic little wretch plucked up courage enough to sniff. 'All the ladies knew. They considered she was a cheat. Though she was very clever; she spoke French very well.'

'But Hirson and this rascal they call Jean-Pierre did not discover it themselves until last Friday or Saturday?'

148

She turned her eyes up at me like a scolded child, but let her rag slip down a bit, and whispered, 'If you please, Jeremee, that I do not know.'

'Keep yourself covered,' I said. 'I'm in no mood for further love and kisses. And there's one thing you should know; you're well in the way for a damned light fitting necklace; and it won't be pearls either. Now then, who and what are Hirson and Jean-Pierre?'

'Hirson is of the committee. There are several of them or many, I think. It is called the Committee of Morality and they say that when Napoleon comes the ladies will be sent to the French Indies. But those who help the cause as they are ordered may be allowed to go free.'

'So you also was doing the best you could for yourself?' She started another tearful protest, but I waved her to silence and reflected on this. Granted they expected Bonaparte to take London it was fearful threat enough. 'Most of the ladies are at Madame Rosamunda's?' I continued. 'Where they dispense their favours to the nobility and gentry, gentlemen of the government, the Horse Guards, and the Admiralty. Be damned, it's a pretty picture. And I fancy this Jean-Pierre's the prettiest part of it. Who's he?'

'Jean-Pierre Labaud. Him I have never seen myself, but he is said to be of a rough appearance and manner and very brutal. An ancient *sans-culotte* and one of Fouché's men.'

'Joseph Fouché? Bonaparte's Minister of Police?'

She nodded. 'That is why I am afraid. He has assumed command of this committee. They say he comes and goes at will, and conceals himself so that he can never be discovered.'

'I fancy he's soon to have a rude awakening,' I told her, and mused, 'Such rascals can never end their reign of terror; and all these pestilential revolutionaries have committees on the brain. But we'll come to Antoine Hirson. Between thirty and forty, sallow and sharp featured, a little pointed beard and masterful manner.'

'That is the person, yes. It is very real of him.'

Recollecting the two men who had gone up the stairs at Coventry Court to see whether Henriette d'Armande was dead,

149

and for whom the woman Grope was later murdered in case she should describe them, I continued, 'There's another villain somewhere.'

The wench was tumbling over her own tits with eagerness now. 'I have told you, there are several, but I have only seen one other; Monsieur Maurice. A younger person, quite handsome, and of a liveliness; very gay with ladies. You might perhaps consider him an Englishman.'

'We're doing famously,' I announced. 'So now pay attention to these names. Monsieur Henri Leclerc. Mr Rodney Pottle. Dr Wilford Caldwell. Mr Cloudesley Merritt, or Popham Snadge. Have you ever heard of, or do you know any of 'em?'

She shook her head once more. 'I do not indeed. That is certain, Jeremee.'

I concluded again that she was telling such truth as she had in her and finished dressing at leisure, putting several further questions. But there was little more she could tell me, not even where the men Hirson and Jean-Pierre were to be found— neither did I expect it, for plainly the poor chit was only on the outer edge of the affair—and at last settling my neckcloth and smoothing down my coat I finished, 'Well then, so far as I can make out you've a pretty fair chance of being murdered yourself.' I wrapped that wicked dagger about in several thicknesses of kerchief so it could do no harm while I carried it away and then added, 'But I'll do the best I can for you. Now lock your doors, keep yourself close, and admit nobody again before I send you word that it's safe.'

My soft heart will be my undoing yet, for the minx came close up to me, letting her shift fall in one hand and standing like a penitent Venus with a pout and one teardrop still clinging to her eyelashes. 'Dear Jeremee, I know you truly love me,' she said. 'Would I not be safest of all in your own chambers?'

'As to that, ma'am, you might be but I wouldn't answer for myself,' I replied; and beat a hasty retreat.

NINE

When I reached the said chambers—still sweating at the thought of Anne-Louise taking up her residence in their philosophical quiet—it was a bit after seven o'clock and Master Maggsy had already returned from his several errands. He was reclining in my own armchair snoring, grunting and twitching, a half finished glass of Madeira beside him and one of my new pipes out of the box fallen from his hand. It was a singularly unlovely spectacle, and as I stirred the wretch with my cane I could not but reflect that for all her tricks that pretty little strumpet would make a more pleasing and domestic picture here. He woke with a snarl like an ill tempered mongrel, and I said, 'Come now, you little monster, we've no time for sottish slumbers.'

'God's Pickles,' he roared, 'I dreamt as we was resurrectioning again and you was turned into that horrible corpuss aclutching at me. Likewise Thomas Jagger declares he won't never forget it neither, for all he likes a bit of sport now and again, and he's gone to stable the hosses and clean the chaise in the hopes you won't take another notion like that tonight.'

'We don't know what may happen tonight,' I told him. 'Save that whatever it is it'll happen fast. So let's have your report just as quick. The man Tooley in Coventry Court first.'

'You been Coventry courting yourself, ain't ye?' he demanded, twitching up his ugly snout in an indelicate sniff. 'I reckoned you'd be having another rattle with the Fireship, being Thursday. God's Whiskers, she must drownd herself in that Oo de Quelckers Flewers the way it hangs about like fried onions.'

He broke off sharp and then continued in haste, 'I'm acoming to it. That whore shop's now all shut and bolted up and all the whores turned out of it, and Tooley ain't been seen since the night the old woman was gutted; bar one cove who declared that he see him peering out from one of the upstairs windows yesterday. But the others didn't reckon that; they says it was just as like to be a ghosk, as after all the fearfuls there last Monday it's sure to be haunted by now.'

'Be damned to ghosts,' I told him. 'What I'm after is does he have a scar on his face or not?'

The pig headed little creature was not to be hurried. 'Some says yes and some contrariwise; some say he comes and goes, and others that he ain't been around Coventry Court only this last few weeks anyhow; if you ask me most of 'em was keeping their traps shut as they reckoned to keep well out of this lot in case throat cutting got catching. We was getting nowhere at a gallop till I hit on a dodge. I let on as there was a titled noble-man as this Henriette was his long lost daughter who'd been carried off by gipsies as a child, and he'd catched up with her at last only to find she was dead and gone, and now he'd give a particular reward for any information about her last hours.'

He stopped to take breath, full of mystery, and continued. 'We always supposed it was Tooley fetched that note to the Brown Bear, didn't us? Well it warn't. It was some kind of footman who upped and volunteered that he'd carried a letter in haste to a Robin Redbreast at the Bear on Sunday. What's more it seems this same cove sees Tooley on the Monday morning after and desires him to tell the lady that he took the letter all right but the Robin Redbreast wasn't present so he left it; and expected to get a pint from the said Robin Redbreast for his pains but never did. And what's furthermore this same foot-man declares for certain that Tooley does have a scar down his chaps.'

'So ho,' I said. 'So now we've a fair notion of who Master William Tooley is; and why they killed Henriette d'Armande on Monday. That note was her death warrant; and that damned fool of a footman signed it for her. You've done very well, Master Maggsy. Did you do as well at Beale's chop house?'

'Bits and odds. They was just setting the tables for dinner, but I catched one waiter and says I got a particular message from Bonaparte for Mr Pottle or Mr Merritt.'

I gazed at the child in fresh astonishment. 'What did the fellow say to that?'

'Why nothing, save that the proper place for messages was on the letter board and then bustled off. But I found a little old cove asitting by himself in a corner waiting for his chop and looking like a pot of piss with snuff on the top.'

'Be damned to the romantics,' I rapped. 'Let's have your findings, quick and short.'

'In a bleeding hurry, ain't you?' he demanded. 'All right then. Pottle's knowed at Beale's well enough, but not regular, though thick with Merritt; and when he turns up him and Merritt don't sit at the common table but go off on their own with their heads close like they're talking secrets. Nor Pottle wasn't at Beale's yesterday, and I says he wouldn't be as Mr Merritt's gone to Chippenham and what's he after there? And this little cove as don't seem to fancy Mr Merritt all that much, says he's wicked ambitious among several other matters, declares that's where his family comes from, or close by.'

'So ho,' I observed, 'and if our other information's correct so did Henriette d'Armande. I begin to see certain daylight, Master Maggsy, but let that pass for now. What did you have of Captain Bolton?'

This gallant old retired mariner spends the most part of his time drinking a fearful concoction of rum, limes and a pinch of gunpowder in the back upstairs window of the Prospect of Whitby and looking out over the Pool of London through his spy glass. There is little moves or breathes along the river from the Isle of Dogs to the Tower without he gets to hear of it somehow, and he and Maggsy have a particular affection for each other; and a nice pair they make between them. But I shall pass over the young rascal's account of the captain's health, manner and general opinions and come straight to the nub of the matter.

'Right enough,' he announced, 'there's a fine gaggle of Frenchies in and about Griffin Street by Shadwell Dock, mostly sailors, but not took a lot of notice of as the place is full of foringers anyhow; though Capt'n Isaac declares there's comings and goings from the ships and the Essex marshes, and says some-

153

thing should be done about it which everybody agrees but nobody knows what. As to the pi'son he claims he's heard of such things in the Java seas, but if you reckons this lot come from the South Americas it's most likely brought by a certain Demerara Jack. This same a seaman who worked the South America trade and got lost and cast ashore on the Demerara coast, but made his way back to Wapping a month or two since. Seems he's gone off again now, but was up and about some several weeks telling the tale of his adventures for a pint or two and selling the heathen curiosities he'd fetched with him.'

'So here's another bit cleared,' I mused, 'though there's still much to do.' By this time Jagger had returned, and despite all Master Maggsy's protests that they were both horse tired and very near asleep on their feet I continued, 'We've a fair night's work ahead of us; but we'll start with an early supper.'

Stopping only to prime a pair of little pocket pistols—not an armament I rely on as a rule, being too light and ladylike, but better than the Wogdons for social occasions as these are somewhat noticeable—I placed one in each side pocket of my coat and we next all three repaired to a modest eating establishment on the way to the Brown Bear. It was a quick and simple meal with little said save for Maggsy's grumbles and cavernous yawns; but I was in haste to hear what Bob Snaffle could tell me, and without staying to smoke a pipe I soon gave the word to move.

He was already awaiting us, leaning back on one of the settles, legs stretched out before him, hands thrust in trousers pockets, beaver tilted over his eyes and surveying our collection of rogues through the haze of candlelight and smoke. 'You keep ripe company, Jeremy,' he observed. 'Be hanged a man does well to have his hands on all he's got here.' He drained his tankard at a swallow and finished, 'I'll take a pint of claret.'

The fellow plainly meant to exact a fee for his science, but I rapped on the table for the serving wench, and then demanded, 'Come now, Bob, what did you discover?'

'God's Blood, how did you dig him up?' the hardened rascal

154

enquired. 'Did you use a herd of wild elephants to have him out?'

'There was a touch of confusion about the affair,' I confessed.

'But did you find anything, man?'

'His own mother wouldn't ha' liked the look of him,' Snaffle declared callously. 'And as to what we found I can tell you in one word. Nothing.'

'Damnation,' I cried. 'I was counting on you, Bob. The man was murdered; I'll swear to that. And I'll swear you found a little cut or prick on him somewhere.'

He nodded. 'On his neck behind and below the right ear. He was murdered right enough; and they meant to make sure of him. There was also a contusion under the hair at the back of the skull. Not enough to kill him; the bone wasn't depressed. But it would have quietened him for a bit.'

'So he was stunned first,' I said. 'Then they used that damned stuff to finish the job. First because it was already handy, and quiet; second as there'd be no mess of blood to clear up or other traces left in the dower house to be seen by Markham or Caldwell next day. But it's the poison I'm after. Are you sure there's no sign or trace of it?'

The wench had brought his claret by then and he put half of it down at a draught before continuing, 'Nothing we could find. Poisons ain't easy unless you know what to look for. I told you this morning, we've got travellers' tales; but they ain't enough. I can't give you evidence, Jeremy. There was no inflammation, constriction or other disorder. All I can tell you is that he'd taken a meal of bread, cheese and a blackish kind of pickle some time before. It's commonly reckoned that food don't start to digest for about an hour, but anybody who tried to swear to it'd be a fool. By the look of this lot say two hours; give or take a bit.'

'The fellow who stopped at the Windmill,' I mused. 'And again at the Waggoners at Mill End, where he took a quick bite, including pickled walnuts. I've always had a notion that's who he'd prove to be, and now we're pretty sure of it. But what about the man himself? We've got to put a name to him; though I can make a fair guess at that too.'

'Names ain't my business,' Mr Snaffle announced. 'We

reckoned he'd be about thirtyish, and well nourished but not fat. Could have been a soldier at one time for there was an old scar on his right upper arm which looked like a pistol or musket bullet just scraping him.'

'What of the clothes? Was there anything in the pockets? And was they English or French?'

'French,' he answered. 'There was a maker's label in the britches and another in the boots; Coignet of Paris, and Leduc. But nothing in the pockets. They'd been turned inside out to strip 'em and left that way. The shirt was uncommonly fine linen and fancy ruffles and stitching. So who was he?'

'I'll not name the fellow till I'm sure of him,' I said. 'But the rest seems plain enough. He made his way to the Dower House to confront Leclerc and the so-called servant. What for we can't say yet, though we may guess at it. Neither can we tell whether he knew where they'd be or had to look for 'em, and we may never know. It don't matter all that much. But confront 'em he did; and they shut him up for good. And there in the laboratory by chance they'd already got a body trussed up for burial next day. It was the simplest matter to change one for t'other. Mr Markham and his other guests was in the habit of flinging the cares of philosophy aside after supper and these rascals could work without interruption. We're told it was raining cats and dogs, so there'd be nobody abroad to see 'em; and the river barely fifty yards away ready and waiting for poor Gipsy Tom.'

Mr Snaffle grunted. 'Be damned, why take the trouble? Why not have the fellow himself in the river and be done with it?'

'Because they dare not take the chance. Lookee, Bob, a pauper simple not even worth the cost or courtesy of a coffin to put him in is one thing. No doubt if by some misfortune he was found, being supposed to be buried, it'd be a country wonder but little more. There'd be no cause to lay it to Monsieur Leclerc and his servant. But let an unknown gentleman in fine French clothes be discovered and there'd be questions asked and to spare. They had to take what seemed the safest way. It's pretty plain they meant to stay quiet at Mill End for some several days yet and only my appearance that afternoon decided 'em on flight. Yet even then they were so careful of Mr Markham's curiosity that they chose to wait till he and the others were safe at their bottles or abed.'

I was somewhat short about it, for I cannot put up with having my explanation of a mystery questioned, but what further debate the critical rascal might have started was checked by Holy Moses then creeping in, sidling on to the settle, and gazing sorrowfully on the company of rogues all about us. 'What a vulgar throng we have here,' he complained. *"Virtutem videant intabescantque relicta"*; "Let them look on Virtue, and pine away because they have abandoned her"; Flaccus.'

But it was plain by the twist of the old canonical's chaps that he had discovered something and was calculating what it might be worth. 'A curious chance,' he announced. 'And well met, Mr Sturrock. I have today walked my suffering feet to the bone, and worn my eloquent throat dry to a hundred of my poor wretched friends; and certain others. But not without success. Yet I have an uneasy rumbling in my bowels which I hope a pot of gin might assuage.'

'God's sake,' I said, 'if it'll set you talking the quicker you shall have even that,' and banged on the table for Nan; a signal which roused Master Maggsy and Jagger from their snores and caused Mr Snaffle to finish his own claret in a hurry.

When that was seen to Moses at last lifted his rosy snout from the pot and condescended to continue, 'One, Polly Lockett, common woman to a James Lamb, stable man at the Belle Sauvage, and also on occasion to Bully Hucker.'

'The stage coach whip?' I demanded.

Moses inclined his head benevolently. 'The same, Mr Sturrock. Reputed or pretends to be the fastest four-in-hand in the country but now unemployed this six months as the coach companies have one and all turned against him. They declare that he gives them an ill name, frightens their passengers, and drives their horses into the ground.'

'Come to it, man,' I rapped out. 'Hucker's tricks're well known. What about him?'

'The woman avows that being in poverty and ugly tempered with it for so long he has this last few days become unaccount-

157

ably flush of money; and furthermore on Monday last deep in his cups, he boasted that he'd show these lily livers some fine fast driving, and had been engaged for a hundred guineas by a Frenchman. But then he muttered something that they'd cut his throat if he blabbed of it and said no more. I do not give his own words as repeated by the woman, but that is the true substance of them.'

'Be damned to his own words,' I answered. 'Where can we find the rascal?'

Moses took another draught from his pot. 'Alas, Mr Sturrock, I fear we can't. He left London yesterday.'

Not for the first time in this confounded tangle I felt my neck cloth start to tighten; but I restrained my rage and observed, 'It's not a lot for a pot of gin. Is that all?'

'The man, James Lamb. He deposes that in the last day or two several *émigré* gentlemen have hired or purchased horses from one livery or another; the best obtainable and paid for in gold. Four to his certain knowledge, but he has also heard of others.'

'You've done pretty well,' I observed, 'but I need more yet. Maggsy, and you Jagger, wake up.' They jerked to with a start and I continued, 'You're to go with Holy Moses. I want this fellow James Lamb questioned, and you may do it how you like. I want anything more you may gather of the man Hucker; in particular where he's gone. And I don't care how you get that either. Be damned,' I roared, cutting short their complaints, 'so am I tired. And we might all be tireder yet before this lot's done. Set about it now, and be quick for I want you waiting with the chaise by twelve o'clock in the Cock Yard opposite James Street in the Haymarket. I hope to God we may not need it; but if we do we shall need it badly.'

It was then a little past nine and early for Madame Rosamunda's—if it were worth going there at all now—neither had Mr Rodney Pottle yet appeared. I was in a fever of impatience, for it was plain that our villains had scattered or were scattering; but I had a notion that the most important of them would not be making for Weymouth. Unless I was losing my wits, which was sufficiently unlikely, they must have some secret hid-

158

ing place in the country. Much now hung on Maggsy coming back with fresh information; and to give the child time to find it I must needs wait till midnight. While I must also contrive to send warning of the danger to His Majesty.

I resolved on my next stratagem, and said, 'Madame Rosamunda must wait for us tonight, Bob. We've other business on hand.'

'Be hanged,' he protested. 'You offered me some entertainment.'

'So I did,' I agreed, 'but the best I can promise now may be a damned long, rough ride. Though you might also hear something of that poison. Are you game?'

'Game enough,' he answered. 'What're you up to now?'

'A call on a celebrated botanist and traveller,' I told him. Then, pausing only to instruct One Eyed Jack that if any other persons were to come looking for me he was to send them to wait in the Cock Yard by twelve o'clock, I led the way round quickly into Drury Lane; where there are always hackneys to be found by the theatre. In another minute or two we were cursing our way northwards against the press of evening traffic and the lamps and torches; but we got through quicker than I might have dared to hope and the event was fortunate, for as we drew into Queen Street I perceived another carriage standing at the doctor's lodging and Dr Caldwell himself there watching the groom carry in his valises. Pulling up our own man sharp, ordering him to wait and dismounting, I wasted no time on ceremony but said, 'By your leave, sir.'

He turned to survey us up and down, not best pleased, before observing, 'Why, Mr Bow Street Runner. What is it now then? Not further experiments with Franklin's Jars, I pray.'

'Experiments with a certain poison, sir,' I told him sharply, 'and four deaths; two being murder. And more to come unless we stop it. I'm persuaded you might help us.'

We stood for an instant more in the darkening street, under fresh storm clouds lowering the sky, until he nodded and without another word turned into the house and up the stairs to a front apartment where the candles were already lit.

It was a strange silence. Still without speaking he threw off his dust coat while I took out Anne-Louise's dagger to lay it on the table. Then regarding me and Bob again for an instant he turned to study the wicked instrument, closely examining the treacly smear in its groove and on the point, even touching it carefully with the tip of his finger, and at last asking, 'Where did you get this? D'you know what it is?'

'I think you can tell us,' I said and, indicating Bob, added, 'This gentleman is from St Bartholomew's Hospital.'

Dr Caldwell nodded curtly, and just as abrupt continued, 'It's known to the Macoushi Indians of Demerara as wourali. It is prepared from a forest vine described botanically as *Strychnos toxifera*, together with certain other plants, roots and ant venom; it may be swallowed without harm, but when introduced to the blood it is inevitably fatal. In its fresh state it is said to kill in a few minutes, but there is some reason to believe that as it stales it becomes less potent. To be plain with you, we don't know. But at any time it's a hell's brew, for it seems to paralyse the motor muscles without bringing unconsciousness; so the victim dies of collapse in an extremity of terror. Is that what you want?'

I gave him a little bow. 'Some of it, sir. Would you be good enough to write that down for me and sign it?' For another instant I fancied he was about to refuse but I added, 'I can speak of the terror; I've seen the victims myself. One of them was a young and lovely girl. I'll stop at nothing to avenge that poor creature.' On that he stared at me once more, but then took a sheet of paper and quill from the writing stand, sat down to write quickly for a minute or two, and then pushed the paper across. Bob watched, but wisely said nothing, while I bowed again, folding it and placing it in my inner pocket. You should never lose sight of the lesser objective in the greater; at least my dozen of Madeira and the humbling of that damn fool coroner were sure.

'I'm properly obliged, sir,' I announced. 'But tell me if you will. You were quick to admit us and explain this. I wonder why?'

'You spoke of murder,' he answered shortly. 'And there was more behind your tomfool antics than play acting at Markham's

160

yesterday. More still behind opening that grave; you were after the body for autopsy.' He regarded me thoughtfully. 'You were seen and recognised; and I'll warn you, sir, Markham's beside himself. He swears he'll have you broke for it if nothing worse.'

I discovered myself conceiving a rare liking for this Dr Caldwell, for I love a man with wits as keen as my own. But there was no time for the sociables; I was more concerned to see him cleared of this business, and not only out of kindness. The last extra morsel I wanted on my plate now was diplomatic conclusions with a neutral American citizen; and I had fancied for long enough that this was the damnation hot chestnut which the gentlemen of Whitehall had set me to pick for them. I resolved on a simple question. 'As to Mr Markham, we must await the issue. But there's one doubt I still have. We don't know whose body it was.'

'Then I can settle that,' he answered readily. 'It was a poor simple fellow they called Gipsy Tom; and an accident. I'm satisfied he found his way into the laboratory and there cut his finger with a scalpel Leclerc had been using. And I may assure you that I spoke my mind in no uncertain manner concerning carelessness with the wourali.'

That it was an accident I was well aware; that Dr Caldwell still thought the body must be Gipsy Tom was a vast relief, for it was plain that he was telling the truth as he knew it, and that it set him clear of any collusion. I made sure of it by desiring further had he been aware of any other unknown visitor, or that Monsieur Leclerc and his servant had left in haste and secrecy last night, and then continued warmly, 'I'm yet more obliged, sir. Is Mr Markham still at Mill End?'

'I fancy not. He spoke of spending a few days at a fishing lodge he holds somewhere. He's a devoted angler along with his several other interests.'

'It's a philosophical art,' I observed. 'Tell me one last thing, doctor. Did you ever hear the names Mr Rodney Pottle or Mr Cloudesley Merritt mentioned by anybody at Mill End? Or the woman, Henriette d'Armande?'

He shook his head. 'I did not. See here, Mr Sturrock, you're asking a plaguey lot of questions, but answering very few.'

'There's precious few to answer yet,' I told him. 'When I've got the business done with I shall beg the honour and privilege of your company to sup with me, and then tell you the whole tale. But for now, sir, I must set to work fast. "At my back I always hear Time's wingèd chariot hurrying near", as some poet or the other remarks.'

I often find that a well chosen jewel of our noble English literature will cloud the issue nicely and, giving Mr Snaffle the nod that there was nothing more to do here, we escaped with little more said on either side. Waking our grumbling hackney driver and his lousy horse I ordered them to turn back for the Haymarket at best speed and we rattled off once more. It had been twenty minutes or so well spent and I was not dissatisfied, though Bob himself was somewhat complaining. 'Be hanged, Sturrock,' he said, 'I thought you promised me some fun.'

'You may see it yet,' I told him. 'We've still got very near two hours to wait for what Master Maggsy may discover. That's enough for a call on Madame Rosamunda after all. You shall have your fun; and fast and furious before we've done with it.'

It was a bit more than half after ten when we reached James Street, and here we found that rumour had not lied in describing the house as an elegant establishment. We were admitted by a pretty blackamoor child, dressed simply in baggy black silk trousers, gilt sandals and a gold turban, to a fair sized hall lit with fine wax candles. There was perfume in the air and a sound of music from above, several fanciful pictures which would not be welcome in a lady's parlour, brocaded hangings, a flight of wide stairs and two footmen standing each side at the bottom of them. Livery and white wigs enough, but a look about them that spoke of other duties besides calling a gentleman's carriage.

The naughty child scampered off to acquaint madame of our presence and before long she appeared, flirting a feather fan at the head of the stairs to survey us from behind it, and then billowing down upon us. The most monstrous fat woman you ever saw in your life, envolumed in a maiden's blush pink Empire gown, topped by a round, rice powdered and raddled

162

face with a little rosebud mouth painted on it, and set off by henna coloured hair glittering in glass jewels and three ostrich plumes. It was like nothing so much as one of Mr Gillray's lewd cartoons, and beside me Snaffle gave a sound like a strangled horse, while I did my best French bow and she let off a simper that would have felled a brewer's drayman; then announcing in a little fluting voice, 'Why gentlemen, I'm fantastical honoured.' What you could see of her eyes swept us up and down, estimating our value. 'But my silly Baba didn't seem to catch your names.'

'Ma'am,' I said, 'Ebenezer Rampole, of Charleston, Carolina, and my very good friend Lord Hampton; lately come into his inheritance,' I added on an aside.

She treated us to another simper. 'Then indeed I'm double fantasticalled. But gentlemen are commonly presented here by another gentleman. In these wild times a poor defenceless lady must mind her modesties.'

'A most proper sentiment,' I agreed warmly, trying a ranging shot. 'And so our good friend Mr Gervase Markham of Mill End warned us. But we're resolved to cast ourselves on your kindness.'

'La, sir,' she cried, 'you're impetuous. But 'tis often the way to a lady's heart and any gentleman sent by Mr Markham is welcome. Will you be pleased to ascend with me, Mr Rampole, and my lord.' She fetched a fresh simper which very near took Snaffle's head off. 'Though I fear you're late for our theatricals. Nothing will satisfy my young ladies but they must entertain their guests with *tableaux vivants*. We've had the Judgement of Paris tonight.'

With several further genteel observations she led us up to a handsome corridor, where there were two more footmen stationed and a little gilt console table on which several black silk masks were arranged. 'Pray be so obliging, gentlemen,' she continued here. ' 'Tis a polite convention. And my pretty rogues affect that they love to be overwhelmed with astonishment when their *beaux* reveal themselves.'

What lewd thoughts that prompted in Mr Snaffle may best be imagined, for he barely suppressed another snort, and madame's

163

simper took a sudden sharp edge over her fan. The rascal was little better than Maggsy in his manners and I trod hard on his foot, saying, 'My lord's fresh from the country, ma'am; a somewhat green and nervous disposition,' and then adding in a fresh whisper, 'but an uncommon large inheritance and a close neighbour of Mr Markham's.'

It was touch and go for a minute, but then she gave a sideways look to the footmen and they opened a pair of double doors to let us into a biggish salon blazing with candlelight; gilt chairs and an opulent cold buffet and wines, two more flunkeys, several musicians discoursing soft airs from a little stage or dais, an archway and portière at one side of this guarded by a pair of negroes as black, naked and polished as ebony; and six or eight gentlemen all dressed in the pink of fashion. Like ourselves they were masked but some of them plainly known to each other for they were conversing and laughing in groups, all most elegant and genteel. None of them seemed to take much note of us, and madame said, 'Pray, gentlemen, accept our hospitality. But I beg you recollect that names are not discreet.'

'Ma'am,' I assured her, 'we're the heart and soul of discretion.

She gave us another flirt with her fan and wobbled her great shire horse arse, ostrich plumes and gown off to do the socials, while we remained more modestly aside for a minute or so to survey the company. An old lecher who by the look of him would have been better dandling great grandchildren by his own fireside, a brace of young bloods and a heavily built ruddy gentleman I fancied must be of the Admiralty, another all lace and languidities with a quizzing glass, and a pair who by their manner and cavalry mustachios were pretty clearly military men. There were two more I studied with some care. The first of these one of the flunkeys, at present with his back to us but whose powdered wig seemed too small and his livery ill fitting; and the second a face made well known to all, and none too kindly, by the cartoonists. Even those impudent rascals have their uses, and despite the mask his lantern jaw and habit of carrying his head a bit to one side—as he might have been half

164

hanged and cut down too soon—were as good as his name. I shall not divulge it for fear of scandal; but I reflected that there was a trick or two here I might take.

'Well then, Sturrock,' Bob Snaffle demanded. 'What's to do? Be damned, we're out of our weight here. I dunno about you, but I've got less than half a sovereign in me pocket.'

'It'll be enough,' I told him. 'We'll take a glass of wine and play to the cards as they fall,' I added, edging into the throng with one eye on Madame Rosamunda. It seemed she had forgotten us for she was now letting off her simper at the two cavalrymen, and I gave her another little bow for luck and took a glass of wine. It was thin, fanciful Rhenish stuff, and not a good gallop with the ladies in a bottle of it though well enough to moisten the throat, and I turned to get a fresh look at that flunkey. He also had moved away however and was concealed behind the naval gentleman and our wry necked political lord; but I was still close enough to listen with one ear to madame and her two gallant soldiers.

'La, Captain Clancy,' she was saying, 'I declare you're a bold rogue; yet I'll whisper a secret. There's several of my naughty minxes are praying and begging that you'll bid high and hard to save 'em from the clutches of one certain other gentleman. But where's Colonel Maskelyne? For he vowed he'd be with us to-night.'

Where Colonel Maskelyne might be I neither knew nor cared; his name was good enough. I moved on again idly, this time to a pretty, indecent mirror set on the wall, its gilt frame embellished with sundry nymphs and Priapian figures most remarkably endowed and performing feats even more remarkable than their natural gifts. It would have sent Master Maggsy into fits, but I paused by it as if to straighten my neckcloth, gazing into the glass; while beside me Bob whispered, 'Hark now, Sturrock. They put 'em up for auction; I've just heard it. And all I've got's but eight and tuppence ha'penny.'

I did not answer, for the man I was seeking had come into the glass. He seemed unaware of me, bowing to proffer a tray to his lordship; but as he had several times been described, rough and brutal with the scar down his left cheek; yet a pair of keen and commanding eyes, a manner of authority even under his wig and livery, and no doubt a brave and resolute rascal after his own fashion. I caught a glance between him and the languid fellow and then another to the two bloods, and said softly, 'Watch now, Bob. I'm about to pass you a pistol unseen, and for God's sake keep it so unless it's called for. There're some damned important people present, and I want to keep it peaceful if we can. That flunkey's the man I'm after. I knew I'd find him here and so I have. But I fancy there's others with him, and we might have a tussle for it.'

What Bob answered was lost for I had other business on hand. So far as I was aware Labaud did not know me to look at, but we could not be sure of it and must work fast. Madame was now billowing herself over to the musicians and I moved behind the two military men; the good fortune of soldiers being here was more than I had hoped for, but I could see a stratagem to make the most of it. Speaking short but quiet over their shoulders I said, 'Gentlemen; which of you is Colonel Maskelyne?'

As of one they turned on me, the first whispering, 'Dammit sir, no names. Don't you know the orders?'

'I've others more important,' I replied. 'From General Garth at Weymouth. Officer Commanding His Majesty's guard.' It was covered by Madame striking a little gong, and I continued, 'I'm instructed to look for Colonel Maskelyne or Captain Clancy.'

'What the devil's this?' the other demanded. 'Maskelyne ain't here. I'm Clancy.'

Madame was mounting the dais amid a new air of expectancy, Bob Snaffle standing close by me concealing the pistol, our two officers torn between suspicion and puzzlement, and I murmured, 'We've a French agent here, gentlemen; I'm advised to call on you for assistance to arrest him.'

'What the devil?' Captain Clancy started again, but by now Madame was crying 'Dear friends, please to take your seats for our auction. Recollect, I beg you, that the higher the bid the more the lady is complimented. But no promissory notes unless approved.'

One of the negroes placed a little stool on the dais, the

fiddlers struck up a lively tune and a bevy of naked children as nymphs and cupids came gambolling on; these followed by two raddled, simpering youths got up as satyrs—and again thank God Maggsy was not there to witness it—dragging a rope of flowers and drawing after them a rout of figures closely veiled from head to toe in several coloured gauzes. It was plain Madame Rosamunda was suffering a severe attack of the classicals, and a pity to have to spoil it. But we could give 'em a minute or two yet, though my soldiers were whispering together and Captain Clancy demanded in my ear, 'Damme, sir, what the devil is this, I say?'

'A conspiracy against the person and safety of His Majesty the King,' I answered out of the side of my mouth. 'You'll deny me your assistance at your own peril. When I give the word I'll have you announce that you've got a squadron of your men surrounding the house.'

His further astonishment was lost in a fresh buzz of anticipation, for the two youths had now carried one of the wenches up to the stool and the nymphs and cupids were doing a naughty lascivious dance about her stripping off the veils one by one. They revealed first the face and then a shoulder and tit, a long thigh and voluptuous belly until a slender creature of olive hue stood disclosed and disdaining modesty. She drew her hands up her body in an enticing gesture, raised her arms above her head and turned slowly about to present her backside, swaying in provocation and time to the fiddles. She was a rare ripe baggage, though for my part I cannot put up with a shameless woman, and the naval gentleman cried, 'Tasty, by God. Built like a frigate. 'Minds me of the starn of the old *Indomitable* before the Frenchies sank her. But not so much gilding, mind.'

'Fifty guineas,' shrieked the old grandad, slavering at the chaps and jigging for lechery.

'Sixty,' said my lord.

'Seventy,' one of the bloods joined in, followed hard by eighty five from the languid fellow who was surveying the trollop up and down through his quizzing glass, as she now turned to face him, working her hips and belly.

'One hundred,' his lordship announced.

167

I could not let him have her, for though the rest of them could purchase their meat and carry it off for all I cared my lord was another unexpected card in my hand and I meant to play him. 'Be damned,' I observed, 'we're insulting the lady to talk of ha'pennies. And twenty-five.'

'You rogue,' screeched grandad. 'Forty.'

Bob was standing dumbstruck and I gave him a sharp kick on the ankle to remind him of his manners. 'Eight and tuppence ha'penny,' he muttered but then called, 'Hundred and fifty,' while behind us Captain Clancy roared, 'Gone away, follow the hounds; seventy-five.'

'Begod, ma'am,' my lord observed, 'we've some thrusters here tonight. Let's see what they're made of. Two hundred.'

By now the wench was striking an attitude that even at its most polite could only be described as indecent, Madame Rosamunda shaking from her tits to her ostrich plumes with excitement, and the old bag of bones and lust very near having a fit. 'Two hundred and five,' he wailed on a despairing note.

'My lord,' the slut squealed, 'you'll not see me so wasted.'

'And fifty,' he answered. 'That should settle it I fancy.'

It was time for me to move. In another minute his lordship would carry the wench off, and I wanted him here. All eyes were on them as she stepped down from the dais, while madame cried, 'Gone for two hundred and fifty guineas. But take heart, gentlemen, we've other precious tidbits left for you.'

'Not tonight you ain't,' I observed softly to Bob, added to the cavalrymen, 'Stand by now,' and called to Labaud, 'You there, my man, wine for all of us; we'll toast the gallant victor and his Venus.'

So far as I could see he was still unsuspicious, for he and the other flunkey set to filling goblets; though the languid fellow had let his quizzing glass fall and was eyeing me. I should have watched him more closely, but behind us Captain Clancy's companion muttered, 'Hang it, d'ye know who that is with the doxy? He'll have our guts if we offend him. How d'we know ye're not some cursed impostor?'

'You don't,' I answered him from the corner of my mouth.

'But I'll have your guts yet quicker than his lordship if you fail me.'

'Oh, be damned, Pinky,' Captain Clancy whispered. 'It's a jape ain't it? The old bitch took a hundred guineas from me last week but I'll have my worth of it tonight. And sup out on the tale for a month to come.'

Our captain was a sportsman, but apart from that the affair went mischancy from the start. Labaud presented his salver to my lord and the pretty naked trollop clinging to his arm and wagging her hips. Madame turned a simper loose on both of them while the disappointed ancient rip tried privately to snatch the veils from another of the wenches. All the others clustered round, the fiddlers tuned a triumphant chord, the nymphs and cupids capered and clapped; and I drew out my pistol and said, 'Hold there, my man. I'm arresting you as a notorious French agent; one Jean-Pierre Labaud.'

For an instant we had silence. Then all was pandemonium. As quick as a snake Labaud flung his tray at my head. My pistol exploded in my hand and before I could grapple with the villain he had tossed my lord one way and his Venus the other— shrieking, cursing and flat on her back waving her legs—to plunge between them for the door. I saw Bob close with him as the languid gentleman forgot his airs and fell on me like a tiger. Him I snouted short and sharp, tossed him into the admiral's arms and turned after Labaud; now engaged in a flying mill with Bob and Captain Clancy, while the captain's bold companion was dancing round the three of 'em with a bottle he had snatched up. But above the screams of the other wenches, the cries of the old grandad trying to get under their veils to hide himself, cupids and nymphs scuttling their bare little arses under the tables, madame was screeching, 'Samson; Jason! Murder and arson!' The two negroes came on laughing as the doors were flung open and the other footmen tumbled in.

It became a somewhat confused affair. I was too busy to watch how Bob Snaffle and the cavalrymen fared, being heavily engaged with the negroes and three footmen myself; though by the fortunes of war our private battle was over by the por-tière, so preventing his lordship's escape. I broke a chair over

169

one negro's head, which sobered the fellow nicely, then with a leg of the same gave a footman his quietus and further discouraged the languid gentleman who came back breathing fire for all his snout was running claret; but I was hard pressed, for they were clinging like dogs to a bull and seemed to have a particular malevolence against me. What with the wenches screaming, gentlemen cursing and madame screeching vulgar abuse, the crack of Bob's pistol exploding and the smash of broken bottles and furniture there was neither space, quiet nor time for studied niceties.

How it might have ended I do not know—though I laid one more footman cold and tossed aside Master Quizzing Glass who was now industriously striving to throttle me—but then there came the sudden thunderous crash of a heavier weapon and a tinkle of splintering glass from the chandelier. There were fresh figures at the double doors and a voice roaring, 'Quiet there. This is the Bow Street Patrol.'

It brought a lull; and gave me leisure to draw back, take a breath, and perceive Master Maggsy, Jagger, and of all people my colleague Mr Ludwell standing there with some surprise on his face; and Maggsy holding my Wogdons one in each hand. 'God's Tripes, what did I tell you?' he demanded in his dulcet tones. 'Didn't I tell you if Sturrock's out and loose there'll be mischief?'

TEN

There was nothing left but to survey the carnage; and a fearful scene it was. Nymphs and cupids peering from beneath what was left of the tables; madame reclining in a chair drumming her heels, shrieking and weeping, with one of her ostrich plumes shot away and a sad end to her classicals. Wenches, flunkeys and customers huddled against the walls, Mr Quizzing Glass tumbled in a heap with no further interest in the matter and myself surrounded by fallen adversaries. My lord's naked doxy trying to wrap herself in one window curtain and my lord in another; Bob Snaffle and Captain Clancy dishevelled but victorious, Labaud lying snoring on the floor as cold as mutton, the captain's friend standing over him flushed but gratified and still clutching the neck of a broken bottle; and Master Maggsy announcing, 'God's Pickles; even for you, Sturrock, this is a rare right un.'

'Put those pistols down before you do a mischief,' I ordered him and continued to Ludwell, 'You're most timely, Mr Ludwell. But how do you come here?'

'Returned from Bath tonight,' he answered, 'and thought to find you at the Bear. Was then advised to go to the Cock Yard, where I discover this little devil; who opined that we'd best come on here as you was out after trouble. And bedamn you've found it,' he added. 'You'll have an account or two to reckon for this.'

'By God he will,' says my lord.

Like all politicians when the battle is safely over he emerged from his hiding place to make a speech; and most eloquent. Among several other more florid observations I understood that the least to be required of me would be my neck. I let him go on for a bit but then said, 'Very good, my lord, I'm properly

171

rebuked. I'll own it wasn't as tidy as I'd have liked it. But by your leave we've more urgent work before us. I'll presume you have your carriage here? Then I'll beg you to drive fast to Whitehall and have post messengers sent out in haste, and the telegraph semaphore signalling to Portsmouth. To the effect of a general state of alert.'

That produced an astonished silence and then a second explosion from his lordship, louder than the first though shorter. For a minute I was concerned for the gentleman's health; but he would carry more authority than I might, for a few words from him would be an order. I hit upon a happy stratagem to hurry him on his way and said, 'Sir, I've not presented this gentleman.' I indicated Bob Snaffle. 'He's apprentice to Mr Gillray; a cartoonist. If he were to set this scene on paper he could have it in the print shops in a day or two. Or if the news sheets got hold of the tale, God knows what they'd make of it. The very thought of what *The Times* might say makes my blood run cold.'

It did little to warm theirs, and I continued, 'Pray, my lord, hear me for a minute.' He was in no case to stop me, and I told the tale as quick and short as I could, to finish bluntly, 'All the information these rascals need has been collected in this establishment for weeks past; from the highly placed gentlemen and officials like yourselves who are entertained here.' I paused to let that shot strike home. 'It has been passed on to this man; Jean-Pierre Labaud, one of Joseph Fouché's officers and ring-leader of the affair.'

My lord was somewhat sallow, but the admiral roared, 'It can't be done. God dammit we're blockading Brest, and we've frigates quartering the Channel by day and night.'

'It will not be a sortie; nor made from the sea. It's to be done by trickery, and to come from inland. It must be brought off tomorrow night to time with Bonaparte's review on the day after. The men about it are already on their way; and we've less than twenty-four hours to find and stop them.' Stirring the still unconscious Labaud with my foot I added, 'This fine fellow thought his part was over and nothing left for him now but to wait here for the news.'

172

'Lookee, my man,' the admiral demanded, 'how's he to bring the news to Boney when he has it? The Devil himself with a cannon ball up his arse could not escape and get to France in time.'

'They don't need the devil. We shall do it for 'em. The Portland beacon's marked on that map. It's to be fired as part of the plot; and one by one so will every other blaze from it all along the coast. In little more than minutes the news will be flaming from Dungeness; plain to be seen from Boulogne.' His lordship nodded at last, though with no great love or kindness on his face, and I continued, 'My lord, if the attempt succeeds Bonaparte has us at his mercy. If it fails he loses nothing but a few lives; and once those beacons are lit the confusion they'll cause will still be worth a victory to the monster. Before morning you'll have the whole of the south coast on the move in disorder; and he could well mount his invasion hard after.'

'The fellow's got a notion, ain't he?' Captain Clancy enquired. 'I don't claim much of a noddle on me, but even I can see that.'

'When I require your opinion I'll request it, sir,' my lord told him coldly and continued to me, 'Very well, my man. I'll have the warning sent. But mark this. If you're mistaken or making fools of us I hope God may have mercy on you, for I'll see nobody else does.'

'We must await the issue, sir,' I answered humbly, even giving a bow as he marched off with the admiral after him.

There remained now the rest of this fine company, for they must all be lodged and questioned and I had no time for it; moreover Master Maggsy was plainly full of fresh news for me. It must be Ludwell's business, and I turned to him with a nice diplomacy and said, 'Mr Ludwell, Henriette d'Armande's your enquiry and you're in command here. I'll ask your leave to be off to take the other rascals in this plot. But first might I ask did you have any good in Bath concerning the woman?'

'Why to be sure I did, Mr Sturrock,' he answered. 'I commonly have good of my enquiries. The Assembly Rooms billet was issued to a Mr Gervase Markham. The young lady concerned was observed on several occasions at these rooms with the gentleman, but then known as Miss Harriet Ashford. The same on further enquiries proving to be governess to a considerable family close by Chippenham; but dismissed from that employment some several months back over one of the older sons of the house—a young person little more than eighteen—calling out Mr Gervase Markham for a duel on her account.'

'And was the family named Merritt, by any chance?'

'It was not,' he replied. 'The name is Mandeville.'

'A pity,' I observed. 'But I'm still obliged.'

I paused for little more. Labaud was still unconscious with Bob Snaffle bending over him, and I added generously, 'I'll leave you the pleasure of questioning Madame Rosamunda and her ladies, Mr Ludwell. But you'll discover that ugly fellow Labaud will complete your case. Known as William Tooley he used the whore house in Coventry Court as he needed it for his headquarters. I fancy you'll find that he murdered the old woman there on Monday night last for fear of her talking too much to me. And he caused the death of Henriette d'Armande by poisoning that same afternoon; details of which poison I shall present to Mr A myself as the occasion arises.' Maggsy and Jagger were waiting by the door and I finished, 'Now then, let's get on our way. And if you feel like joining us, Bob, you're welcome. I can do with all the men I may find.'

Captain Clancy rose to the bait like a pike. 'Then we're with you,' he cried. 'We'll not be out of it now. What d'ye say, Pinky? Back to the barrack, rout up our grooms and be after 'em, eh? Where are ye bound for?'

'Chippenham first, or near by,' I flung back over my shoulder already hastening down the stairs with Jagger, Maggsy and Bob at my heels. 'We shall go by way of Staines and Windsor to the Bath Road at Maidenhead.'

It was by then a bit after midnight, the streets near enough clear and by the Grace of God an open moonlight night. True to his instructions Jagger had our chaise waiting in the Cock Yard, and coming to it pretty well in a trot we set off once more; but first to Soho Square to take up my powder flask, pistol balls and other necessities for such an excursion as this promised to be. Then at last I had leisure to ask Master

174

Maggsy, 'Now then, what did you discover?'

'It's Savernake Forest you want,' he answered. 'We went alooking for word of Bully Hucker, as I says there was a gentleman seeking him to drive a four in hand as he was running off with a titled lady from her husband and there'd be murder done if he was catched. Went down very well that did, and in the end we discover a stableman at the Three Cups who says to ask at the Swan with Two Necks in Lad Lane, as Hucker'd been boozing there this last several weeks. Well then that was right enough as we found an ostler who says Hucker was off about some such job already and a week back had been asking what was the roads like from this Savernake Forest down through Wiltshire and Dorset. He says he was to go there beforehand and drive the roads up and down to see how long it'd take, and he'd be doing a moonlighter. Wasn't no more to it as this ostler turns nasty over half a sovereign as he seems to reckon I promised and tells us to sod off; which we done.'

By then we were clattering at a fine clip through Kensington, and I said, 'Savernake's close by Marlborough; and little known and wild. We shall be hard pressed to do it in time.'

'I don't see what you're after,' Bob Snaffle observed. 'You've passed the warning and you know what your poison is. Ain't that enough? Not that I mind. Save it looks like being a damnation longer ride than I'd have got at Madame Rosamunda's for eight and tuppence ha'penny.'

'God help any man who trusts to Whitehall,' I answered. 'I've passed the warning as in duty bound. But we've an audacious crew here; and they'll continue with their plans for they've no means of knowing that the plot has miscarried. Moreover I'm damned if I'll stand aside and see 'em taken by the militia, with our whoremongering lordship announcing to all that he's the fine fellow who bottomed the conspiracy. I want those rascals myself and mean to have 'em. I mean to know what Mr Gervase Markham's part in the matter is; and what Mr Rodney Pottle and Mr Cloudesley Merritt are up to.'

For the rest there is little to tell of that fearful journey but Master Maggsy's curses and complaints; swaying, rolling and rattling, Jagger kept up a hammering pace, roaring and singing to keep himself awake. We made short stages to have our cattle lively and changed first at the Apprentice in Isleworth, where by good chance the landlord and his ostlers were about some mysterious business rolling casks out of a barge on the river. This I intimated was no concern of ours so long as we were off fast about government business, and they were as thankful to see the back of us as we were to leave them behind. Then on with a rush to Staines, where we had a brisk exchange of views with a sleepy, surly rascal whose rude opinions on the several exalted names I bawled up at him should have got the fellow into Newgate.

Half way to Windsor there was a fresh thunder of hoofs hauling up, and then a perfect troop about us; Captain Clancy, his companion Pinky, another confounded reckless young rascal and three mounted grooms all riding like steeplechasers. I was forced to address several observations to the gentlemen which even as cavalrymen they listened to with respect, and somewhat chastened after that they rode more orderly, but still very fast, with four of them around us like an escort and Captain Clancy and his friend spurring on ahead to rouse the next staging post. What tales, cajoleries or threats they used I did not enquire, but from Windsor and every house after there were lamps lit in the stable yards, men and horses ready waiting and a fine air of urgency; indeed several times I caught myself referred to as "the general". So Maidenhead and Reading fell behind us, one sleeping village after another with the clatter of our passage echoing back from the buildings, the Angel at Woolhampton and the Pelican of Newbury, and a grey and misty morning found us pulling up in a steam at the Black Bear in Hungerford. By my reckoning we must have been travelling at the incredible speed of near ten miles an hour.

Here Captain Clancy called a halt, advising a blow and provender for men and beasts, and then bringing over the third gentleman who had ridden with us through the night, a fresh faced young fellow I had scarcely noticed; a diffident manner, little stutter, barely years enough to support his mustachios, and a further surprise, for on appearing at the door to survey our cavalcade the landlord cried, 'Why, my lord,' in evident pleasure. 'Young Capper's guv'nor's got a seat close by,' the adventurous captain explained. 'Fetched him along as he might be useful. There's precious little afoot from here to Marlborough and even on to Chippenham that his folk won't have heard of.'

'Sir,' I announced warmly, 'you've a most excellent headpiece on you. But it's not Chippenham we make for now. We want Savernake Forest; and the fishing lodge of a Mr Gervase Markham.'

'Suss-savernake's on the doorstep,' the young gentleman answered with a wicked glint in his eye. 'Not eight miles.'

'There you are then, Capper,' Captain Clancy told him kindly. 'Cut off now and see what you can snout out, there's a good fellow. And bring back as many of your men as you can raise; and some decent mounts.' Without another word my Lord Capper raised one finger, wheeled his horse, and went away at a canter; while Captain Clancy added, 'He's a regular roaring young devil, is Capper; and his guv'nor keeps some rare fine hunters.'

It was now coming up to seven o'clock, and though I was in a fever to be on with the hunt there was sense in Captain Clancy's advice. A wise general knows when to rest his forces and we settled to a short breakfast of steak, mutton chops, black puddings, and ham washed down by a quart of home brewed ale apiece. It was time well spent for barely was that done before a clatter of hoofs in the yard announced the return of my Lord Capper on a lively chestnut, at the head of half a dozen other well mounted fellows each leading a fresh horse, and my Lord himself full of news. 'Mum-markham's lodge lies about three miles this side of Suss-savernake village, off the road in the forest,' he announced. 'My guv'nor swears it's a cuc-cursed ill favoured place.'

'Then let's go to find it,' I said.

With Capper and his man ahead for guides, Captain Clancy and the rest of our troop behind, we passed through the village at a brisk trot. The mist of early morning was now thickening to drizzle, a deserted countryside fading into greyness on either side as we turned off to more remote lanes, and before long the

177

dark forest starting to close about us and add mystery to melancholy. I composed several philosophical reflections on the scene while looking to the priming of our pistols, but neither Master Maggsy nor Bob Snaffle seemed to take much account of them and we all fell into a silence broken only by the muffled beat of our hoofs and the jingle of harness.

We came at last to a long straight ride flanked by ghostly beeches and glimmering away to dusk, where far ahead there was a speck of grey light as it might be at the end of a tunnel. Capper and his groom were riding fifty paces in front, little more than shadows themselves, and here Capper pulled his horse and turned to look back to us, his pink and white face and golden mustachios strangely innocent in the sinister dusk. He beckoned us on, and then when we came up with him whispered like a conspirator. 'The gates're another hundred pup-paces on the right. But you can view the house from here; and there's soldiers about it.'

It could just be seen through an open glade; a stone built edifice such as are common to this part of the country, standing well back on a little rise and in open ground with a high surrounding wall about the park. And it seemed we were barely in time for there was a coach and four in hand team standing at the front, its driver already on the box gathering his ribbons, another man in uniform getting up beside him, one more entering the carriage and some half dozen more mounting escort horses. Captain Clancy was now beside the chaise and he muttered, 'That's Hanoverians; the King's German Legion.'

'Or at least the uniform,' I replied.

For the first time the good fellow seemed somewhat uneasy. 'And by the cut of him that's a full colonel getting in the coach. Lookee now,' he asked, 'are you certain sure you ain't mistook about this? By God there'll be hell to pay if you are.'

'If I am I'll take the reckoning,' I answered. 'It's a damnation clever plan and they must needs have a colonel for it. Those men are impostors, and I mean to stop that coach and arrest them. You gentlemen may follow me or not as you please.'

It comes hard for a cavalryman to take orders from a mere civilian, but it comes harder still for gentlemen to be put to a dare. 'God dammit, Clancy,' Capper demanded with the naughty gleam in his eye again, 'are you jibbing? I ain't had such a jape since the day I tipped my tutor in the horse pond at the age of six. Besides my guv'nor curses Markham for a confounded radical Whig.'

'I'm obliged, sir,' I said. 'Then be good enough to follow me,' and cried, 'Now then, Jagger, make it brisk.'

They fell in behind and brisk it was, for we swept on to pass along the outer wall and reach the gates just as some fellow was pulling them open, very near bowling him over as we turned sharp in with the drive clear before us. Jagger took the gentle rise at a sharp trot, while I observed that at several corners within the walls there were rough wooden platforms constructed, and at a height to allow firing with a musket or pistol over the coping. It looked as if they were turning this lonely house into a fortified point. The boldness of their plan, and its certainty had they been allowed to carry it so far, took my breath away but there was no time to examine more as by now the carriage and its escort were coming down the hill towards us at a steady gallop. Behind the chaise Master Capper let out some wild hunting cry, Captain Clancy called, 'Extended order, line abreast!' and as they had been on a parade ground our horsemen drew out on either side pounding up on the turf. I could only thank God that they were not carrying sabres or there might have been a particular mischief. As it was Jagger cried, 'Does I ride slap into that coach, or does they ride smack into us? Either way there'll be a pretty mess in a minute.'

'Keep on,' I answered, 'I want them flustered.'

'You want 'em flustered, do you?' Maggsy screeched. 'God's Whiskers, what d'you think you're doing to me?'

Bob Snaffle also said something I did not catch for I was all eyes on the carriage, now at a hundred paces and the coachman already hauling on his ribbons bawling something which was lost in the general thunder of hoofs, the man beside him likewise screaming, another sticking his head out of the window, six more riding doggedly behind, and consternation on every face. I had also perceived a shallow ditch on either side of the drive and whichever one got his wheels in that would travel no further; but it was to be a close thing and a trial of dare or die. 'Keep straight, Jagger,' I roared. 'He's pulling.'

'I hope to God he does,' howled Jagger, 'or we'm dog's meat.'

'God's Tripes,' yelled Maggsy, 'you're cracked.'

'D'you call this fun?' demanded Snaffle.

Fifty paces, thirty and then twenty; carried by its own weight the coach now could not stop, and it was the Frenchman on the box who ended the matter, as foreseeing a dreadful future hard on him he snatched at the ribbons himself and pulled their leaders to the right. In the next instant they were through the ditch and in one more the coach was in after them, Mr Hucker flying off the box all legs and arms, the other fellow tumbling with him, and the third tossed halfway through the window, where he hung bellowing and cursing. But by some kindly intervention of Providence the horses somehow kept their feet and were not injured; though Captain Clancy was displeased and cried, 'By God, sir, that was damned uncivil; you might've upset them animals.'

I had no time to answer as by now the affair became a sudden battle. All Frenchies are well known to be excitable, and no doubt resolved to sell their necks dear they came down upon us like a whirlwind; and they were armed with holster pistols as heavy as my Wogdons. What with me roaring to the brave but hopeless rascals to surrender, explosions, shouts, curses, a welter of horses kicking and rearing, Bob Snaffle using strange medical oaths and Master Maggsy leaping clean out of the chaise with a screech to go about his own mischief, it was a pretty confusion.

Hemmed in on my own side there was little I could do, though I blew one fellow's shako off his head and then crowned him with the barrel of my Wogdon. But hard on that Jagger's own beaver went flying away and so discomposed the good fellow that let out a roar which was the last start to our horses. Already rearing and dancing they went off at a bolt. For a minute more we jostled in the *mêlée*, and then they broke clear to set off in a mad gallop with Snaffle and myself swaying, tossing and clinging to everything we could find to grasp. Only the hill and Jagger's strength saved us from careering straight over the forecourt, up the steps and into the open door of the house itself, but somehow he managed to swing the wild creatures, pull them in and bring them to a halt; and in the sudden and blessed stillness Bob Snaffle announced, 'Well, by God, if that's a ride with you for eight and tuppence ha'penny I hope I may never have a sovereign's worth.'

'It turned a bit unruly,' I confessed, 'but we'll soon have it done with. I want you and Jagger in the house now. Go by the back doors and reload and take the pistols if you like,' I said to encourage him. 'We're still seeking two other gentlemen; by name Mr Rodney Pottle and Mr Cloudesley Merritt. Below on the drive Captain Clancy and his bold fellows seemed to have settled their business for the impostor Hanoverians were all dismounted and surrounded. Only our last answers were wanting now and I finished, 'I mean to find Mr Gervase Markham myself.'

The door was open to a big hall, with a wide fireplace and unlit logs on the hearthstone, a handsome wooden staircase and dark panelling. For a minute I regretted my generosity in letting Bob Snaffle and Jagger take the pistols, but reflected that their need might be greater than mine; and there was nobody in sight and never a sound but an ancient clock somewhere ticking heavily. Then a little rustle on the staircase caught my ear; and, as it might have been a ghost, a figure coming out of the shadows down to the landing. It was Miss Geraldine Markham and now dressed decently as a woman, in a travelling habit. Her face was pale against the dark stuff of her clothes, but her voice was light enough. 'La, Mr Sturrock, you visit early. It's barely half after eight o'clock yet.'

'I've urgent business, ma'am,' I told her. 'With Mr Gervase Markham.'

'And such a crowd of odious rascals invading our grounds.'

'They're gentlemen of the cavalry,' I said. 'And I should tell you also that I have the house surrounded by forces of the country volunteers.'

She laughed. 'Old Capperdown's clod hoppers? My brother will be vastly diverted. I'll call him.'

Another voice spoke from a door which had opened unseen

to my right. 'There's no need.' Markham himself was standing there and another gentleman beside him; the sharp features and little beard several times described of Monsieur Antoine Hirson. I had found my men well enough; but Mr Markham was carrying a brace of duelling pistols, their silver mountings catching what little light there was. And fresh trouble to come; for up on the gallery above the stairs I caught sight also of another wicked face peering down through the carved banisters. It was Master Maggsy. How he got there so quickly I shall never know, but he can move as fast, silent and unseen as a cat when he pleases and is twice as inquisitive. But none of the others were aware of him, and Miss Markham descended the last few steps to stand beside her brother, watching me.

They were all three as cool as any villains I've ever seen, even when I announced, 'I am here to arrest you severally on matters of conspiracy to kidnap and abduct the persons of His Majesty the King, Her Majesty Queen Charlotte, and Her Royal Highness the Princess Augusta-Sophia from Gloucester Lodge, Weymouth; to bring them to this house and hold them here as hostages.' It was a handsome charge.

By this time Lord Capper, Captain Clancy, Pinky and their men were crowding about the open door and Mr Markham said, 'Why, gentlemen, it's over early to propose a glass of Madeira.' They stopped short at that and he came on a bit to stand a few paces from me with his back to the great empty fireplace. 'I wonder now, would we have brought it off?' he asked as one gentleman of another at their club.

'By its very boldness,' I answered. 'His Majesty is living as a simple country gentleman and retires to bed at ten o'clock. Your plan was to fire the beacon on Portland first; then in the general alarm and the militia concentrating on the harbour and seaward approaches a carriage would come to Gloucester Lodge. A colonel and escort of the German Legion would present their credentials and within minutes they'd be off. Given the rumours and confusion nobody would have a notion of what was happening. The whole of the coast would be on the move in minutes, nobody to stop and look for a coach and escort, and once in this house, even were Their Majesties discovered here,

182

none would dare attack you. You could have made your own terms,' I concluded. 'But still had you failed only setting off the beacons would have been mischief enough.'

'All come to nothing,' he mused, 'for a mere thieftaker. And you'll hang me for it. Well then, a man can only hang once.' He cocked one of the pistols as he raised it. I counted it my last instant. With all lost, and surrounded, the man could see he had no more at stake. Vain gesture it might have been, but nothing could have saved me; for all present were struck to stone, we were a bare five paces apart, and the first move I made he would fire. But like a fool he paused just long enough to savour the moment himself; and in that moment Master Maggsy descended.

Whether the child fell down the chimney or climbed is uncertain, but he appeared like a demon in a cloud of soot and dust spitting, sneezing and cursing. The unfortunate gentleman could not have known what had attacked him for my little monster was on his back in a flash. Even Miss Markham was womanly enough to scream. He went down backwards and helpless, with one pistol exploding and the ball flying harmless overhead; all done so quick that none of us had time to move, but could only gaze at him lying there in a reeking cloud of soot and gunpowder smoke. 'I knowed it,' Maggsy screeched, standing over him. 'Soon as I see them pistols I knowed what he was at; but he never reckoned on me being a chimney sweeper's boy at one time. Why I knows my way about chimneys better'n you lot know your way about whore shops.'

I helped Mr Markham to rise myself, and took the unexploded pistol away from him. There was no more fight in any of them now, though for a minute the lady looked as if she might fly at us, but then thought better of it and turned aside. The hall was full of our men and their prisoners, and Markham himself said, 'Be damned then; let's have an end of it.'

'In a minute, sir,' I promised. 'But I want a private word or two first.'

'I'll have no words of any sort with you,' he answered.

'Dr Wilford Caldwell is still in London,' I told him, 'and I'm satisfied he's innocent of any part in this affair; as I've a notion he'd prove a kindly gentleman if his help were asked.' I looked back at Miss Geraldine and then round at the others, and went on, 'There's none of us here would wish to see a lady in such a strait as this. We could help her out of it.'

She made several observations which surprised me, coming even from a hoyden, but Mr Markham interrupted, 'No, Gerry; it seems we're forced to bargain with the fellow.' He looked me up and down as if I were the criminal waiting for a rope and added, 'We may go in here.'

'You watch it,' Maggsy shrilled from his coat of dust. 'He'll have your guts if he gets the chance.'

Mr Markham cast him one further look and then turned back to the room while I stood aside to let Miss Markham pass in before me; at which she drew her skirts aside as if I had the pox, the plague, yellow fever and stinking with it. But carrying the duelling pistol I followed them in and closed the door. It was a comfortable gentleman's sporting cabinet with leather easy chairs, cases of fowling pieces and angle rods, and Mr Markham stopped by the table again for all the world as if I were the villain and asked, 'Well, what is it you want?'

I was feeling my weskit button straining but said, 'Sir, I was set on from Whitehall to snatch two damnation hot chestnuts from the fire. The first being yourself as a man of wealth and influence who might well pull the government down. The second a reputable American citizen who could start a devil's dance of diplomatic trouble or worse. If a mere Bow Street thieftaker got his fingers burned it would be no great matter; they could afford to cast him aside and declare they'd never heard of the impudent rascal so long as they had two or three official agents already at work to unearth the plot itself.' I paused to let him digest that before continuing, 'It'll suit everybody best if the matter never goes to court. I'll have a written and signed statement if you please; addressed to Jeremy Sturrock of the Bow Street Patrol and setting out your whole part in it.'

'I'll be damned if I will,' he answered.

I laid his pistol down on the table observing, 'If the London mobs get their hands on you they'll not wait for a hangman.' Miss Markham caught her breath, and I added, 'Or if it comes to trial and your affairs with Henriette d'Armande or Miss Harriet Ashford are disclosed they'll not make pretty hearing. I can prove she was your mistress till she lost her employment with the Mandeville family. And I know that when you cast her off she found her way to the Haymarket whore shops, where she assumed the French name and so fell into Monsieur Labaud's net. I can tell that when they discovered she was an Englishwoman and about to split on what little she knew they murdered her; and in as dreadful way as I've ever seen.'

'God damn you,' he burst out. 'I knew nothing of it. I never expected that any innocent people might be killed. Nor did I hear that Harry was concerned until it was too late.'

'I doubt you did,' I agreed. 'But you'll not find a judge and jury to believe it. And the mob will tear the court down to get at you.' Miss Markham was as pale as chalk, but she did not speak, and I finished, 'There are further matters, Mr Markham. One being the murder of another man by the same wicked poison at Mill End on Tuesday night last. You might or might not have known of that, and it's no great matter now; but I'll have your statement. Only tell me one thing first. How did you get into this affair?'

He answered with the strange pride of all such crackpots. 'I'm of republican and Bonapartist sympathy, and was approached several months since as owning this property. We could hold it as long as need be; and what's George the Third but a sick, mad old man?' I fingered the pistol, for nobody shall speak to me so about as kindly a Christian gentleman as I've ever known; and he stopped short at my look, yet still added, 'I'll not bandy opinions with you. But unless this war is stopped it will continue for ten years and tear Europe apart. Even America may be brought in; and we shall be defeated in the end.'

Offering a silent prayer for protection against all such righteous addle-wits who know better than we do ourselves what is good for us, I said, 'Pray desire Miss Markham to retire and prepare for her journey. When I have your statement there'll be no charges laid on her; and I'll repeat that Dr Wilford Caldwell is still in London.'

185

What she might have said to that I do not know, for then there was a fresh clamour from the hall, Master Maggsy's angelic tones, Bob Snaffle and Jagger. There had been talk enough now, and I went out to have an end of it.

And to have an end of the whole affair, for as I expected they had found Mr Rodney Pottle and Mr Merritt; dusty and dishevelled, scarce able to stand, and as crestfallen as beaten fighting cocks. 'Well, my fine fellows,' I said, 'my cunning government men who thought they'd take the tricks while Johnny Mumpkins dealt the trumps for 'em, a pretty mess you've made of it. Where did you flush this brace of pheasants, Bob?'

'Found 'em in an attic,' he grinned. 'Trussed up, ready for roasting.'

'It was cursed ill luck,' Pottle started.

'It was a pair of damnation simpletons. Begod with wonders like you on our side Bonaparte don't need an army; and to save you the trouble I'll tell you who you are myself. Mr Rodney Pottle, otherwise known as Edward, the man Mr Grimble had supposedly never seen; and Mr Cloudesley Merritt who I fancy was trying his hand as an agent for the first time. I hope it may be your last, sir, or you might get yourself into trouble before you've done.' It is not in my kindly nature to crow over the misfortunes of others, more especially with our cavalrymen standing about and listening, but I wanted to give Mr Markham time to make up his mind, and asked, 'How did you come to get yourself taken?'

'How was we to know we'd ride slap into a whole damned garrison?' Merritt demanded. 'We'd a notion we might find Mackenzie here.'

I gazed at him in wonderment. 'Mackenzie, your agent in Boulogne who first got wind of the plot? We'll come to him in a minute. Let's have this much clear first. You, Mr Merritt, came to Chippenham on Wednesday, being sent by Mr Pottle who told you he'd had information that Henriette d'Armande had been seen there. Yesterday I showed Mr Pottle a certain map, and also requested him to ride out to Maidenhead to make certain enquiries. But Mr Pottle perceived what that map was, and perhaps even a bit of the plot and concluded to push on to

186

Chippenham to find you.'

Mr Pottle was recovering his spirits quickly. 'And a confounded hard ride it was.'

I listened at the closed door but could hear no sound from within and continued, 'We'll go further. When you came to Chippenham, Mr Pottle, Merritt related what he'd discovered of Henriette d'Armande and Mr Markham, and told you of this house. By now you perceived that Markham was in some part concerned and concluded to ride on here in a fine flush of heroics.' Mr Merritt only nodded, more crestfallen than ever, and I turned to Bob Snaffle. 'Now we may come to Mr Mackenzie. Bob, be good enough to describe the corpse you examined.'

He did so with some relish, and Merritt said glumly, 'Aye, that'd be Mackenzie right enough.'

I next added what had befallen the unfortunate man. 'It's plain Markham never knew the fellow was at Mill End,' I finished. 'Mackenzie thought simply to have the matter out with Labaud and Leclerc himself. But why in God's name was he so rash as to go there alone?'

'Because he was that sort,' Merritt growled. 'When he was told you were called in he swore he'd have no damned Bow Street thieftaker poaching his game.'

I pounced on him like a terrier at a rat. 'When did he return to London? You'll recollect that in my conference with your Mr Grimble he was said still to be in Boulogne.'

Pottle winked at Maggsy and gave me one of his saucy grins. 'Easy with your leaders. You shall have the whole tale. Mackenzie came back unexpected on the Monday, by way of a smuggler's boat to Essex. We met him in Beale's chop house, Merritt and me, and he had not yet reported to Grimble; a man he never could put up with.'

'And what was your reckoning then?'

'Mackenzie thought, as we all did, that it was a plot to assassinate Mr Pitt. Begod he flew into a fine rage and damned Grimble from here to hell and back when Merritt told us a Bow Street man was to be brought to the business. So it was determined that Merritt might come to the Brown Bear to make himself known to you, while I went to Henriette d'Armande as already appointed. It was true enough, what I told you of my meetings with her. Then Merritt was to give us an account of your call to Grimble the next day; and after that Mackenzie himself would ride down to Mill End to finish the matter before you'd started on it.'

What observations I might have made on these disclosures were cut short by the door opening and Miss Markham appearing. She passed through us as we had not been there and started up the stairs, but then stopped at a step or two higher to look down over her shoulder. 'My brother desires me to take your safe conduct,' she said with a face of ice. 'I shall wish to leave in a few minutes.'

We watched her pass along the gallery in silence, neither was there any other sound from behind the door yet, and I continued, 'So I was to get my fingers burned on the politics while you goose-wits followed my discoveries and reckoned you'd be set up for life. By God, you should be in the government yourselves; that's where your half cock talents lie best. Was Grimble party to this?'

Mr Merritt answered with a sour laugh. 'Grimble was in a cleft stick. He dare not let Mackenzie's warning pass. But neither could he move too plain, for Markham has some high placed friends. They could well see him out of his office and broke if he went a step too far with nothing proved.'

'It shall be proved clear enough,' I promised, pausing to listen once more and then adding, 'There's but one last thing. We'll have the whole of it clear. When you let yourself get caught last night, like the nincompoops you are, did they not question you? Did you not warn them that the plot was discovered?'

Pottle regarded me warily. 'We had to reckon our own lives. There were some of 'em for shooting us there and then, but I'll say for Markham that he wouldn't allow it. Merritt here was out like a dead duck from a blow on the head, and Markham promised if I told all we knew he'd see us set free when they'd finished their business. I reckoned it more like that if I did they'd murder us despite Markham and then go to ground.

188

Whereas with you in the hunt and close on their heels there was little danger that they'd bring it off now. It seemed best to let 'em have their heads to run into a trap, and I pretended some reluctance but in the end confessed we'd reason to believe they were after Mr Pitt, who's taking the waters at Bath.'

'No doubt thanking God for Bow Street,' I observed. 'You've the wits of a lawyer at least.' Hard on that came the sound I had been waiting to hear. Muffled, but plain enough; the bang of a single pistol shot. It startled all the company and Master Maggsy let out a fresh screech, but I said, 'I fancy that concludes the matter; and to the best interests of most of us concerned.'

There is little more to relate. By arrangement with my Lord Capper our prisoners were carried off to be lodged at his father's residence until more official arrangements could be made for them; and I am informed there was much ado to prevent the excitable old gentleman from trying and condemning them all himself. Mr Pottle and Mr Merritt were left to their own devices—which I fancy were to drown their disappointments in the Pump Room at Bath—while Captain Clancy and Mr Pinky volunteered gallantly to escort Miss Markham back to London, where she was much befriended by Dr Wilford Caldwell. I learned some little while after that now being a considerable heiress from her brother's estates she took herself off with the good doctor when he returned to America; and there no doubt learned the virtues of womanliness and the folly of radical politics.

For myself, Maggsy, Bob Snaffle and Jagger we went on to Weymouth. All being somewhat weary we travelled at leisure and arrived only by nightfall to find that pretty, elegant little town alive with soldiers, the royal yacht in Portland Harbour, and our fine British frigates standing close in. But ten o'clock passed and then eleven without alarm, and at last we retired to a modest lodging for our well earned rest. Nevertheless we were early astir that next morning to join the fashionable throng on the Esplanade, and to doff our hats in loyal respect when the band struck up the National Anthem as His Majesty entered the water for his daily bathe. I was content. My part would remain unknown; apart from Mr Markham's written and signed confession to save me from further embarrassment I had little out of it but a dozen of Madeira and a post-chaise—while for some time after my master, Mr A, was to wonder why he did not receive the knighthood he so coveted—but I was content. I cheered as loud as Master Maggsy when His Majesty emerged from the sea.

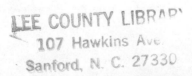